PARADISE

A Post-Apocalyptic Thriller

Aftershock Series
Book One

****

MICHAEL R. WATSON

Paradise: Aftershock Series, Book One
Copyright © 2016 by Michael R. Watson.

All rights reserved. No part of this book may be reproduced, stored in a retrieval system or transmitted in any form or by any means, electronic or mechanical, including photocopying or recording, without prior permission of the author, who is the copyright holder.

Printed in the United States of America.

Cover design by Deranged Doctor Design.

This book is a work of fiction. References to real people, events, establishments, organizations, or locales are intended to provide a sense of authenticity, and are used fictitiously. All characters, incidents, and dialogue, are drawn from the author's imagination and are not to be construed as real.

ISBN: 978-1533213266

Dedication

To my grandchildren, Ethan, Paige, Kinsey, Lilly, and Macie. May you always be prepared.

Acknowledgements

I'd like to thank my family and friends who 'volunteered' to be beta readers throughout the writing, review and revision process.

Prologue

Earthquakes in America's heartland had been so rare an occurrence and their magnitudes so low most weren't even considered newsworthy. Then, that all began to change. The first tremors were weak and barely perceptible, but within weeks it became difficult to ignore ripples on the surface of a glass of iced tea or glasses clinking together in the kitchen cabinet. Even though these early signs lasted only a few seconds, their cause was undeniable.

Gradually, over the next few months, the frequency and magnitude of the tremors continued to rise as did a growing apprehension among those affected. It then became almost commonplace to hear a brief mention about the most recent one during the evening news. Strangely, the tremors weren't occurring everywhere across the region, but only in isolated clusters or swarms.

A growing concern and curiosity brought a handful of

respected earth scientists together to study the anomalous occurrences. Within a matter of weeks they had completed their evaluation of the data and reached a unanimous conclusion, something no one expected.

The data was re-evaluated again and again, but it became obvious there was a common culprit, the disposal of wastewater from the oil and gas industry into deep injection wells. Favorable prices had resulted in increased production, which in turn had led to an increase in volume of wastewater. It was suggested that the surge in volume of the contaminated water had pressurized and "lubricated" known and previously unknown fault zones, making them susceptible to movement, inducing the earthquakes to occur.

By the time the governing bodies accepted the results of the study there was still the question of what could be done about it. Or was it already too late? Through news outlets the public was made aware of the cause, who then demanded the disposal wells to be shut down. The oil and gas companies vehemently opposed such a drastic action. As a compromise, the first response was to curtail the amount of wastewater being placed down the disposal wells nearest the strongest quake occurrences. The action appeared to have had no immediate effect as the frequency and magnitudes of the quakes continued to escalate. Perhaps too much had been expected too soon or it had been too late to stop the process already set in motion. The state officials were in a quandary as to what to do next. Safety, of course, was *a* priority, but not necessarily *the* priority. After all, the oil and gas industry was a major source of revenue for the region.

PARADISE

* * *

Thousands of miles away, a series of simultaneous and massive earthquakes struck areas all along the Ring of Fire from New Zealand to Southeast Asia, to Alaska, and back down along the Washington, Oregon, and California coastline to Chile. The devastating results were compounded by the tsunamis that followed with mountains of flood waters being driven into the coastal areas, creating even more destruction. For those who had survived the earthquakes and had remained along the coast, there was no hope. The death toll soared into the tens of thousands.

Earthquakes along the west coast of the U.S. were a common occurrence. It was an unfortunate but eventual consequence of living near the San Andreas Fault system and the Cascadia subduction zone. But, this time, something was different; the magnitudes being reported in California were even higher than the historically devastating ones from the 1906 and 1994 earthquakes.

As a result of these quakes, there were reports of widespread chaos and devastation. The government and local law enforcement lost control, collapsing and becoming non-existent. Then all communication with the west coast came to a halt. With no radio, television, phone service or internet, one could only assume the worst.

The people of the heartland could only attempt to relate to what the people were going through on the west coast, recalling their own experiences with tornados and flooding. But the destruction the quakes and tsunamis brought encompassed a much larger area and affected a great many more people. Some of the hardest hit places were so decimated they would possibly never recover. The moderate quakes taking place in the heartland seemed almost insignificant in comparison.

Then, according to reports, something even more unbelievable appeared to be taking place. The massive quakes and aftershocks had triggered a chain reaction of quakes, releasing stored up energy from interlinked faults as they spread slowly and steadily inland. The migrating movement was like a series of surging waves approaching a shoreline. Public announcements attempted to warn those ahead of their path of the impending danger and the potential for even stronger shockwaves to come. But nothing like this had ever been experienced before, so no one listened, resulting in the avoidable loss of even more lives.

*   *   *

Even though the quakes occurring in the heartland were a significant increase in both numbers and magnitude from previous years, the moderate magnitudes were not enough to convince the majority of the people they were a legitimate threat. And the idea they were in danger was a ridiculous notion and treated as a joke. After all, they lived in a safe zone, the west coast was over a thousand miles away, and the effects of an earthquake there would never reach the central plains.

In this part of the country, earthquakes hadn't been expected or planned for. They were something that only happened to other people, like those living along the west coast. None of the buildings had been built or designed

PARADISE

with any consideration given to withstanding an earthquake. And why would they? Earthquakes in the region had been a rare and insignificant occurrence, and quake-resistant design and construction would have been a ridiculous notion as well as a waste of money.

Afraid and confused by the bizarre aftershock waves, there was a group who prayed to be spared from a similar devastation being experienced to the west, that somehow the Rocky Mountains would intercept or dampen this new anomaly's spreading force and momentum.

It took only a few days to realize their prayers had gone unanswered. Without warning, shockwaves struck the heartland with magnitudes higher than any previously recorded, propelled even higher in the "lubricated" cluster areas. Tremors that had at first been just mild curiosities were now frightening and dangerous anomalies.

As subsequent waves struck, and their magnitudes increased, the damage to buildings and the infrastructure progressively grew worse. The increase of magnitude had also included increases of duration, lasting thirty seconds to over a minute, resulting in the greatest damage. It became evident a collapse was coming.

The first physical and obvious indications of the seriousness of the threat came when cracks appeared in both interior and exterior walls and windows began to shatter from the shifting and heaving of foundations. Structural damage couldn't be prevented and there was nowhere safer to go. The surrounding communities were all dealing with the same dire situations. The people could only watch as their communities crumbled around them.

By the time the third major wave hit, the schools and

many of the businesses had already closed, the buildings too dangerous to be occupied. Communities rallied together with both friends and strangers helping one another with a willingness to share what little they had. Food and clean drinking water were the priority.

However, as those essentials began to run low, the aforementioned willingness to share came to an abrupt halt as families turned to self-preservation. It didn't take long for neighbors to turn on one another.

The people of the heartland were at the mercy of the earthquakes, and each other.

* * *

Chapter 1

A month had passed and the earthquakes continued to move toward us in waves, each subsequent one increasing in frequency and magnitude. Unfortunately, according to the few news reports we'd received, there was nowhere better or safer to go. And since the quakes struck randomly, without any set pattern, it was impossible to predict exactly when the next one would hit. The waiting and anticipation were almost as bad as the actual quake, adding to the stress and placing many of the people on the verge of panic.

Based on the assumptions of the investigating earth scientists, a quake with a projected magnitude of 8.0 or higher could hit at any time without warning.

I was worried for my family. They stayed home while I walked downtown to look for answers. They began to sort out what we could take with us if or when we had to leave.

MICHAEL R. WATSON

Even though the car had almost a full tank of gas, I was on foot, the precious fuel in reserve for if and when we needed to leave in a hurry.

Near City Hall the street was full of people, anxious to see what, if anything, was being done to help our desperate situation. I recognized several people in the crowd as the same ones who in the beginning had scoffed at the idea of earthquakes causing any damage in our community. Panic and fear were on many of the faces, helpless, not knowing what to do, looking for any kind of help or guidance. Some had already lost their homes. Small groups consoled one another while others, I learned, had already left town, gambling that there were answers and help elsewhere.

My attention was drawn to the sky above by a growing sound, surprised to see a helicopter hovering directly overhead. Perhaps we were finally going to receive the help we so desperately needed. But, instead of landing, the helicopter continued to hover overhead as an arm began to throw papers out the side door. Confused, we watched as they fluttered down to us.

I grabbed one of the papers out of the air. It was a flyer, an invitation to a place offering help. I was immediately suspicious and crumpled it up, about to throw it to the ground. Then, I considered that Sarah, my wife, might like to see it and stuffed it into my pocket. The ground was littered with the flyers, others reacting just as I almost had. I heard comments from both those who were overjoyed that someone was offering to help and others, like myself, who were skeptical of a helping hand coming out of nowhere. I could sense the crowd's frustration building with a few individuals becoming excessively

PARADISE

vocal, working up the others, while yelling for the helicopter to land. I was sympathetic; we were all in the same boat. When I looked back up, the helicopter was gone.

Its sudden disappearance without offering assistance of any kind brought out the worst in the crowd. Angry chants began to fill the downtown area. Maybe it was the idea that someone was able to fly around in a helicopter while we were struggling for the bare essentials for survival.

I wasn't surprised to hear the City Hall's doors were locked. And no one had been able to reach the Mayor or any of the Town Council for over a week. I was startled when a brick shattered a large pane of window-front glass. That was my cue to duck away. They weren't going to accomplish anything other than to release some of their stored up frustration. As I walked away, others from the community, some of them my neighbors, joined in with the destruction, breaking windows of storefronts, grabbing and carrying away whatever they could get their hands on. The community was falling apart and things were getting ugly. My only thought was to get back to my family.

Walking back home, I avoided a group who appeared to be intent on causing trouble by crossing to the other side of the street. They were traveling in a pack, breaking out car windows as they walked down the other side of the street. As I passed by, I recognized some of their faces. They were just kids, maybe fifteen. I was pretty sure one of them was the boy who sacked my groceries. They moved on and so did I.

I noticed the owner of the corner convenience store,

Bill Flask, was hurriedly placing plastic bags over the pump dispensers. It was a common practice when a dispenser needed repairs, but he was covering all of them. He was the last business holdout. Curious, I walked over.

"Bill, are you out of gas?"

"I might as well be. My tanks are almost empty and I just received a call. The fuel trucks won't be coming. The quakes hit the refinery we use pretty hard. They've been fighting fires and trying to make repairs, but they're fighting a losing battle. They're abandoning the plant. It's too dangerous for anyone to stay. Even if the refinery was still operational, they said delivery would be impossible with the roads the way they are now. Cracks and crevices have opened up across the roads, the asphalt and concrete have buckled, and many of the bridges have already collapsed. Even the rail lines have been damaged beyond use. Airports are at a standstill with fuel supplies exhausted and runways too damaged to be used. That's when the phone line went dead. Now, I can't reach anyone."

I pulled out my cell phone and checked for a signal. There weren't any bars. It came as no surprise. Reception in town had always been hit or miss, but this time there could be a good reason, the cell towers could be down due to the recent quakes. It was difficult to believe all this was happening, here, in what should have been a safe zone.

The pack of boys was now headed back in our direction and it was larger now. It seemed as though their courage was growing too, becoming even more arrogant, destructive, and loud.

"You'd better get on home," I warned. "Trouble is on its way."

PARADISE

He looked past me, seeing the agitated and destructive group of boys moving in our direction. He nodded agreement and ran back to the store, locking the doors. I'm sure he knew as well as I did it wouldn't matter. I avoided the boys once again as I made my way home.

As another shockwave hit, I watched as people struggled to stay upright, grabbing hold of whatever was close. I grabbed onto the trunk of a nearby tree and held on until the tremor subsided. Reaching our house without injury, I was shocked to find one wall had already collapsed during my absence, the roof sitting cockeyed. Sarah was sitting on the ground in the front yard, surrounded by piles of our belongings, crying and trying to console our frightened and confused son and daughter, Christopher, 9, and Cindy, 7. When she saw me, she jumped to her feet and ran to me, throwing her arms around my neck. Chris and Cindy were right behind her. I tried to comfort all of them with a prolonged hug.

"Oh, John," Sarah exclaimed. "Our home, it's gone."

"It'll be alright," I told her, trying to soothe and reassure her, not knowing if it was true or not. "At least we're all safe."

She looked up at me with red and mascara smeared eyes, forcing a weak smile.

"You're right. I don't know what's the matter with me." She wiped away her tears and took a deep breath. "What do we do now?"

"I'm not sure, but we can't stay here. Tell me what you need and I'll try to get it out of the house. "

"Leave our home?"

"Just look at it. It's not safe and it's only going to get

worse. I'm surprised there's still any electricity in town. Soon there won't be. And once the gas lines break, it'll only be a matter of time before the whole town goes up."

A good friend and neighbor, Jerry Wilson, excitedly ran over to us from across the street. It appeared their house had suffered as much damage as ours.

"Did you hear?" he asked excitedly.

"Hear what?" I asked.

"A helicopter flew over earlier and dropped flyers inviting all of us to a safe place in western Oklahoma where we can go to get help. Here, I got one for you. See, it's even got a map."

I pulled my crumpled copy out of my pocket. "I've read all about it."

"It says it's an old prison," he continued, "with walls strong enough to stand up to the quakes and they have their own solar panels and wind turbines for power. It also says they have plenty of food and water. I'm going to load up my family and go there. Most of our neighbors are going, too. How about you, John?"

"Jerry, you know everyone's not going to be able to stay in this prison," I pointed out, still skeptical, trying to be the voice of reason. "No matter how large it is."

"Probably not, but at least there will be food and water," countered Jerry. "Before long, that'll be more than we have here."

I had my doubts. Like I'd always heard, 'If something sounds too good to be true, it usually is.' "We're going to have to talk about it. You go ahead. Maybe we'll see you there."

"Jerry, hurry up!" yelled his wife, Judy, from across

PARADISE

the street.

"Okay, John," he said, as he backed away. "But don't wait too long. The first ones there will get the best spots." He waved a goodbye to us as he ran back to his wife. There was no point in trying to change his mind. They had already loaded up their car and were ready to leave. His wife waved just before she and their young daughter piled into their car. Sarah waved back. With the roads in their current condition, I wondered just how far they would be able to drive before having to abandon their car and go the rest of the way on foot. We waved back as they drove away. Panic-driven, a procession of cars and pickups packed full with family keepsakes and comforts of home paraded by, horns blaring and tempers flaring at anyone who got in their way.

"Are we going to follow them?" asked Sarah.

"Is that what you'd like us to do?" I asked. "I'm more than a little suspicious of such a generous offer coming to us out of the blue. And did you see this?" I said, pointing to the flyer. "It's signed by Governor Davis. I've never heard that name before today."

"But should we ignore it completely?" asked Sarah. "We've lost our home and this town is dying. You said we couldn't stay here. So, where else can we go?"

There was a loud explosion and the earth shook. Instinctively, we reached out to steady each other.

"Another quake?" asked Cindy, on the verge of tears with terror on her face.

I looked toward the downtown area where the sound had come from. A large black column of smoke was already rising into the sky.

"No, a gas explosion," I said. "It's begun. Gather only what you absolutely need and load it into the car. We'll see how far we can get."

Sarah nervously smiled her approval and nodded. I wasn't sure where we would end up, but for the moment leaving with the others seemed to make her happy and there weren't a lot of alternatives anyway. If we went to the prison, we knew we would at least be with our friends and neighbors. And she was right; we did have to go somewhere. Hopefully, it would be a safe haven or sanctuary, as advertised, until we found something better.

The roads were packed with vehicles, driving along at a snail's pace. We picked our way along the damaged roadways, at times having to drive through farmer's abandoned fields. Hundreds of columns of smoke rose in the air across the landscape. The acrid smoke-filled air burned our throats and made our eyes water. We slowly passed house after house, collapsed or burning, and dozens of abandoned cars and trucks, either with a mechanical breakdown or more likely out of gas. Groupings of tents had popped up all along our route. People with helplessness on their faces held up signs asking for food, water, or a ride. We rode along in silence, not believing our eyes, not able to help. I looked at our gas gauge. We would be joining them soon. I glanced at Sarah. Her eyes were closed and her lips were moving silently. She was praying. I just didn't know if it was for them or for us. This was our new reality. Things would never be the same again.

*   *   *

Chapter 2

It had been five long years since leaving our home. Tomorrow, my time would be up. I had been dreading this day since Governor Davis had implemented his plan for population control four years earlier. You might think knowing when your time is up, without any recourse, would allow you the time to make peace and prepare for it with a certain amount of acceptance. But the last few weeks had actually been torture, not knowing the exact day or time when they would come, knowing I would have to leave my family behind, to never see their faces again. When I had seen my name posted for the next removal, it had almost come as a relief. There would be no more waiting.

I knew it hadn't been easy on my family. Sarah, Christopher, and Cindy had avoided talking about it. I guess it had been easier to pretend it wasn't going to happen, until now. Tomorrow, a team would be coming to the mill to collect the governor's share of the season's harvest, and with them the disposal squad to remove me and a handful of others who met the age criteria, to transport us to an unknown location deep within the wasteland. There was no coming back.

* * *

The governor's mandate specified everyone, upon reaching the age of forty, had reached the end of their usefulness, and before becoming a burden on the food supply, would forfeit their life for the well being of the remaining population. Then, on a quarterly basis, those fitting the criteria would be collected and delivered to an unknown location within the southern wasteland for disposal where they would be left to fend for themselves, if they could, or die. The intent was to maintain a delicate balance between the necessary workforce and a sustainable food supply. The reasoning was the brainchild of Governor Davis, enforced without any regard to humanity, ironically for the good of the people. The first year had been especially terrifying and horrific, with anyone displaying gray hair or age wrinkles automatically culled out.

The country we knew had gone downhill quickly with little reason for hope. After suffering through almost a full year of earthquake activity with magnitudes ranging from 4.0 to as high as 7.0, they had mysteriously stopped.

With few places to go to for safety, tens of thousands had lost their lives. Those who had survived had done so by leaving the cities, going to the flatlands, far from any

PARADISE

structure, natural or manmade. Even basements and caverns were avoided out of fear of being killed by their collapse.

A tent city had popped up overnight with our family in one of the tents right outside the walls of the governor's compound. That had been five years ago and since then there'd been a reluctance to rebuild, afraid the quakes would return and it would all start over again. If attempted, recovery would take decades, if not longer. But some, like the governor, seemed to like things just the way they were, a new world with new opportunities.

* * *

I was graciously allowed to stay home from work today, to spend my last hours with my family and to say our final goodbyes. Sarah and myself sat in our tent with our two children, Chris, now 14, and Cindy, 12, in silence, not knowing how best to spend this final time together. Cindy's eyes were red and moist. For now, she had stopped crying, but her sobs continued to escape at random. Chris remained silent. He knew what was expected of him after I was gone. He would be the man of the family.

Sarah leaned against me, wrapping her arms around my arm. This was not how I wanted to spend my last hours with them. I thought about suggesting we go for a walk, but decided against it. I didn't want to spend our final time together outside where our neighbors would be able to watch and pity our situation. I preferred our remaining time to be joyful and meaningful, and private.

I began to tell stories about the happy times I recalled

about our children as they were growing up. The stories were bringing smiles to all their faces and the mood in the tent began to change for the better. Soon we were all exchanging stories, laughing and enjoying ourselves. This was how I wanted to spend our final hours together.

Sarah was only a few months younger than me, but since children were involved, she would be given a reprieve when she reached the age limit. She would be allowed to stay in Sector 4 an additional two years and continue to work in the fields until our youngest, Cindy, reached the age of fourteen, the age when all children graduated to adulthood and were placed into the workforce. At that time, Sarah's future, and fate, would be the same as it was going to be for me.

*   *   *

Sarah and I stayed up late into the evening recollecting the wonderful life we'd shared together and with our children. We had been so happy at our home before the quakes, and had been so disappointed on our arrival here. When our car had run out of gas, we'd been forced to abandon it on the edge of the road with all the others, having to walk the last ten miles. Our hopes had vanished as the prison had come into view. The prison and the surrounding grounds had already become crowded and overflowing with people just like us, looking for the promise of a safe haven.

"I'm sorry," I told Sarah. "If I hadn't decided …"

"Don't," she was quick to say. "We both chose to come here."

PARADISE

I looked into her eyes and forced a weak smile. I didn't want to argue, but I knew it had been my fault, my decision to come here. My gut had told me not to. We should have stayed near our hometown. In hindsight, I would have preferred to have attempted survival there somehow.

Sarah changed the subject, helping me remember some of the good things I had forgotten from long ago. And it helped talking about the kids. We hadn't talked like this in quite a while. I'm not sure why. I guess life had just gotten in the way. It was a shame the threat of death was the element bringing us closer. I glanced over at our children. Chris and his sister had fallen asleep earlier while listening to our stories. Sarah and I exchanged a smile at their innocent and peaceful sleep.

Later, Sarah had fallen still and silent as she lay beside me. Her warmth and the sound of her relaxed breathing were comforting, but I wasn't able to sleep. I couldn't help thinking about what awaited me the next day. I glanced over to look at Sarah's face as she slept. She was looking back at me with a smile spreading across her face. From the sliver of moonlight filtering through the tent flap, I could see a small glint of light reflecting off the moisture in her eyes.

As the sky began to lighten ever so slightly, I got up to dress and make final preparations. I looked out the tent flap. It was surprisingly quiet and peaceful outside with the streets empty. I wasn't exactly sure what to expect today, after being taken away. No one had ever come back to tell the tale. The people taken to the wasteland weren't expected to survive, intentionally taken far enough away to make it impossible to return on foot. They were expected to slowly die of dehydration in its dry and harsh environment or suffer at the hands of those who lived there, the Raiders or other scavengers.

The governor showed his mercy by providing an alternate method of death, allowing a person to self-terminate. It was a pill, and said to be pain free and quick with no suffering, which to a few had been the terrifying, but preferable choice. The obvious down side was that it was final, there was no coming back. It wasn't for me. I was no quitter. I was a survivor. Even with being dropped off in the middle of nowhere without adequate resources, as long as there was still even the slightest possibility of survival, I would try.

I was being allowed to take one gallon of water and anything else from a provided list of acceptable items that would fit into my backpack. It was of little consolation. I wouldn't last long after my food supply and water were gone, most likely suffering a long and agonizing death within a matter of a few days. I'd heard of people who had gone up to three weeks with next to no food, but had suffered system shutdown from a lack of water. If I was fortunate enough to last a few days, perhaps it would give me enough time to find a means of survival. In that amount of time I would try anything and everything available to me. I was determined to see my family again, somehow.

The bell at the gate began to clang. Possibly the signal that the governor's men were there. If so, it was sooner than I'd expected. If not, it could be a warning. Even though we were near the prison and guards were posted at the gate, the community still had to protect itself from

PARADISE

marauding bands of criminals, ready to take whatever they could from a weak community with their hit and run tactics. As a precaution, a crude fence and gate had been erected using the Tent City dwellers' abandoned and useless vehicles. The governor had been extremely cooperative in providing aid in the construction. His reason was two-fold, to keep his workers safe from marauders, and to discourage his workers from leaving.

Today, there was little doubt as to why the bell was ringing. The collection and disposal squads were expected and had been seen leaving the prison gates. Hearing the bell and unable to control herself any longer, Sarah broke down, crying uncontrollably, running to and grabbing hold of me with all her might, as though she would never let go. I knew how hard she had tried to remain strong for me and our children, but she wasn't able to keep it hidden any longer. The sound of the bell signaled the reality she had hoped somehow would never come. Cindy joined in the embrace with no attempt to hold back, her tears and sobs flowing freely. I, too, was trying to stay strong for them, but my eyes filled with tears, knowing I would probably never see any of them again. Chris took after me, slow to show emotion. But now, both of us were finding it hard to hold back.

"I have to go," I whispered into Sarah's ear. "I don't want them to have to come and get me."

Sarah loosened her grip and I grabbed my backpack and a blanket to use as a bedroll. I checked the list of acceptable items again for the hundredth time. The list included very few items that would actually be useful; being mostly a list of what was excluded, making the likelihood of survival even more remote. Any kind of weapon was a definite exclusion, but I decided it was worth the risk to attempt to smuggle out a kitchen knife. It wasn't much, but it could be the difference between life and death. Besides, what could they do to me if they found it? I had already been sentenced to death with no chance of reprieve. I rolled it up inside the bedroll.

My family and I left our tent together, walking slowly toward the gate. Our path was lined with neighbors and friends. It had become a tradition of sorts, to say 'thank you' to the person for their sacrifice and to say 'goodbye.' We had stood along this same path many times before. From this perspective there was no comparison. A few of our closest friends were among the few to make eye contact and nod as we passed. Words were not exchanged. There was nothing to say. I held my head up high, facing the likelihood of death in a way I hoped would make my family proud.

Three wagons were waiting outside the gate, two already being loaded with sacks of grain from our summer harvest, the governor's declared taxes. I approached a man holding a clipboard and yelling orders, the one I assumed to be in charge. It was odd the man appeared to be older than I was, an obvious perk of working for the governor. The man looked up from his clipboard and then looked me over from head to toe.

"Name," he asked.

"John Thomas."

The man looked down his list, showing acknowledgement and making a checkmark.

He looked over my family and then looked directly at

PARADISE

the children. Leaning down slightly and smiling, "You know, you should be very proud of your dad. He's making a very necessary sacrifice to make sure you get enough to eat."

The children didn't make any response, only staring back at him with hatred in their eyes. They were old enough to realize he was taking their dad away forever.

He looked at me, his smile quickly disappearing and with a jerk of his head told me to say my final goodbyes and get in the wagon. They were almost loaded and they would be leaving soon. Cindy began to cry again. We all hugged and kissed for the last time. I pulled away as Sarah kept her arms around the shoulders of our children.

I knelt down to Chris and Cindy.

"I know what they say, that this is the end. But I don't want you to count me out yet. Whatever it takes, I'll do everything in my power to be with you again. Okay?"

They nodded slightly.

The leader was standing nearby; close enough to hear my remarks. He smiled and shook his head, almost imperceptibly, but just enough for me to notice. I imagine the man had heard those same or similar words come from the mouths of countless others and was probably amazed and amused that there were so many who believed they could survive.

"Third wagon. Make yourself comfortable."

I gave Sarah one last kiss and embrace then walked over to the wagon and climbed into the back, seeing three others were already there. I exchanged awkward smiles with two of them and gave them a nod as I entered. There were two men and one woman. The woman hadn't looked up, sitting in silence with no show of emotion. She looked too young to be here. I noticed she wore a wedding ring. There either was or had been a man in her life. Perhaps he had already been taken away. If she was older than him and they hadn't had any children, it was possible that she could go first. Another explanation could be that if she had had children, they could have already reached the age for the workforce. Either way, it wasn't any of my business. There would be plenty of time to talk on our trip to the wasteland, if any of them felt like it. I didn't know any of them by name, but the faces were familiar. At the moment, introductions seemed pointless. I took a seat on the floor of the wagon next to the men. From some distance away, we became aware of a man screaming, getting louder as he came closer. Two of the disposal squad appeared at the back of the wagon, dragging the man between them, hands bound.

"Please don't make me go! I'll do anything! I'm not ready to die!" he screamed, trying to break free from his escorts while kicking at the wagon, trying to brace himself from being lifted inside.

Having had enough, one of the disposal team clubbed him over the head, knocking him unconscious. The two men then picked him up and tossed him into the back of the wagon followed by his bag, closing and latching the backboard. They had left his hands bound. The woman moved quickly to his side, sitting on the floor and cradling his head in her lap.

"A friend of yours?" I asked.

She shook her head slowly. "No. I've never seen him before," she said softly.

PARADISE

As I watched the woman comfort the man, I thought about the words the man had screamed out. I had thought the very same words, but had kept them inside. There was no use in fighting what was happening, what was inevitable. And suppose I had considered putting up a fight, would there be consequences that would affect my family? I couldn't risk it.

I heard the leader tell the others to get ready to leave. Almost immediately I heard the words "Move out!" and the wagon lurched forward. The two wagons carrying the governor's share of the grain split off from the disposal wagon, immediately returning to the prison compound. As our wagon circled away from the gate to leave, I could see the crowd of family and friends who had come to the gate to wave and say their goodbyes for one last time. Over the sounds of the creaking wagon, I continued to hear loud crying and screaming from loved ones well after leaving the gate behind, but then they ended abruptly, presumably from the gate being closed behind us. At that instant I was unexpectedly filled with an all-consuming emptiness and overwhelming doom. Tears welled up in my eyes. I turned my head so the others couldn't see.

* * *

Chapter 3

So far, our journey to the wasteland disposal site had taken a week, mostly in silence. And all of our questions to the three-man disposal team had gone unanswered. The man who had gone berserk on day one had regained consciousness that same afternoon and since then had remained fairly calm, apparently coming to terms with his predicament. The leader of the team had the man's bindings removed, no longer deemed necessary.

Only five of us were being taken away this quarter, a far cry from the numbers taken in the past. The first trips had included multiple wagons, each crowded with unfortunate souls. This was either an off quarter, or the number of those reaching forty was dwindling.

We had traveled in a southwesterly direction, but I wasn't sure how far it had been. My guess would be between fifteen to twenty miles per day, depending on the

PARADISE

changes in terrain and how often we stopped to rest and water the horses.

The wagon stopped unexpectedly mid-afternoon and I was almost glad. The heat inside the enclosed wagon had been unbearable, each of us drenched in sweat and beginning to smell fairly ripe. My traveling companions and I were instructed to unload with our possessions. We exchanged looks, assuming this to be the end of the road. We stepped out into the scorching and bright sun to see a flat, sandy, and essentially barren landscape in all directions as far as the eye could see. A slight breeze against our sweat soaked clothing gave us a brief moment of relief.

Individually, we were taken away from the group and searched, both in our clothing and in our bags. It appeared all of my companions had followed the rules. The man frisking me nodded to the leader that I was okay. I smiled inwardly. I had gotten away with hiding the knife. The leader waived for me to rejoin the group, but the other man grabbed my bedroll, untying the binding.

"I almost forgot about this," he said, looking for a reaction. I didn't give him the satisfaction.

When he rolled it out, the knife fell to the ground. There was no point in denying it was mine.

"Wait here!" demanded the man, running to the front of the wagon. The other man pulled his side arm as he kept watch over me.

The first man came back with the leader. "There's no need for that. Put it away," he said to the man with the gun.

"Mr. Thomas. It appears you're not able to follow the rules, no doubt a troublemaker. We have come up with a way of dealing with your type. Take off your clothes."

I looked at him with disbelief.

"I can't survive out here without any clothes," I replied.

"That's the whole point of this exercise, now isn't it? Do it!"

"I don't think so."

"Either you do it yourself or I'll have these two men help you. You might as well cooperate. It's going to happen."

I looked at the others for support. They remained silent, sheepishly looking at the ground, refusing eye contact, not wanting the same to happen to them.

"Fine!" I spewed out.

I began by removing my boots.

"You can put your boots back on after you've stripped. It's not like we're savages." His men snickered. I swung around catching the closest man squarely in the nose, drawing blood immediately as the man fell backward, hard to the ground. The other man quickly stepped in before I could react, clubbing me with his rifle butt along the side of my head, dropping me to my knees.

"Now, if you don't mind, off with the clothes," redirected the leader.

Slowly, I stood and disrobed. Then, standing butt naked, I slipped my boots back on. I'm sure I was a sight. I glanced at our woman member, Jill. Gratefully, she had turned away. I reached down for my bedroll.

"Sorry, John. That's part of your punishment, too. You won't need your bedroll after a couple of days out here anyway."

PARADISE

"Then what's the point of taking it and my clothes?"

"The rules have to be followed, John."

"No one's going to know. Besides, according to you, we're all going to be dead soon anyway."

The berserk man, who we now knew as Paul, had a relapse and fell to the ground sobbing. The woman, who had been silent for the last three days, except to tell us her name, knelt down to comfort him.

"True," said the leader, "however, my men and I would know and I can't jeopardize their integrity. I'm sure you can understand. So, I think we'll say goodbye here. John, even though you pulled that stunt, I'm going to let you keep the provisions you brought." He paused.

I had to bite my tongue to keep from giving him an excuse to change his mind. I almost felt as though he was baiting me, hoping I'd say something.

He continued, "We won't be seeing each other again, so I'd like to take this opportunity to thank you for your sacrifice." He flashed us a large, toothy smile.

I wondered how many times he'd delivered that same little farewell speech.

"Don't count on never seeing us again," I said. "By the way, what's your name? I want to know who to come looking for when I get back."

The leader seemed to smile with amusement. "Morgan. If you do happen to make it, it'll be a pleasure to see you again, Mr. Thomas. Good luck, or rather goodbye." He began walking back to the front of the wagon. "Let's go, men!"

In a matter of only a few minutes, all five of us were standing alone, watching the wagon make a large half-circle as it turned to return to what they called civilization. Paul, now recovered with Jill's help, reached into his bag and pulled out an extra shirt, handing it to me, catching me completely by surprise.

"You're going to need this," he said.

"Thanks."

"My pleasure," he said. "I guess we need to look out for each other, at least for a little while."

I placed it around my waist, fastened some of the buttons, and tied the sleeves together, creating a skirt of sorts. It wasn't pretty, but it was functional. And it protected the one place where I didn't relish getting a sunburn. I was pretty sure Jill appreciated it too, not running around with my altogether hanging out.

"Where to now?" asked Gary, one of the other men. We all looked along the horizon in all directions. There was no sign of life, it was mid-afternoon, and the sun was beating down on us. It felt like it was 100 degrees and then some, without a hint of a breeze. Our surroundings were dry and barren with sparse vegetation consisting of cactus, yucca, and the occasional mesquite. There was complete silence and not a bird in the sky. It was as though we had been dropped off in a dead zone.

"We've been heading southwest for the past week, anyone have a problem with heading due west?" I asked. "It appears there may be some hills in that direction along the horizon."

"Any other reason why we should go in that direction?" asked Dan, our other male companion.

"None whatsoever," I said. "I just don't think there's a reason to keep going south. I do have another question we

PARADISE

need to discuss though."

"What's that?" asked Gary.

"Do we want to stick together or does anyone want to strike out on their own?"

My companions exchanged looks, but no one spoke up.

"Stick together?" I asked. Each nodded in agreement. "Okay then, we should probably keep our eyes open for some sort of shelter before dark."

* * *

After walking for two hours, we stopped to rest. The terrain was exactly the same as where we'd been dropped off, without a single tree in sight. We hadn't seen wildlife of any type either, not even a lizard or a vulture circling overhead. And the hills in the distance didn't appear to be getting any closer. The sun beat down on us mercilessly, and without any sign of shade, there didn't appear to be any hope of relief. Our water wouldn't last long under these conditions. Each of us was already showing the effects from the heat and the sun's direct deadly rays, especially me, already turning a bright shade of red where I was exposed from the waist up.

Paul noticed. "I'm sorry I don't have another shirt for you."

"I'm just glad to have this one, or I'd be suffering a whole lot worse."

Since sunset was drawing near, we decided this was as good a place as any to stop and make camp for the night. The setting sun would give us an evening of reprieve from its heat. We placed our possessions together near a small mesquite bush and split up to search for something to burn in the campfire. Once the sun went down, the temperature would begin to cool off quickly. Then we'd need to worry about staying warm. We set out in different directions to search for anything that would burn. Finding very little, each of our group did return with something, consisting mostly of dried dead weeds and a few twigs from mesquite bushes. I had been lucky, finding several long-dried-out cow patties that would burn slow, provide some heat, and having little to no smell. It was evident cattle had grazed the area at some time in the past, most likely wild ones since no rancher in his right mind would intentionally put cattle on ground like this.

The fire started easily with the extremely dry tinder. Thanks to Sarah's suggestion, I had brought matches, which was fortunate, because no one else had. She had always been a good planner. Thankfully, they had been one of the acceptable items on the list.

Not knowing how long we would last under the scorching sun, we were still optimistic enough to ration our provisions, wanting them to last as long as possible. There wasn't much diversity in what we'd brought, or more correctly, what we'd been allowed to bring.

The sun had zapped us pretty good resulting in mild cases of heat exhaustion, a loss of appetite, and mild nagging headaches, but we nibbled a little anyway to keep up our strength. Dead tired, we settled in around the fire, looking forward to resting and recuperating. We each sat in silence, staring into the crackling fire. We had agreed to keep it small, not wanting to draw attention to ourselves,

PARADISE

not knowing who or what lived out here.

In the brief time we'd been thrown together, I came to believe every member of the group had the willpower to fight to stay alive. No one seemed ready to give up, lie down, and die. We decided to take turns tending the fire and to keep watch. Watching for what, we didn't know. Perhaps the Raider's territory extended this far. And if it did, rumor was that they were a ruthless and dangerous bunch of cutthroats. Fortunately, we hadn't seen anything or anyone, dangerous or otherwise, all day. I took the first watch.

None of the group felt they would be able to sleep even after spending a week in the wagon and walking in today's relentless beating sun, but the journey had taken its toll. I watched as each of them eventually nodded off. My watch was quiet and uneventful. Paul volunteered for the second watch, telling me to get some sleep. He didn't have to tell me twice. I must have gone to sleep as soon as I closed my eyes.

The next thing I knew I was waking up and the eastern sky was just beginning to lighten. I noticed immediately that the fire had been allowed to go out during the night. The coals were still slightly warm. I wasn't sure who'd taken the last watch and I wasn't going to accuse anyone for the mistake. As tired as we had been, it could have happened to any one of us. I did a quick head count. One of our group was missing. Paul.

"Has anyone seen Paul?" I asked.

The others sat up and looked around, then shook their heads.

"His bag is still here," Jill pointed out. "Maybe he's

taking care of his business."

"Maybe."

We had a bite to eat and a sip of water while waiting for Paul to return. Refreshed from a well needed rest, our hunger returned, but not knowing what lay ahead we decided rationing was still the right thing to do.

There was still no sign of Paul after half an hour. It was time to do something instead of just sitting around.

"Let's split up and take a look around to see if we can find Paul or at least try to determine which way he went," I suggested.

"Let's do it," agreed Gary.

"I don't know what good it's going to do," grumbled Dan. "We made footprints all over out there when we were looking for something to burn."

Dan was right. It would be hard to determine whose footprints belonged to whom. The sandy soil didn't reveal a distinctive footprint, only a slight depression where each of them had taken a step.

"Don't you want to find out what happened to Paul?" asked Jill, not understanding his attitude.

Dan didn't answer.

"Let's check the perimeter further out from the campsite," I suggested. "Work progressively bigger circles. Yell out if you see anything."

After only five minutes, Gary called out. "I think he may have come this way," waving us over. We all gathered there to take a look. The footprints were leading directly away from their campsite in a straight line back to the south. Though we couldn't be sure, it was a pretty good guess it had been Paul.

PARADISE

"First, I don't understand why he would take off and leave all his provisions behind, and secondly, why would he go south?" I asked.

"I think I know," said Jill. "I saw indications and should have said something, but I didn't think he would do this."

"What do you mean?" I asked.

"I think it's obvious," said Jill. "He gave up. He went south to die, because we had concluded that direction to be the worst way to go. And he left his provisions for us, to help us survive."

It was looking like I'd been wrong about Paul coming around.

We stood in silence looking at the depressions in the sand, letting what Jill had just said sink in. Had Paul actually sacrificed himself for us?

"I didn't see this coming," I commented. "What do you want to do now?" I asked the group. "Keep moving in the direction we'd been going or try to catch up with Paul and perhaps save his life, even if only temporarily?"

"I say if he wants to kill himself, let him," said Dan.

"Dan, that's a terrible thing to say," rebuked Jill.

"I'm being honest. It's just the way I feel," he said with a shrug. "We'll all probably be dead along with him before long."

"If you believe that, then I guess it doesn't really matter which way we go, does it," I pointed out. "So, why not go south after Paul. If it comes to it, he shouldn't die alone."

"I agree," said Jill. "South."

"I'm game," agreed Gary.

I looked at Dan, wanting his approval, preferring we were all in agreement.

"Like I said, we're all going to die anyway, so sure, whatever you guys want to do. I'll go along."

We went back to our campsite, collected our possessions, and headed south. None of the group was overly optimistic about finding Paul alive. Making the assumption that he'd left as soon as everyone was asleep, he had a good head start. If he had truly given up, who knew what actions he might have already taken.

Our group followed what we believed was Paul's trail for nearly two hours until the unexpected happened. His footprints were joined by others and wagon tracks. Our first thought was that the disposal team had come across him and had taken him again. But that didn't make any sense. The whole purpose of bringing us out here was to let us die, not to rescue us.

Now, our group had another choice to make since Paul no longer appeared to be alone. We needed to decide whether to risk continuing to follow Paul and whoever had picked him up or return to our westerly course. There was a risk in either direction, with no way of knowing if one was any better than the other. As a group, we decided to follow the wagon, more out of curiosity about Paul than anything else. There was also the chance his new companions could be friendly and help us too. It didn't make any sense to think they were the ones who had dropped us off.

We followed the wagon tracks for two days. We had agreed from the beginning to share what we had, but with each person's rations running dangerously low, it was becoming irrelevant. Dan had grumbled about sharing his resources from day one, but his attitude had changed as they ran low, having brought less than anyone else. And contrary to Dan's wishes, we had initially left Paul's pack alone, knowing he would need whatever was in it if and when we caught up to him. But after learning he was no longer on his own, we had given in. There hadn't been much variety in our provisions, only what had been allowed.

Surprisingly, however, Paul had come better prepared than any of us. His pack included such delicacies as nuts, dried fruit, candy bars, and tins of specialty items usually reserved for the privileged, like canned peaches. It was obvious he had had connections, but even he couldn't escape complying with the forty year age limit. Perhaps that had been the reason for his 'fit' on the first day, believing he was exempt. We were glad there was still some equality left in the world, but we were sorry for Paul. We had gotten to know him and liked him. I assumed he had been allowed to bring these specialty items as some sort of a consolation.

On the third day, the tracks turned toward to the east. We were now completely out of food and had very little water. The outlook was grim. We continually attempted to encourage each other to keep going, hoping the wagon we were trailing still led to help or rescue. We began to wonder why we should keep going. Jill, the optimist of the group, reminded us there was always hope as long as we were still alive. With her repeated words of encouragement, she refused to let us give up.

As the sun began to set, I was surprised to see what I

thought was a covered wagon in the distance, directly ahead. I didn't trust my eyes, asking the others to take a look. The object was distorted through the rising heat waves, but we all saw something. It gave each of us hope and a boost of energy as we picked up the pace. We hoped it was the wagon we'd been following.

As we came closer, we agreed, it appeared to be a wagon very much like the one that had dropped us off a few days earlier and now it was stopped. Perhaps we had been wrong to dismiss the notion it was the disposal team's. But why would they be out here, headed in this direction? Where could they be going? We approached cautiously. With evening approaching, we assumed they had stopped for the night. As we approached, an individual, a man, appeared from within the wagon, lowered himself to the ground and turned to face us.

"Paul?!" yelled Jill, afraid her eyes were playing tricks on her.

Paul smiled and waved. "It's good to see you, old friends."

He appeared to be in good health and even better, in good spirits. Then, as we came up close, two men stepped out from the front of the wagon and joined Paul. We came to an abrupt stop approximately fifty feet from them. Both seemed to be friendly with broad smiles on their faces. And we were relieved to see they weren't in uniform as the disposal team would have been. They were dressed simply with dark pants, white shirts, and wide-brimmed black hats. And they were old, both with full gray beards. I hadn't seen anyone of their age in four years. The senior residents of Tent City had begun to disappear soon after

PARADISE

we'd reached Sector 4. We'd heard rumors that all the older people had been taken to other sectors where they could be cared for more easily. Then the governor had implemented his disposal plan and it didn't take much of an imagination to figure out what had actually happened.

"We've been waiting for you," one of them said.

"I knew something like this was going to happen," mumbled Dan, as if to say 'I told you so.'

"You knew *what* was going to happen?" I asked, turning on him, tired of his attitude. "Nothing has happened yet."

"He's right, Dan," said Jill. "We came looking for Paul and we found him. So, what are we waiting for? Maybe they have something to eat."

One of the men motioned for us to join them. Still hesitant, Paul called out, "It's all right. C'mon. They're friends."

"We might as well," said Gary. "What else are we going to do and I could use something to drink and eat."

We moved forward in unison. Jill, the least concerned about any danger, took the lead. We had become fairly well bonded for the short time we had been together. Relying on each other for survival would do that. Jill ran up to Paul and gave him a hug. I could see by the expression on his face that he had been caught completely off guard by her and taken aback a little. Overcoming his initial surprise, he returned the hug, a huge smile appearing. The two men watched, also smiling, recognizing and appreciating the joy of the reunion.

One of the men extended his hand to me. "Hello. My name is Samuel and this is Eli."

It seemed as though a barrier had just come down. We all began to exchange handshakes. Paul continued with the introductions.

"We saw people behind us when we stopped to water and care for the horses," explained Eli. "Paul was sure it was you. Until then we didn't know anyone was behind us. When we found Paul, he was in pretty bad shape. It wasn't until the next day, after he'd recovered from dehydration, that he mentioned he had been with friends. But by then it was too late to turn back."

"I'm sorry, guys," replied Paul.

"Care to join our little group?" asked Samuel.

"Of course," I said. "Out of curiosity, where are you headed? I didn't think there was anything out this way."

"A place where you are welcomed and where you'll be safe," responded Samuel.

We were given apples to eat and all the water we wanted before climbing into the back of the wagon with Paul. Apples, or fruit of any kind, had been another delicacy reserved for the privileged, a favored group of the governor's friends and select staff members. None of us had had any kind of fruit since moving into Tent City. We savored every mouth-watering bite.

As the wagon began to move, Jill anxiously asked, "Paul, why did you take off like that?"

"I just wanted it to end. I believed it was inevitable anyway, so why prolong it."

An uncomfortable silence followed. Each of us had been forced to deal with what was intended to happen, each in our own way.

Then Paul, smiling from ear to ear, sat up straight,

PARADISE

"But, now I'm not worried any more."

"How did you end up with these guys?" I asked.

"I had fallen to my knees, thirsty, tired, and not wanting to take another step, waiting for the end to come, praying it would come swiftly. Then I heard a wagon creak as it came up behind me, and then stopped. I raised my head to see Samuel and Eli standing over me. I thought they were angels coming to take me away and I was ready. I think I must have passed out." Paul paused, head bowing, tears coming to his eyes. He looked up at the group. "Sorry." He took a deep breath as he wiped the tears away. "When I came to, I was in the back of this wagon. It took awhile, but they finally convinced me they weren't angels. Funny, isn't it? They told me later I had been a little delirious. Samuel assured me they would take care of me and get me somewhere safe, and here we are. They saved my life."

"And you saved ours. If you hadn't left your provisions behind, we might not be here," said Jill.

"I wasn't going to need them," said Paul. "And I knew you could."

"That was very dumb of you, Paul, but thank you," said Jill, placing a comforting hand on his.

Dan opened his mouth and started to say something, but I gave him a look that let him know to keep it to himself. This was no time for grumbling or some smart-ass remark. It was a time of thanksgiving. Our deaths had been postponed for at least another day thanks to Eli and Samuel.

We traveled two more days. On the second day at mid-afternoon the wagon came to a stop. Our group assumed it was to care for the horses since it was about the same time we had stopped each day. We exited the wagon to stretch our legs.

"Come and see," said Eli, motioning for us to join him. He had a look on his face and a twinkle in his eyes we had not seen before. It appeared to be pure happiness. Whatever it was he wanted us to see had to be something special.

When we reached his and Samuel's sides we understood why. The dry and desolate desert dropped away to a valley nothing less than a green paradise. In the valley we could see a small settlement with a lake, surrounded by farm plots and trees.

"Welcome to Paradise," said Samuel, with a sweeping motion of his arm, "your new home."

*   *   *

Chapter 4

We could see across the expanse of the valley to the other side, perhaps half a mile, to where the landscape returned to the same desolate type of land as where we were standing. Below was an unexpected oasis in this barren wasteland, easily overlooked by anyone passing by. We stood awestruck and in a daze for I'm not sure how long, attempting to take it all in, not knowing a place like this still existed.

Samuel interrupted our trance-like state, "How about a closer look?" It was a redundant question. He knew our answer by just looking at our expressions of wonder, beaming with excitement and anxious to see everything up close.

We climbed back into the wagon and within minutes we were descending into the valley along a series of switchbacks. We couldn't believe our good fortune, first of all, knowing we probably would have been dead by now if it hadn't been for Samuel and Eli, and secondly, to be brought to a place like this. Once we reached the bottom and proceeded toward the town, we could see, through the back opening of the wagon, men and women of all ages coming toward us, many who were well past their fortieth birthday. And best of all, there were children of all ages. Newborns had been a rare observance at Tent City. None had wanted to give birth and raise a child in that environment.

The growing crowd shouted greetings to Samuel and Eli, thankful for their safe return. They followed the wagon as it continued to roll on. All appeared to be very glad to see us as well, smiling and waving with repeated shouts of "Welcome!"

From the greeting we were receiving, it must have been a rare occurrence for the community to see outsiders. There was excitement and celebration in the streets. But, no matter how perfect this place appeared, it occurred to me how separated and isolated they were from the rest of the world, such as it was. Though the valley was an obvious paradise and sanctuary at first glance, I couldn't help thinking how some might see it as confinement. Once here, where could one go. I hoped I wasn't becoming a pessimist like Dan.

The valley was amazing and beautiful with huge mature trees providing a shady canopy over a central lane, with green grass, a couple dozen small houses, and a small lake. A picture-perfect postcard community, reminding me of the home I'd known years ago before the earthquakes had destroyed it all. The big difference was that this

PARADISE

postcard appeared to have been taken in the 1850's.

There was no sign of overhead utilities with no electric or telephone lines cluttering up the skies, and no motorized vehicles, only horse-drawn carts and wagons. But, on closer examination, small wind turbines could be seen on many of the rooftops, evidence that the community did have electricity, an extremely useful commodity.

We came to a stop and the crowd was quick to gather at the back of the wagon, joined by Samuel and Eli.

"Okay, give them room," said Samuel, motioning for us to climb down. "C'mon out folks. This is it."

As we came into the sunlight and stood at the back of the wagon, Samuel introduced us to those gathered nearby, explaining how they'd obviously been successful on their journey. He encouraged other members of the group to introduce themselves in the days to come. Then he asked us to follow him. As we did, members of the crowd patted us on the back and told us how glad they were we had been found and were safe. At Samuel's request, the crowd began to disperse to go about their own business. Samuel and Eli led us up to a rustic two-story building in the center of town with the words 'Town Hall' carved into a wooden plaque. I paused a second outside the door, looking and listening all around. The town was surprisingly quiet and peaceful, with only the sound of a breeze through the rustling leaves of the trees and the sounds of children playing. Inside was a long wooden plank table in the center of the large room, surrounded by hand-crafted wooden chairs. Two globe lanterns were burning on each end of the table. There were no windows.

"Sorry, we haven't added electricity to our new Town

Hall yet," said Samuel. "Please, have a seat."

A short plump woman entered the room. She was dressed like many of the women we'd seen earlier with a dark colored dress and a white head covering. Like everyone else we'd met, she smiled warmly toward us, as though she was genuinely glad we were there. She remained silent as Samuel introduced her as Emma, his wife, and she curtsied, making me smile.

"Emma, could you bring our new friends something to eat and drink?" asked Samuel. "I'm sure they're famished from their journey." She nodded and left the room.

"First of all, let me say welcome to our little community and you're welcome to stay as long as you like. However, there are certain conditions you need to be made aware of."

We all exchanged looks of concern. Dan was nodding slightly, mumbling repeatedly, "Here it comes, here it comes."

"Dan!" I whispered loudly, shaking my head once I had gotten his attention.

"Everyone is expected to contribute by helping out in some way, whether it's with the crops, providing some service, or applying your time to a beneficial craft. We are firm believers that idle hands are indeed the devil's workshop. Can we agree?" asked Samuel.

Jill raised her hand, which amused Samuel and Eli. "There's no need for that. What would you like to know?" asked Samuel.

"Did you ..."

"What if we don't want to stay?" asked Dan, cutting Jill off.

PARADISE

"You're free to leave whenever you like," answered Eli, "but I think you'll find that there's no reason to do so and besides, there's nowhere else to go, not within walking distance anyway."

Dan fell silent, appearing to be thinking it over.

"Like I was about to ask," continued Jill, "did you know we would be out there?"

"Not you specifically, but yes, we knew someone would be dropped off."

"How?" I asked.

"From my son, Ryder," said Samuel.

"And how did your son find out?" I asked.

"He was a member of the Guard when the governor's plan was announced."

"Your son is in the Guard?" I asked with surprise. How could anyone leave a place like this for that cesspool?

"*Was* in the Guard," Samuel clarified. "Let me start from the beginning. Ryder left the valley about five years ago, restless and anxious to see what he was missing in the outside world, ending up at the governor's compound, enticed into joining his Guard. I guess it sounded exciting at the time. While there, he discovered he had access to the stockpiles of supplies hoarded in the lower level of the prison, and never distributed. So, he began to remove small amounts of the things we needed the most, like medical supplies, and smuggled them to us. I objected to the risk he was taking, but he wouldn't take no for an answer. Ryder had rationalized that the stored items were for the people and he was just helping to distribute them, without the governor's knowledge of course. After having success the first time, we started making a trip there every six months."

"It was during one of the first supply runs four years ago Ryder told us about the governor's forty-year death sentence and that the people would be dropped off to die every three months at or near where we found Paul."

Eli began to shake his head. It was obvious he still couldn't believe it. Samuel continued, "At first, we didn't know whether it could be true or not. It sounded too crazy. Who would believe people were intentionally being taken out in the middle of nowhere and left to die of thirst and starvation at any age, much less at forty, in the prime of life?"

"It was decided then," said Samuel, "to try to save as many of those people as we could, so we began to make our supply run every six months to coincide as best we could with the one of the disposal team. The first time out we failed, but we have continued to try. This was only the second time for us to be successful. That's one reason why everyone was so glad to see you. It's a miracle that we found you."

"Thank you for continuing to look for survivors. We owe you our lives," said Jill.

"I must give credit where credit is due," said Samuel. "We had help. Since we never know exactly when or where it'll take place, there was a lot of faith and prayer involved in finding you. All we know is it happens every three months around the first of the month, in the same general area. It would seem this time our prayers were answered."

"Then your son is no longer with the Guard?" Jill asked.

"That's right. After the enchantment had worn off and

PARADISE

Ryder had had his fill of the injustices being carried out by the governor, he decided to leave, to live in the wasteland. But before he left the Guard, he made sure someone he could trust was in place to continue with what he had started, by helping us. Ryder now lives in the wasteland with quite a following. He's found his purpose and accomplished some great things."

I could see the pride in his eyes.

"So, are there other people here from Sector 4?" I asked.

Samuel smiled warmly. "There are a few people living here who were once in your same predicament, brought out to the wasteland to die. Those were the first ones we picked up. As I said before, sometimes our prayers are answered as we'd like, sometimes they aren't."

"And you've been doing this every six months for four years?" Jill asked.

"That's right, ever since we were informed by Ryder," answered Eli, looking to and receiving a nod of confirmation from Samuel.

It occurred to me, if they made a supply run every six months and the disposal team went out every three months, there were two trips every year when the people had no chance of rescue, forced to survive on their own or die. "Have you considered going out there the other two times of the year?"

"Of course we have. But, it takes time, manpower, and supplies to take on one of those searches. And those are resources we don't always have." He paused. "I know it sounds callous, but we're trying to survive with a growing community the best way we can with the resources we have."

I nodded that I understood. I didn't want to sound critical. After all, he had just saved our lives and we were extremely grateful.

Dan wasn't through. "In the last four years, has anyone ever left?"

"Yes, there've been a few," answered Samuel, without elaborating.

"And?" pressured Dan.

"We don't know. We never saw them again," answered Samuel.

"So, then, as far as you know, they safely made it out of here," continued Dan.

Dan was beginning to get on my nerves, again. "Even if you decided to leave," I confronted, "where would you go? If you, by some miracle, made it back to Sector 4, don't you think they'd just send you out here again or shoot you on the spot? Can't you get it through your thick skull, they don't want us anymore?"

"I just like to know what my options are," said Dan, trying to justify himself. "I don't want to feel trapped, which is exactly how I'm beginning to feel now."

Jill felt he was being rude to their hosts. "Dan, what you should be doing is thanking these people for saving us. Without them, we could very well be lying dead or dying out there right now."

"She's right," added Paul. "As for myself, I couldn't be happier. It's quite a realization to have given up and know you're about to die and then be rescued by two guardian angels." He smiled at Samuel and Eli and they nodded in return. "I've been given a second chance and

PARADISE

I'm better off now than I was at Sector 4. I'm not afraid here. As long as they'll have me, I'm staying."

Feeling as though he was being ganged up on, Dan blurted out, "Who the hell do you people think you are to tell me what to think or what to do?"

"That's enough!" exclaimed Samuel firmly, slamming his hand down on the table, looking angrily into Dan's eyes. Dan flinched and drew back. This was the first time for any of us to see this no-nonsense side of Samuel. "Profanity is something not to be tolerated here. It is one of the things, if done repeatedly and without regard for others, that will lead to you being asked to leave. And you should also know slothfulness will not be permitted here either." He continued to look at Dan. I wasn't sure how, but in our short time here, it appeared he already suspected Dan of having that character trait. "We are a God fearing people and we attempt to live according to his word. If you can live within his guidelines, you're welcome to stay. If not, we'll provide you with provisions, wish you well, and send you on your way."

There was an uncomfortable moment of silence.

"How tolerant are you?" I asked, breaking the silence. I knew my own shortcomings and knew from time to time I was likely to slip and step outside the rules, even though it would probably be unintentional.

Before Samuel could answer, Gary, who had been sitting still and quiet all this time, spoke up, "You mean to say if anyone breaks your rules they are asked to leave?"

"They're not my rules. But, to answer John's question, we are a tolerant people. No one is perfect and mistakes will be made. To paraphrase the scriptures, no man is without sin. For the infrequent indiscretion, forgiveness is the first choice. However, if the act is committed repeatedly, without any sign of remorse, the person will be asked to leave. The saying that one rotten apple spoils the entire barrel is an old one, but an accurate one. We'd like to keep that very thing from happening here."

Emma entered the room followed by two other women. They were carrying bowls, a cast iron pot, fresh bread in a basket, and a pitcher of water with glasses.

"Looks like your meal is here," commented Samuel. "We'll leave you so you can eat and talk freely. We'll be back in a little while to show you where you will be sleeping tonight. Enjoy. Emma is an excellent cook." Her cheeks blushed a bright red from the compliment.

The food had been left on the table. I lifted the lid on the pot to see a stew with an aroma that made my mouth begin to water. At that moment I realized how famished I really was. A smile even came to Dan's face. If it tasted only half as good as it smelled, it would be the best thing I'd ever put in my mouth. We each grabbed a bowl and dug in. With the fresh bread the ladies had brought and what I assumed was freshly churned butter, it was a meal fit for a king. The stew had chunks of potato, carrot, tomato, and some sort of meat. We believed it was beef, but we couldn't be sure. It had been years since any of us had had any kind of real meat.

Soon after arrival at Sector 4, supplies had begun to diminish as demand grew, with rationing quickly excluded meat of any kind. But, according to rumors, beef, pork, and chicken were still going to the rich, the only ones who could afford the governor's prices.

PARADISE

There was silence around the table as we all dug in to the best meal any of us had had since arriving at Sector 4. When we asked Paul about the availability of meat in his former life, he didn't seem to want to talk about it. By some of the items we'd seen in his bag, we had presumed he had been one of the privileged back there and probably had access to such things. We didn't push the issue. Perhaps he didn't want to come across as a braggart.

No one seemed anxious to be the first to start a discussion about our current circumstance, but some things needed to be discussed before Samuel returned.

I decided to break the ice. "We came here as a group, but I think each of us should make up their own mind on whether to stay or go. I for one am glad to be here and I think I can live with their rules. So, I'm willing to give this place a chance. Besides, the alternative isn't very appealing."

"I think you already know how I feel," said Paul. "I'm staying."

"Me too," said Jill.

"And me," said Gary. "I don't see an option. I'm not willing to head across country into the same wasteland we were just rescued from and just hope for another place like this."

"I'd like to keep an open mind though," I added. "If another opportunity presents itself, I'm not opposed to looking at it. How about you, Dan?"

"I haven't decided yet. I don't like the idea of having to live by their rules or being told what I can and can't do."

"From what I can see, it's still better than where we just came from," I offered. "And I know for a fact you were told what to do there too." I hadn't known Dan very long, but I could make an educated guess that he had been a complainer back at his hometown as well, never satisfied. And nothing I said was going to change that. His attitude would most likely be the same no matter where he was, whether there were rules to follow or not. He would most likely always find something wrong.

Samuel entered the room. "If you've finished with your meal, I'll show you to where you'll be sleeping. I'm sure you're all tired. We can talk further in the morning. Please follow me." He picked up one of the lanterns.

We were led to a closed door at the rear of the room. Samuel opened it, revealing a rustic staircase leading upstairs. The procession of shoes and boots on the wooden stairs created a series of loud clunking hollow sounds as we climbed to the next floor. At the top of the stairs Samuel opened another door revealing a large open room with two rows of cots. It wasn't exactly what we had been expecting, but it was still a vast improvement from sleeping outside on the ground.

"Hope you all have a restful sleep and I'll see you in the morning for breakfast," said Samuel, setting the lantern on a small table. He turned and left, closing the door behind him, followed by the sound of the door being locked from the outside.

We all exchanged looks of surprise at the unexpected act.

Dan rushed to the door and pulled hard on the handle, but it refused to budge. We looked around the room, noticing for the first time there weren't any windows here either.

PARADISE

"I knew this was going to happen!" Dan yelled, anger in his voice. "Now we're trapped! I knew something like this was going to happen!" he repeated.

Whatever Samuel's reasons had been, we weren't going anywhere until morning.

"Calm down," I said, sitting on the edge of a cot.

"Don't tell me to calm down!"

"You're alive aren't you?" I stated.

"But for how long? I don't like it!" yelled Dan with no sign of calming down. He began to pace back and forth in front of the door, like a caged wild animal.

"Dan, I think we're safe," said Jill. "We were just given a fabulous meal. Why would they do that if we were in danger? For one, I'm ready for a good nights sleep."

Dan didn't bother to respond or even look at her, continuing to pace, still agitated.

"I'm with Jill," agreed Gary. "Besides, there doesn't appear to be any other way out of this room."

"Tomorrow, we can find out why we were locked in," I said. "But I have a feeling it wasn't as much a trap for us as it was for their protection. We're the strangers here. They don't know if they can trust us and we don't know if we can trust them. Look at it another way, Dan, if it'll make you feel any better, they're locked out."

Paul gave a chuckle.

Everyone but Dan had picked out a cot and had laid down.

"Dan, when you get ready, could you blow out the lantern?" asked Jill.

He didn't answer, but we could hear him continue to pace back and forth. I closed my eyes and was quickly lulled to sleep by the sound of his continuous footsteps on the wooden floor.

*   *   *

We were all wide awake when we heard the door being unlocked. There was a knock and the door opened, Samuel stepping into the room.

Dan immediately rushed up to him, face to face. "I want out of here right now!" he demanded.

Samuel kept his composure and smiled. "I was just coming to get you. Breakfast is ready downstairs."

Dan brushed past him and ran downstairs. The others followed, but in much less of a rush. I waited behind to talk with Samuel.

"Why *did* you lock us in last night?" I asked.

"Just a precaution for both your protection and ours. We don't know each other. Not yet."

"I assumed it was something like that."

"I hope you're going to stay, John. I think you're going to fit in here just fine."

We followed the others downstairs. When we entered the main room, Gary and Paul were seated at the table eating what appeared to be oatmeal. Jill was standing at the open door, apparently upset about something.

"What's wrong?" I asked.

"Dan ran out, yelling he was going to get away from this place. I'm afraid he's going to do something stupid."

I turned to Samuel. "Can you help us find him?"

Always calm, level-headed, and in a cheerful disposition, Samuel patted Jill on her shoulder. "Don't

PARADISE

worry. We'll find him before he can leave the valley. He's not the first to have this reaction. In time, he'll come to know us and accept us. If not, we'll send him on his way, because if he doesn't want to be here, we won't force him."

* * *

Dan didn't know where he was going. He just knew he had to get away from there. Something was wrong with this place. He didn't understand why the others couldn't see it. He ran past several people on their way to work, each smiling and greeting him with "Good Morning, Dan." He found it odd no one attempted to stop him or question him about where he was going. He was sure everyone in this community knew each other and they knew he was a stranger. They had probably seen him and his group when they came in the previous day.

He stopped running, but continued to walk at a fast pace, taking in his surroundings. It *was* a beautiful little place - quiet, clean, green, and charming. If it wasn't for the rules, it might not be a bad place to start over. But then, looks could be deceiving.

"Where *was* he going?" he asked himself. He didn't have a plan, just the need to get away at all cost. He couldn't shake this gnawing feeling that something wasn't right? It wasn't just being locked in the room overnight, even though that wasn't a great start. It was something else. But he couldn't put his finger on it. He hadn't been threatened. Just the opposite, everyone had been extremely friendly. Maybe too friendly. It wasn't normal, at least not like where he had come from anyway. Maybe he was overacting because it hadn't been normal, not the normal he had known. Perhaps he should try giving it a second chance. Maybe following their rules wouldn't be so bad, temporarily anyway, until he knew more. Rules suggested structure and a purpose. That couldn't be all bad.

Two young men stepped out from one of the buildings directly into his path. He could tell it wasn't a coincidence, they were there for him. There was no sense in running again, he would be patient and wait for a better time, after he was better prepared.

"I think your friends are worried about you," one of them stated, both smiling and cordial. Neither man attempted any show of physical force. He headed back to the town hall as his stomach began to growl.

* * *

We were all waiting outside the Town Hall when Dan returned with his escort. The two men smiled and nodded to Samuel, then turned and walked away.

"Thanks, men," he called after them.

I got the feeling they had done this before. Dan sheepishly rejoined our group. The table had already been cleaned and he had missed out on breakfast, placing him again in a foul mood. He had messed up and there was no one to blame but himself. I didn't feel sorry for him. However, Jill did, handing him a biscuit she'd saved. I saw him mouth the words 'thank you.' Maybe he wasn't a lost cause.

There was no point in asking why he had run off, we already knew, and why make him even more uncomfortable. He had been a pain from the very beginning, but he was one of us. If he wanted to talk about it, we'd let him bring it up.

"While we have everyone together, how about a tour of our community before you decide on whether to stay or leave us?" asked Samuel, the invitation directed especially to Dan.

Paul perked up. "That would be great," he said eagerly.

As we gathered on the front porch, I motioned for Samuel to lead the way with a sweep of my hand. We were first led through a small downtown area with storefronts showing off some of the craftsmen's wares: such as clay and metal pots, dresses and shirts from a seamstress, and breads from a baker. The fantastic aroma from the bakery let us know loaves had just been recently removed from the oven. One shop contained miscellaneous second hand items like one would see at a flea market, and then at the end of the street we passed by a stable where the blacksmith was noisily working at his anvil.

"You won't find a cash register in any of these businesses," commented Samuel. "We conduct our business by the barter system, trading items or services. Nothing is free though. If you choose to work in the fields, a portion of the harvest will be given to you to exchange for whatever else you may need. I'll have my other son, Levi, come by tomorrow. He'll talk with each of you and see what you would like to do or what you are suited to do. We'll try to find a place where you'll be happy. Okay?"

I nodded. We continued at a casual pace down the center of the main street into an area with small houses on both sides. I was surprised at how quiet it was and that there were no other people out and about. Other than the clinking sound coming from the blacksmith shop, the town seemed to be deserted.

"Why is it so quiet this morning?" I asked. "And where is everyone?"

"Working. They are all working, men and women, either in the fields or at their craft. Just like I told you, everyone works."

"Where are the children we saw yesterday?" I asked.

"School, of course. Just like a real town." Samuel seemed to be slightly amused and at the same time slightly offended I would ask such a foolish question.

"Are there many children here?" asked Jill.

"Not many. Most are from our people, but a few are from your people."

"What do you mean by "our people"? asked Jill.

"The people like you who we've brought here. Some have met and started new lives together, followed by babies. It's a good place for a new beginning."

"How long have you and your people been here then?" asked Dan.

"Our family left your world behind many years ago when the country's problems first started, and I'm not just referring to the earthquakes. My ancestors traveled here from Pennsylvania, praying for a safe place to start over. And then they found this place, and they knew their prayers had been answered. My family has been here for five generations now, and from the stories we've heard about your world, we haven't missed anything."

"It appears you've thrived here. You have a nice little

PARADISE

community," I replied.

"Thank you."

"If you're so against the rest of the world, why do you help outsiders like us?" asked Jill.

"We're not against it, we just choose not to be a part of it. And we help because we can," answered Samuel. "It's not your fault where you come from. It wouldn't be right to know we could help and not even try. It would be as bad as us putting you to death ourselves."

"But you said if we couldn't agree to follow your rules we would have to leave," I pointed out.

"That's right. But it would be your choice, now wouldn't it? We have to maintain certain rules to maintain our lifestyle. We won't sacrifice that for anyone. Period. Like you said, we have a nice little community here and as it stands now, most of us, for the most part, are of a like mind."

We fell into silence as we continued to follow Samuel on a tour of the community. He brought us to the edge of town.

"This is our primary source of food," he said.

There was a huge garden where several people, both men and women, were collecting a variety of vegetables including tomatoes, carrots, cucumbers, squash, cantaloupe, and lettuce. The soil appeared to be a dark loam, rich in nutrients. Beyond the garden we could see two fields, one with wheat, the heads beginning to turn a golden brown, the harvest maybe still a couple of weeks away. The other field had been planted in corn, the young stalks about two feet tall.

Samuel gave us time to take it all in.

Then he informed us everyone in the community helped to bring in the harvest, regardless of what they normally did. Without any modern equipment, the harvest was gathered by hand and horse drawn equipment, taking more time and effort.

"We also have a few cattle, sheep, hogs, and chickens. I'll show them to you another time. It'll be lunch time soon, so why don't we go back to Town Hall so you can get cleaned up and rest. I'm sure Emma is preparing something for you."

Samuel led the way back. We had been gone most of the morning with Samuel anxious to show us their community. We'd been just as anxious to learn about the place by bombarding him with questions. When we got back to Town Hall, Dan was hesitant to enter, but he'd missed out on breakfast and was starving. His stomach had been heard growling while on the tour. Otherwise, he'd been surprisingly quiet during our tour without a single negative comment. I could only guess he had temporarily accepted his situation, going along just until he could plan his escape. Whatever the reason was for his silence, I was grateful.

Jill, Paul, and Gary had already entered the building, without hesitation, anxious for more of Emma's cooking.

Samuel pulled me aside before going in. "I want you and the others to feel free to go out and become familiar with the community and talk to whoever you like about whatever you like. I believe you'll find everyone living here is very happy and I hope it'll help you make the right decision for you."

"I've been thinking about something. If I decide to

PARADISE

stay, I'd like to go back to Sector 4 and bring my family and two children here."

"I'm afraid that's not possible. To do so, someone would have to take you and we'd have to provide a wagon, horse, and enough food and water for the trip both ways. At the very least, it would be a three week round trip, if there weren't any complications. It's just too much to ask. I'm sorry. Maybe one of these days we'll pick your wife up too."

"I'd be willing to work extra hard. I'll do the work of two men, whatever it takes."

"I'm sorry, John. It's not possible." Samuel turned to leave. "I'll check on you tomorrow," he said over his shoulder with a wave of his hand.

The others jumped when I slammed my fist against the door. I saw the concerned look on their faces. "Sorry."

It was true. Sarah would be sent to the wasteland once their youngest, Cindy, had reached the age of fourteen in two more years. I wasn't willing to wait that long.

* * *

Chapter 5

"Mom!" yelled Cindy, poking her head inside the tent flap.

Sarah stepped out from behind a sheet serving as a partition. "What is it?"

Cindy stepped inside, pulling the flap closed behind her. "There's a strange man outside asking for you."

"Did he say what he wants?" asked Sarah, smiling at Cindy. Her daughter could be overly excitable at times.

"Just that he wanted to see you."

"We just got home from the fields. Ask him if he can come back another time."

"I already told him. But he won't go away."

"Okay. Tell him I'll be right out."

Cindy relayed the message, standing directly in front of the flap, blocking any line of sight inside. It seemed to amuse the man.

PARADISE

"You certainly are a pretty young lady. Cindy, isn't it?"

She was uncomfortable with the fact he knew her name. She didn't answer. She had been taught not to talk to strangers, especially here.

"And twelve years old?" he asked.

She wondered how he knew about her.

"Before long, you'll be all grown up."

She didn't like this man at all. His smile made her uneasy and suspicious.

Sarah peeked through the slit of the tent flap. He wasn't an unattractive young man, perhaps in his mid twenties, but she'd never seen him before, which was unusual since she knew most of the faces in Tent City. She threw the flap back and went out, stepping protectively in front of her daughter.

"I'm Sarah Thomas. Can I help you?"

"My name is Taylor Grey. I'd like to talk to you. Alone if possible."

Cindy grabbed her mom's arm, not wanting to be separated.

"I don't think so. What do you want?"

"I assure you I'm not a danger," he said. "I'm just here to help, in any way I can. I know your husband is gone and I'm here to help you and your family out."

"Well, Mr. Grey, I appreciate your offer, but we'll be just fine. Now, if you don't mind, we've had a long day and we're very tired." Sarah and Cindy, arm in arm, turned to go back inside.

"You know, it can be very unsafe without a man around. Someone to keep the scavengers away."

"And are you that someone or are you one of the scavengers?" asked Sarah, not really expecting an answer. They entered the tent, closing and securing the flap.

"You'll be sorry!" he shouted, before turning and stomping away.

"Mom?" asked Cindy, not understanding.

"I guess it was just a matter of time. I've heard about men like him. They're sent by the governor to dig deeper into our pockets. Scavenger is a good word for them. They offer their 'protection' services for a portion of our grain allotment, which goes right back into the governor's pocket."

"But I don't want him here," said Cindy.

"Neither do I. "

"How did he know Daddy was gone?"

"The governor keeps records of everyone. I suppose some women, if left alone, might be willing to pay for the protection. But I'm not alone. I have you and Christopher."

"Christopher will take care of us now," proclaimed Cindy.

"You're right, we'll be fine. But I want you to let me know if he comes around again when I'm not here."

* * *

It had been three weeks since the disposal team had taken me from Sector 4. Sarah would probably think me dead by now. At least that had been the governor's objective when I had been taken away. Not to return and most assuredly not to survive. And she would have no reason to think otherwise. Maybe it was best to accept my

PARADISE

situation and let her get on with her life. Then I realized it would only be another two years until Cindy turned fourteen and Sarah would be in the same predicament as I was in now. No. I couldn't just accept it. Not since I knew there was still the possibility for a long life here together with my family. Somehow, I had to get back to her and my children and bring them back here, or die trying.

I would try to talk to Samuel again and try to convince him to change his mind. I didn't know if it was possible to make it back on foot or whether I'd be able to carry enough water and food to make a trip that long. I wasn't positive about the direction either. A few degrees off course and I could miss home by miles. It seemed odd now to think of back there as home. It had never seemed like a home, just a place to survive. But I could see this as becoming our new home. This evening after work I'd look for Samuel.

* * *

Levi had met with each of us and work had been assigned according to our past experience in Sector 4 or to what we had done before the quakes. I had worked for a small engineering firm, wearing several hats, and based on that had been put into a leadership position of maintaining the irrigation systems at Sector 4. Samuel was thrilled when he heard, telling me they could use someone with my experience. I agreed to do what I could to make sure water continued to reach the crop plots and garden area. Jill had been a librarian, so she had been asked to help the school teacher, which she was thrilled to do. She loved being around children. Gary, as a carpenter, was asked to help with general maintenance and new construction. And if people continued to be brought here, housing would always be in demand. Paul's past experience had come as a surprise, but it helped us to understand how he had come by some of the specialty items in his backpack. He was an entertainer. He could perform a soliloquy, quote poetry, tell stories, or sing a tune. In doing so back in Sector 4, he had been in demand to perform at many of the governor's gatherings and other functions of the privileged. Even though he wasn't one of them, it gave him access to those items reserved for the elite. Apparently, the way he told it, he was very popular. But even so, when he turned 40, he was just as expendable as we were, dragged away without any hope of reprieve.

Samuel seemed to be pleasantly surprised to learn of Paul's background. There was no one else in the settlement with his abilities. He would be valuable in providing an avenue of entertainment they'd never experienced before. Paul was just as thrilled at the idea of performing for a whole new audience. Dan was another story. He had been unemployed when the collapse occurred. In Sector 4 he'd been given tasks requiring little more than a warm body and physical exertion, which I learned he was perfectly happy with and seemed to make him a more agreeable person. He seemed to enjoy the mindless task of pulling or hoeing weeds in the garden and fields, being able to work alone and at his own pace without anyone looking over his shoulder. And from what I heard, he was good at it. It didn't take long for the members of our group to become acclimated with the community. Dan was even having second thoughts about leaving.

PARADISE

* * *

When the work day had ended, I went in search of Samuel, finding him in the downtown area, visiting with the storeowners. He saw me coming and raised his hand to stop me.

"John, I know what you're going to ask. The answer is still no," said Samuel. "Right now, when we're about to begin the harvest, I need everyone to help who's able."

I wasn't getting anywhere with him and I was becoming more frustrated each day.

"You'd be conducting the harvest whether I was here or not," I attempted to reason.

"That's true, but with your help we'll be able to bring it in that much faster. The weather is perfect right now, but it could change in an instant and we could lose part of the crop."

"If I decide to leave anyway, will you force me to stay?"

"Of course not, John. You can leave whenever you like. I just hope you'll decide not to. But if you do, is there a reason why we should welcome you back?"

"I can't answer that. I just hope I've already shown you I can be a contributing member of the community. But there's nothing more important to me than getting back to my family. And with your approval, I'd like to bring them back here."

"You can't have everything your way," explained Samuel, a slight smile appearing. He was the most pleasant man I'd ever met. The only time I'd seen him get angry was right after our arrival when he objected to Dan's language. Other than that one time, he'd always been a man of reason rather than emotion.

He already knew me better than I knew myself, even though he hadn't known me but a short time. I wasn't going to desert them if they really did need me, especially since I owed them. They had saved my life.

"I'll stay long enough to help, but you already knew I would, didn't you?" I didn't expect an answer. He just gave me a wink and a smile. "Will you help me get back after the wheat is in?"

"It would be easier then, but then the corn will be ready for harvest in about six weeks."

"I could be back by then," I said, testing his reaction, hoping for a favorable response.

He stood there, staring at me, presumably thinking about it. At least he hadn't immediately said 'no' this time.

"Please?" I pleaded. I decided to give him a little push. "I'm going after the wheat harvest anyway. And with your help I can be back in time and with extra hands to help."

"You're making an assumption," he said.

"And what's that?"

"That you won't have any trouble finding your family and bringing them here. First of all, they think you're dead. And secondly, they may not even be in the same place where you left them. And what if the governor won't let you take them away?"

"I don't intend on asking permission."

"They're going to try to stop you. The governor depends on them as laborers to work in his fields."

"Like you?"

"I hope you see there's a difference. For one thing, we

PARADISE

all work together for the mutual benefit of everyone, and you won't be taken out and left to die when you've outlived your usefulness."

"And who determines when we're no longer useful? When we no longer toe the line? When we don't follow the rules? When we become a burden?" I was taking my frustration out on Samuel. He'd done nothing but treat me with kindness since day one. He didn't deserve the way I was acting, but I couldn't seem to keep myself from venting.

"I'm having a hard time trying to talk to you today," said Samuel. "Maybe we should do this another time, after you've cooled off and had time to think."

* * *

Cindy met her brother outside the tent as he returned from work, anxious to tell him about the man that had come to their tent, offering protection. Chris was puzzled. He was the man of the family now. They didn't need help. He quickly entered the tent in search of his mother.

"Mom! Cindy said a man came around offering to protect us," stated Chris, bristling, wanting confirmation.

"Don't worry about it. I told him we didn't need his help," she said calmly.

That seemed to help relax Chris slightly. "I can take care of you, Mom. We don't need some stranger coming around here."

"I know, Chris. I've heard about men like him. They're sent by the governor to take advantage of the women left single after their husbands have been taken away to the wasteland. It's a form of blackmail where a man will promise to keep a widow safe in return for a portion of the widow's allotment. And I want no part of it."

"Just let me know if he comes back, okay?"

Sarah had used those same words to Cindy. She knew he took his new role as man of the family very serious. She smiled. He was only fourteen and already as tall as his dad had been and filled-out almost as much, and still growing. But he was still just a boy and no match for the man who had come by. It gave her a sense of pride though at his willingness to step forward to protect both her and his sister.

"I don't think he'll be back," she said, attempting to ease his mind further.

"Mom," said Cindy as she peered out through the front tent flap. "Come here."

Sarah went to her daughter, looking over her shoulder. "What is it?"

"Look," Cindy said, pointing.

A short distance away, standing near the corner of another tent, was the man again, watching. Chris came over and saw him too. "Is that the same man?" asked Chris.

"That's him," said Cindy.

He slid past his mother and sister to the outside of the tent. "I'll talk to him," he declared, starting to walk toward him with quick deliberate steps.

"Chris!" his mother called after him. "He's not doing anything, so leave him alone. Come back here."

The man, Grey, became alert and stood up straight at seeing his approach. Two more men stepped out from the edge of the tent. Chris came to an abrupt stop, his bravado

PARADISE

disappearing. One man was one thing, but three would be suicidal. And the two men looked considerably rougher than the first man. Chris stayed motionless, neither retreating nor moving forward, unsure of what to do, whether to stand his ground or not. He didn't want to appear as a coward to his mom and sister. The three men stayed where they were too, smirks appearing on their faces, knowing they had the upper hand. The situation resulted in no more than a staring contest. Grey said something to the others and then suddenly all three of the men turned and disappeared, laughing and glancing back at the boy.

"I don't like them hanging around here, Mom," said Chris, as the men disappeared.

"Do you think they'll be back?" asked Cindy.

"No, probably not," answered her mother, trying to be reassuring. The truth was that they probably would be back. She wasn't sure how far they would go in an attempt to persuade her to change her mind, but she was sure they wouldn't give up so easily.

*   *   *

I was determined. Now, I knew there was life and hope and a future in the wasteland, I couldn't keep my mind on anything other than my family and how I could bring them to this place. But there was a problem. As it stood with Samuel now, if I left before the wheat harvest and was able to return with my family, we may not be allowed back into the community. Just as Samuel had learned to read me, I also thought I had learned a bit about him too. I had my doubts about whether he would actually turn me and my family away. It seemed an action like that would be contrary to his beliefs. Otherwise, it would be as though he was condemning us to death and it didn't seem likely. So, I was counting on Samuel's good nature and beliefs to accept us back. That was just the second part of my concerns. First of all, I'd have to find my way back to Sector 4 and get my family out of there without detection. There were a lot of 'ifs' involved. But if I could pull it off, I could once again be with my family.

If I was able to accomplish my family's escape, if you could call it that, I could make a future for all of us here. Escape, perhaps, wasn't the right word. My family, to the best of my knowledge, was actually safer where they were, unharmed and unthreatened, at least until the age of forty. They may be safer where they are instead of fighting to survive in the wasteland while I tried to get them back to the valley. One of the potential dangers would be becoming lost, which could end badly. Another would be running into the Raiders, described by the governor as a band of cutthroats and thieves. It had been said they regularly attacked and stole goods from the governor's collection patrols sent out to scavenge for supplies. Without any regard for human life, the Raiders were said to kill without mercy. I had no idea what we would do if we encountered them.

I hadn't asked Samuel yet, but often wondered if there were other settlements like this one in the surrounding area. But even if there were, the people may not be as hospitable as these people had been. This place was already well established and I liked the people. My

PARADISE

companions and I had been welcomed with open arms, with only minimum and reasonable expectations. Not only did I hope to reunite here with my family once again, it would give me the chance to watch my children grow up and to perhaps one day see my grandchildren, which would have been impossible back in Sector 4. I had already made up my mind. I was going. But, right now, timing was the big issue. I had to work something out with Samuel, his help would be essential if I was going to be successful.

* * *

Chapter 6

Four men approached Sarah's tent. The one leading the way was dressed in black as one from the governor's inner circle, escorted by two of the governor's Guard. Following them was the man who had paid her a visit two days previously, Taylor Grey.

Cindy and Chris were outside the tent, washing up after a long and dirty workday. Cindy was the first to see them coming, nudging her brother. Chris was quick to move in front of the tent entrance as Cindy ran inside.

"Mom!" she yelled, anxiety in her voice. "Some men in uniform are coming with the man from the other day."

Sarah came out from behind a partition. "Calm down. There's no need to worry. We haven't done anything wrong."

Sarah peered out through a break in the tent flap. Chris maintained his position in front of her, arms crossed and

PARADISE

defiant. The men came to a stop directly in front of him, ten feet separating them.

"Mrs. Thomas?" the leader called out, after seeing her peeking past her son.

"Yes?"

"May I have a word with you?" he asked, taking a small step forward. Chris stood his ground, refusing to let the man past, puffing out his chest as a warning.

The man smiled, amused at and admiring the boy's courage. He stepped back to where he had been.

Sarah stepped through the tent flap placing herself between the men and her son. She would protect her children no matter what. Chris didn't like her making herself vulnerable and he started to say so. It was his job now to protect his mom and sister. His mother gave him a familiar look, stopping him from objecting. He wouldn't argue with her.

"Who are you and what do you want?" she asked.

"Forgive me. My name is Counselor Damon and I'd like to talk to you about Mr. Grey here." Grey stepped out from behind the guards to where he could be seen better. "It's my understanding you have refused his services. Is that correct?"

"We don't need his kind of help!" blurted Chris, pointing at Grey. The two guards moved in next to Damon in a protective posture.

"Mrs. Thomas?" he asked again, wanting an answer.

"That's right," she confirmed in an evenly controlled voice. "I tried to explain to Mr. Grey we could take care of ourselves."

"I do wish you'd reconsider. Mr. Grey is only offering

this service as part of the governor's program and it's been working quite well for the last two years. I assure you that with his help you'll find it much easier to cope since your husband left."

"He didn't leave! He was taken away!" shouted Cindy from behind her mother.

"I think we're coping just fine," said Sarah. "As you can see, I'm not alone. I have my son and daughter to help out."

"But you must be able to see the benefits of having a man around to provide protection for you and your children. Mr. Grey could even be a father figure."

"Father figure?!" Her voice began to give away her increasing anger. "No, we don't need his kind of help. I told Mr. Grey and now I'm telling you 'no thank you' as politely as I can. We'll be fine."

"There's no reason to be upset. I'd like you to think over what I've said. I know your family's safety is a very big concern. We'll be back in a few days for your final answer."

"But ...," started Grey, but stopped when Damon shot him a dagger-like look.

"I've already given you my ...," began Sarah, no longer trying to conceal her frustration and anger.

"Don't be too hasty, Mrs. Thomas," warned Damon, cutting her off. "There is something else you should keep in mind. Your son here, Christopher isn't it, may not be around much longer since he's turned fourteen. I happen to know he's been identified as a prime candidate for the governor's Guard. He could be called to serve at any time and when it happens he'll be expected to reside inside the compound in the Guard housing." He paused. "And then there's little Cindy. She's already twelve and very pretty. It's possible she could be taken at any time for training for the governor's personal staff. Then what would happen, Mrs. Thomas? You would be all alone and almost forty." Cindy held tightly to her mother's arm.

Sarah knew what he was trying to do. She had no intention of falling for his tactics or accepting Grey's services. She was reasonably sure he was bluffing, a tactic he probably used successfully on a regular basis. He had planted a seed though, one she would think about continually over the next few days. There was always a slight chance he wasn't bluffing. As counselor, it was within his power to do just as he said.

"I'll worry about it when the time comes," she answered defiantly.

The two groups stood observing each other with an awkward silence. At an apparent impasse, there seemed to be nothing to add.

"Very well, Mrs. Thomas. But, I *will* be back in a few days. Think about what I've said. Good day, ma'am."

After having his say, Counselor Damon and the others turned and walked away, Mr. Grey obviously upset, his face now a bright red, arguing his case to Damon. The counselor lifted a hand for him to stop, resulting in his immediate silence.

"What are we going to do?" asked Cindy.

"I don't know. We'll think of something."

"What if we just left this place?" asked Chris.

"And where do you suggest we go?" Sarah asked sharply, frustration in her voice. She took a deep breath.

"I'm sorry." She paused. "I wish your father was still here. But the reality is he's gone and he'll never be back. We'll have to figure something out on our own."

* * *

I had held my tongue over the last couple of weeks, not saying any more about leaving to Samuel. I had decided to put the matter on the back burner at least until the wheat harvest was completed. Then, with or without his blessing, I was going.

During the harvest, I helped collect the grain and was given the job to oversee storing it away. Jill was asked to take a break from the school to help with the inventory.

"Are you still leaving after harvest?" she asked. "It's almost over."

He looked around to see if anyone was listening, even though he expected word had already spread about his intent.

"Yes. I have to. I'll go crazy if I don't do something. And I can't bear the thought of my family having to provide for themselves back there when we could all be here together."

"I understand," she said, sounding a bit sad. "I hope you make it there and back safely."

I had become aware of her attachment to me, undoubtedly a result of my watching over her, making sure she was safe. Unfortunately, I began to feel she might be expecting more than a brotherly love.

* * *

PARADISE

It was sunrise of the day following the last tally of the wheat harvest and I was ready to go. I had already made preparations the night before, packing enough food and water to get me started on my journey. I was counting on finding water along the way by looking for working windmills. I met Paul, Gary, and Jill at Town Hall for breakfast. Emma was still preparing our meals until we were permanently settled in. We sat in silence around the end of the large table. When we were done, they followed me back to the small shack Samuel had assigned to me, watching as I slipped my backpack on, adjusting the weight on my shoulders until it felt comfortable. In one of the pockets was a simple head-covering I'd made out of an old t-shirt to protect me from the scorching sun. I'd pull it out once I got on the trail.

I was glad they had come to see me off. Dan was a no-show, which wasn't surprising. But I was a little surprised when neither Samuel nor any of the other townspeople had come. I was relatively sure everyone in Paradise knew I was leaving. News typically traveled fast in a small community. Perhaps my leaving had upset some of the townspeople somehow. There was no guarantee I'd make it to Sector 4 or get back. Actually, there was the distinct possibility I wouldn't make it at all. But, I was determined to stick to my plan to bring my family back here, and with Samuel's permission, stay and make this our home. I refused to consider any other option. My friends walked with me to the foot of the trail leading out of the valley. No one had much to say. Everything had already been said when they had tried to talk me out of it.

I was surprised and pleased to see Samuel and Levi

standing next to a horse and wagon at the edge of town.

"What are you doing here?" I asked. "Did you change your mind about letting me and my family return?"

Samuel ignored the question. "You're not going alone. Levi's going with you. He'll make sure you get there and back safely. It'll be up to you though to get your family."

I couldn't help breaking out into a smile. "Then we *can* come back?" I asked again, looking for a definite confirmation.

"The sooner you leave the sooner you'll be back," he stated, matter-of-factly. I guess I wasn't going to get a direct answer, but I got the message.

Samuel's gesture took a huge weight off my shoulders. There had been a lot of ifs floating around in my mind over this trip. With Levi along, my chances of pulling it off successfully had just increased tenfold.

To help even further, in an attempt to hasten our return, Samuel was providing a wagon, already loaded with food and water, not only for Levi and myself, but enough for my family too. There appeared to be concern in Samuel's eyes. I knew he didn't want me to go and was probably questioning whether he was doing the right thing by helping me. If things went horribly wrong, not only would I not be back, but he could lose a son as well, and of far less importance, but still important resources to the community, a horse and wagon too.

"We'll be back as soon as possible," I said, in hopes of re-assuring him. "Don't worry and thank you."

"I'm not worried," he said. "Just make sure you're back in time for the corn harvest." He forced a slight grin.

Levi had already climbed up onto the wagon seat. "We

PARADISE

need to go," he said.

This was going to be a long and silent trip. The short time I had been around Levi, I had never heard him say more than half a dozen words in a row at any one time. Perhaps I could get him to open up on the trip. I was grateful for his coming, regardless. Whether it was voluntary or not, I had no idea. If I had to guess, it was probably Samuel's idea. Maybe the subject would come up.

I threw my pack into the back and climbed up beside him.

"Be careful," said Jill with a warm flirtatious smile as she stepped back.

Levi gave the reins a flick and the wagon began to move toward the trail that would take us out of the valley, back to the wasteland above. I exchanged a last wave with my friends. I turned back around, facing forward, with a sense of satisfaction at finally beginning the long anticipated trip. I knew without a doubt I was going to see my family again. We couldn't get there fast enough.

*   *   *

Sarah, Cindy, and Chris spent another long, hot, and tiring day in the fields. Cindy worked alongside her mother as Chris had done with his father, learning from their parents so they would be able to take their place some day. Sarah's job during the growing season was to continually weed the fields, as many of the women did. Each was responsible for one row at a time under the watchful eye of a guard. Chris's father had been one of the men who maintained the irrigation system for the corn and garden plots. For the last two weeks they had been busy with the wheat harvest. Without any modern agricultural equipment, due to a lack of gasoline or diesel, the work was either performed by hand or by horse-drawn implements. Either way, it was a slow process. The long thin stalks of wheat were collected and delivered to the threshing shed where the grains of wheat could be separated out. The entire process was labor intensive with few breaks allowed by the governor's Guard.

The three returned to their tent, sweaty, filthy, and exhausted. The guards had been especially demanding today, pushing to finish the harvest. It had been rumored they wagered on the amount of grain their group collected each day. The workers could tell when certain guards had lost by being driven even harder the next day. One good thing had come out of it today. They had finished.

As they washed up at a small metal basin in front of the tent, Counselor Damon approached again with his Guard escort of two and Mr. Grey, just as he had promised.

Chris started to go and meet them. Sarah grabbed him by the arm.

"Chris, don't." It was all she had to say for him to stop.

Damon was all smiles, in a sleazy, over-friendly way. "Mrs. Thomas, I told you I'd be back. I do hope you've changed your mind since we last spoke." It was more of a question than a statement and he waited for her response.

"Nothing has changed. We don't need or want anyone's assistance. But thank you anyway." She could be just as persistent as he could. She saw something in

PARADISE

Damon's eyes change. They seemed to go black as his smile disappeared.

Grey, waiting behind the guards, uttered one syllable, but with one quick glance from Damon, closed his mouth and let his eyes drift to the ground. Sarah got the feeling Grey had already been warned about any outburst.

"Now that the wheat harvest is over, I have also come to give you your voucher for your share of the grain." He pulled out a small notebook and wrote in it, tearing a slip of paper out and handing it to her. "You may pick up a portion or all of it whenever you like."

She took the paper. A puzzled look appeared on her face as she studied it with disbelief. "What is this?"

"It's your payment, of course," he replied matter-of-factly.

"This isn't nearly enough. I have two children to feed and support."

"Don't you remember? I told you if you refused Mr. Grey's services, Christopher and Cindy could be going to start their new training, and that's exactly what we've decided to do. So, that leaves only yourself to care for and the amount there should be more than enough for you to get by on. And you needn't worry about your children, I will personally see to it they're well taken care of."

Cindy's grip on her mother's arm tightened. Christopher for the first time took a step backwards, closer to his mother.

"You can't do this!" Sarah shouted through gritted teeth, her voice trembling. There were no tears of sadness, only frustration and outrage. A few of her neighbors poked their heads out of their tents to see what all the commotion was about. At seeing the counselor and his guards, they retreated back inside, minding their own business, but mostly to avoid drawing attention to themselves.

"Children, go inside!" instructed Sarah.

"That won't do any good, Mrs. Thomas. They can't escape us. Of course, if you were willing to change your mind about Mr. Grey, I have the authority to leave them here with you for a while longer and I can increase the amount on the voucher. What do you say, Mrs. Thomas?"

He had a smug smile that infuriated Sarah. She fought to keep from telling Counselor Damon exactly what she thought, but the consequences were too high.

He remained silent, waiting for her reply. He knew he had her right where he wanted her, allowing her a moment to realize it and accept it.

Cindy and Chris remained standing next to their mother. "Go inside like I told you!" she snapped. She realized immediately what she had done, regretting it. They had never seen her like this before. They were worried. "I'm sorry," she told them both.

"We're not going anywhere!" stated Chris. "Don't do it, Mom," he pleaded.

"They're going to separate us," she said softly with resolve, turning to look directly into the eyes of her children. She gave them each a kiss before turning around to face Damon.

"What exactly am I expected to do?" Sarah asked.

Damon produced a large toothy smile, as did Grey from behind. "Now, that's more like it. Can we go inside to talk about it in a civilized and private manner?" he asked, stepping toward the tent entrance, followed by his escort

PARADISE

and Grey.

Sarah stepped directly into his path. "Just you," she said with determination in her eyes. "This is still my home, and I won't have them in there."

Grey, his face turning red with anger, pushed his way past one of the guards. "I have every right to be present for this. It involves me you know."

With a nod from Damon, one of the guards struck Grey in his gut, dropping him to his knees gasping for air.

"That'll be fine, Mrs. Thomas," he agreed as he followed her in. He turned to his guards. "I should be out shortly. Please keep Mr. Grey comfortable and outside." Both of the men nodded and responded with a "Yes, sir."

Sarah directed Damon to a simple, wooden chair and sat across from him on the ground. Cindy and Chris kneeled by her side.

Damon was hesitant to start, eyeing her children. "I think this is a matter better discussed between adults," subtly hinting she should have the children leave.

"Just tell me what's expected and I'll tell you if it's acceptable," she said.

He smiled and snickered. "Mrs. Thomas, I'm afraid you still don't quite understand your situation. This is not a negotiation. I'm here to tell you how it's going to be."

Sarah remained calm, showing remarkable restraint, not wanting Cindy or Chris to see her lose her composure again. However, Chris was another matter. His frame had become rigid and his face was twisted into an undeniable expression of disgust. He remained by his mother's side. Damon noticed Chris' expression, but remained unconcerned. Sarah waited patiently for Damon to continue.

"Mr. Grey will watch over you and your children during the evening hours in return for a portion of your allotment. I will determine what the amount will be and I'll deduct it directly from your share along with your taxes. You will not be responsible for payment of any kind to Mr. Grey. I will take care of it myself. However, I'm sure he'd appreciate the occasional meal." He paused. "You should know, some women have found the arrangement to be very beneficial."

"I can assure you, that will *not* be the case here. I don't want him setting foot inside this tent," she said.

"That is entirely your prerogative, Mrs. Thomas. This is going to work out very well for both of us. I will explain the arrangement to Mr. Grey. And if there are any matters you feel should be reported, please feel free to contact my office. I think that concludes our business."

"I believe you were going to fill out another voucher," she mentioned, handing him back the previous one.

He tore it in half and pulled out his notebook, filling out a new one and handing it to her. "Satisfied?" he asked.

It was still less than she felt it should have been, but the conditions were better than she had expected and she would be able to keep her children with her. She nodded.

He pulled another paper out of his coat pocket. "Then, I need you to sign this document to show you have agreed to Mr. Grey's services."

She signed and handed it back.

Damon folded it, stuffing it back inside his coat pocket, then abruptly stood. "Thank you, Mrs. Thomas. It's been a genuine pleasure. Mr. Grey's duties will begin

PARADISE

immediately." He abruptly headed straight for the tent flap and was gone.

Sarah went to the flap and peered out, wanting to see Grey's reaction. Damon appeared to be explaining the terms of the agreement to Mr. Grey. He responded by kicking at the dirt and shouting a string of obscenities as he stepped up close to Damon, nose-to-nose. One of the guards quickly stepped in and pushed him back. It was curious to Sarah how Damon never seemed to show any anger, always in control.

As Damon left with his escort, Grey found a wooden box and situated it near the tent entrance and sat down in a position to keep watch as intended, continuing to mumble to himself, grabbing a rock up off the ground and throwing it nowhere in particular. Sarah could only speculate that Mr. Grey must have expected to move in and make himself at home. The conditions as explained to him must have come as quite an awakening.

* * *

Chapter 7

I attempted to start a conversation with Levi several times the first day, but all I received in return were grunts or one-word responses. I didn't know if he was just trying to be the strong silent type or if he had something against me. Maybe I just rubbed him the wrong way or maybe it was because he didn't like the idea of being forced to accompany me. Even though I had tried to be as subtle as possible, I hadn't been able to learn which, if either, was the case. Perhaps both applied.

His silence was making the trip drag on endlessly. I was looking forward to when we would stop to rest and water the horse. Anything would help to break up the monotony.

As we continued to the northeast, our line of direction didn't seem to vary much at all. I noticed we were following the well-worn impression of wagon tracks in

PARADISE

what appeared to be a straight line as far as I could see. Occasionally, we would cross the crumbled remains of what had once been an asphalt road, now overgrown with weeds, a reminder of earlier days.

"I see you've been this way before," I mentioned, hoping once again for more than a one-word response. He gave no comment at all.

"Am I right?" I persisted.

"Yeah," he replied.

"How often do you make this trip?" I continued. From what Samuel had told me, I already knew they came this way every six months to pick up supplies for the town. Then, learning about the disposal drop-offs from Ryder, they had attempted to coincide their trips with those times.

Levi shrugged.

I knew he knew the answer. Evidently, he didn't want to talk and avoided it by playing dumb. I wondered if this was the route they usually took to Sector 4, which led to another question.

"You've been to Sector 4 before, haven't you?" I asked, already knowing the answer to that question too.

I finally got a response. He looked at me like I was crazy. "Yeah, why else would I be taking you?" he snapped.

I almost preferred he stay silent, which was exactly what I got as he once again fell silent.

He wasn't volunteering any additional information. My frustration could have been compared to a dentist trying to pull teeth when a patient refused to open their mouth. I was getting nowhere.

"I suppose you have contacts in Sector 4 that help you

out?" I continued, not giving up.

He turned his head slowly toward me with a deadpan expression. "Yeah."

It took a while, but I finally took the hint. He didn't want to talk and nothing I did or said was going to change that. I sat back, willing to temporarily give him a break from my questions. But I wasn't going to give up entirely. There were things I needed to know. There was too much at stake to go into this blindly. I refused to rely solely on this young man without the information I needed. At some point we would need to work together. Perhaps he'd be more willing to exchange information when we got there.

On the third day we came across a less traveled trail that forked off to the west as the main trail continued straight ahead. We stayed on the course straight ahead. When I asked, Levi confirmed with a grunt that the other trail led toward the area where we had been left for disposal.

*   *   *

As we drew closer to Sector 4, I began to recognize the surrounding area. The landscape contained an increased spattering of old farmsteads, now abandoned and in ruin from the quakes and subsequent fires. It was hard not to wonder about the families that had lived there. Levi pulled back on the reins and stopped the wagon.

"This is as far as I go," he stated. "I'll be over at that partially standing barn tomorrow at sunset. You'll have approximately twenty-four hours. If you're not back here by then, I'll assume something has gone wrong and I'll be

PARADISE

heading back."

Those were the most words I'd ever heard him string together at one time.

"Can't we get a little closer?" I asked. "We're still a ways out."

"No. This is near where I meet our contact with the supplies. And Dad was very clear about not taking any undue risks. I don't have any papers and neither do you. If we were to be stopped, we'd be arrested."

I knew what was coming next. It had been covered in our outcast orientation. If anyone was unfortunate enough to make it back and was discovered, the penalty was death by execution. No appeals, no reprieve. And as a deterrent to others, the punishment would be dealt out swiftly during a public execution. To the best of my knowledge, it had never happened before, and I had no intention of being the first.

I was still about a mile from my family by foot. I could almost smell Sarah's hair.

"I'll be here, with my family," I said as I jumped down.

"You might need this," he said, handing me a knife and scabbard.

"Does Samuel know about this?" I asked. I didn't see Samuel condoning its use.

"No."

"You mentioned you had contacts here. Can I get in touch with them if I need to?"

"No, it's too risky. You're on your own." And that was all he had to say.

I understood the need for secrecy, but not knowing

who I could count on made me uncomfortable.

I decided I wasn't going to get any more out of him, so I nodded a thank you and started the walk toward Tent City. I was going in blind, but my desire to see my family far outweighed any of my concerns.

"Good luck," he called out and then headed the horse and wagon toward the barn.

* * *

"Mom," said Cindy. "That man gives me the creeps."

"I know, honey. Me too."

"I can hear you in there!" shouted Mr. Grey, standing just outside the tent entrance.

"I don't care!" Cindy shouted back.

Sarah couldn't help smiling, but at the same time holding her finger to her lips.

The tent flap was thrown back and Grey rushed in. He stopped just short of the two. "You should be showing me some gratitude and respect instead of constantly belittling me," yelled Grey. "I'm out there every night giving you my protection."

"The only one we need protection from is you," blurted Cindy.

"You should leave now before I'm forced to report this to Counselor Damon," said Sarah.

He took a step back. "There's no need for that. I'm not going to hurt you. I need this job."

For the first time, Sarah began to wonder if Grey was possibly in a similar situation as they were, being forced to comply with the governor's manipulation.

PARADISE

"What do you mean? Are you being forced to do this?" she asked.

He didn't admit it, avoiding the question all together. There was a noticeable change in his demeanor to one of timidness with downcast eyes. "I'll be outside if you need me." He ducked back out, pulling the flap closed behind him.

"Mom," whispered Cindy. "What was that all about?"

"We may have been too critical of Mr. Grey's part in all this. What do you say we try to be a little nicer?"

If you say so, I'll try," said Cindy. "But I'm not sure Chris will go along with it."

"I'll talk to him. Let's try to show Mr. Grey we do appreciate him. Can you take him a glass of water?"

"Do I have to?"

"I think he'd appreciate it."

"Okay. But I hope he doesn't start to expect it."

Sarah was beginning to see Grey in a new light, but refused to drop her guard. She would remain cautious around him until she knew more about the dynamics behind their situation. For one thing, how far would Mr. Grey go to keep any negative reports from reaching the counselor's office? Just from what he said and how he said it, he needed this job.

* * *

The prison and governor's compound appeared in the distance on top of a hill overlooking Tent City. The anticipation was overwhelming, my pace quickening. Lights began to flicker into existence as the last sliver of the setting sun disappeared behind the horizon. The darkness would be to my advantage, but I would still have to be careful. The last thing I wanted was to be recognized and reported. I worked my way easily through the crude barrier of vehicles around the perimeter of Tent City. I stayed in the shadows whenever possible and kept my head down, avoiding eye contact with anyone. I heard my name called out once, but kept on the move, hoping the person would assume it had been a matter of mistaken identity. And why wouldn't they. I was dead.

It was almost completely dark now. Everyone should have been home from work by this time with meals being prepared over the open fires outside the entrance to their tents. The smell of the meals cooking made me realize I hadn't eaten since morning. But food would have to wait.

I was getting close now. I'd have to be especially cautious. My neighbors would be able to recognize me at a glance, if they could believe their eyes. And, even more importantly, I had my family to think of. It would come as quite a shock for them to see me unexpectedly alive. It probably wouldn't be a good idea to just throw back the entrance flap and step inside.

When I was within sight of my family's tent, I decided to watch for a while, waiting for the right moment when I could catch Sarah alone outside. Then, after she had gotten over the initial shock of seeing me alive, she could gently break the news to Cindy and Christopher. I knelt down behind the back edge of a nearby tent where I had a clear view. Immediately, I saw something I hadn't expected. There was a man sitting just outside the entrance. Then, Sarah came outside, carrying a pot and setting it over the fire. She poured something into a cup and handed it to him. It seemed very cozy.

How long had I been gone? I tried to remember. Two months? I hadn't thought she'd replace me this quick. I hadn't even considered it. I'd expected everything to go back to how it had been before. Maybe she won't want to come back with me at all. Perhaps she'd already started a new life. I didn't blame her, she had herself and a family to think about.

* * *

Grey saw a man not far from the tent. He could tell the man was looking them over, trying to be inconspicuous. He stood and took a couple of steps in his direction. His role, as he saw it, was more of a visual deterrent, a protector for appearances sake rather than one of actually having to do anything. But he needed the job and if it came to it, he knew he was expected by the counselor and the governor to do whatever it took to fulfill his contract. The man didn't move.

"Hey, you!" shouted Grey, taking two more steps.

The man stood and began to walk toward him. Grey had a twinge of panic as he swallowed hard. He was going to be forced into action.

Sarah stuck her head out of the tent. "Taylor, what's wrong?" They had come to terms, both in a forced situation. Now, they were on a first name basis.

"There may be trouble. You better stay inside," he said, motioning for her to stay back.

She saw the man coming, but the faint flickering light

of the fire wasn't bright enough to make out any of his features. Cindy pushed past. "What's going on?"

"Go back inside the tent!" Sarah said forcefully, sensing danger from Taylor's reaction. Cindy saw the man striding directly toward them and darted back inside.

"Hold it right there, mister," instructed Grey.

The man kept coming. Grey looked around quickly and picked up a stick of firewood the size of his arm. "I'm warning you. We don't want any trouble. Just go away and leave us alone."

Sarah stood behind Grey, too curious to go inside. There was something familiar about the way the man walked. His features were becoming clearer the closer he came.

* * *

I stopped near the fire with its glow lighting my face.

"John?!" Sarah murmured with disbelief. She looked harder.

She burst into tears, running past Grey, throwing her arms around my neck.

"What is this?" asked Grey, not understanding what was going on.

Christopher and Cindy came out, wondering what all the commotion was about. Instantly, they broke into a beaming smile, running to their father and throwing their arms around him too.

Grey felt out of place and uncomfortable. It didn't take long for him to figure out who this man was. But how was that possible? He had been taken out to the wasteland. No

PARADISE

one ever survived out there.

Finally, Sarah released her grip and looked into my eyes, "John, how? We thought you were dead."

"I'll explain everything, but right now we need to get inside," I said, looking around. They had already drawn the attention of some of their neighbors. I could only hope they wouldn't say anything and was thankful when they turned away, minding their own business. They all began to go inside, except Grey, who stood at the entrance, not sure if he should go in or not. Sarah noticed. "C'mon in, Taylor. It's okay."

"I'm John, Sarah's husband," I said, introducing myself and offering my hand to Grey.

"I figured as much," said Grey, shaking my hand. "Shouldn't you be dead?"

"You'd like that, wouldn't you?"

"Yeah, I would."

"Boys!" said Sarah.

We all sat on the ground in the front room of the tent, Cindy and Sarah at my sides.

With me showing up, I could tell Grey's mind was racing with questions.

"John, this is Taylor Grey. He's been helping out," said Sarah.

The first question entering my mind was "So, Taylor, what kind of things have you been helping out with?" Realizing after the words had left my mouth I may have sounded a bit like I was accusing him of something, which I was.

"John," said Sarah, recognizing jealousy in my question, answered for Grey. "Taylor is part of the governor's program to keep an eye out for us, to protect us from any undesirables, after you were taken away."

"Then, I guess I owe you my gratitude," I said, without an ounce of sincerity. "So, how long have you had this arrangement?"

"First," interceded Sarah, "I want to know what happened to you and how you are here."

"Yes, John. I'd like to know myself," commented Taylor. This man could ruin his situation and security.

"Daddy, are you going to stay with us?" asked Cindy, excited and smiling.

"No, honey, I can't stay here." I wanted to tell my family everything, but I couldn't let Grey hear what I had in mind. I was still confused about what all was included in his role and how much time he spent there. I had a bad feeling about him and had no reason to trust him.

"Taylor," I asked," would you mind giving me a moment with my family?"

His face flushed red, angry at being excluded. He looked at Sarah, who nodded that he probably should go. I thought it odd he would look to my wife for her approval. He quickly rose and stormed outside.

"Tell me again, what is he doing here?" I asked.

"Why John, are you jealous?" asked Sarah with a hint of a smile, already knowing the answer.

"Of course not, but why *is* he here?"

"Just like I already said, he's here to keep strangers away. It's okay, we have an arrangement."

"I'll bet you do."

"Now, John, you know better than that."

I took a deep breath. "Yeah, I know. Sorry."

PARADISE

"It was the governor's idea. He provides a man to protect widows and their families and in return he takes a portion of our grain allotment."

"I've never heard of such a thing."

"I had heard stories, but I didn't believe them. Not until we were paid a visit by Counselor Damon in person, explaining everything."

"Couldn't you refuse? Christopher is the man of the house now."

Christopher sat up straight, chest out, beaming with pride at the faith his dad had in him.

"I tried, but we didn't have a choice. If I refused, they were going to take Cindy and Christopher away from me."

I couldn't believe my ears. "They can't do that!" I shouted. "And Taylor works for those people?" I asked, already knowing the answer.

"The counselor would have done it," Sarah said calmly. She paused to gather her thoughts.

"It's turned out alright," she said. "Taylor has been a perfect gentleman. I'm afraid we gave him a pretty hard time at first. Since then, I've learned he was placed in a similar predicament to the one we were in, forced by the governor to go along." She paused. "Now, it's your turn. Did you escape from the wagon? I want to know everything."

Cindy and Christopher moved in closer, anxiously waiting for the details.

"I'll give you the short version," I started. "We were taken out into the wasteland and dropped off, just as expected, after riding in the wagon for ten days. We started walking toward a low silhouette of high hills to the west.

After two days of walking, with our supplies almost gone, we were rescued by two men who picked us up in a wagon. They took us further south into the wasteland and after two more days we came to a green and luscious valley where there were other people, young and old, and a town. They call it Paradise."

Cindy was wide-eyed and full of excitement. "I wish I could see it, Daddy," she said.

"That's why I'm here, to take you back with me."

There was a moment of silence while they looked at me in disbelief and then at each other.

"But how?" asked Sarah.

"There's a wagon south of town waiting for us."

"But John, will they let us go?"

"They won't know you're gone until it's too late."

There was another moment of silence, not only from Sarah, but also from Cindy and Christopher. I didn't understand their hesitation.

"Kids," I asked, "you'd like to get away from all this, wouldn't you?"

"Well, sure, Dad," answered Christopher.

"Cindy?"

"What will happen to Mr. Grey?"

I was beginning to get frustrated. Why did Mr. Grey have anything to do with this at all? "I'm sure Mr. Grey will be just fine." I didn't really care whether he was or not. All I cared about was getting my family out of here so we could be together. "I thought you'd all be happy to get away."

"It sounds wonderful, John. But it could be dangerous for the children," said Sarah, with concern.

PARADISE

"You're right. It could be dangerous, but wouldn't it be worth the risk? We can be together again. And we can watch them and our grandchildren grow up. I can't believe I have to convince you to do this."

"I'm sorry, John. It's just so much. First, we find out you're still alive and now you want to take us away. And I'm worried if we're caught, we'll never see our children again."

"I'm thinking about them too. It's one of the reasons why I want to get all of you out of here, away from this cesspool. This is no way to live."

She sat thinking in silence. From my perspective, there wasn't anything to think about. I couldn't stay here and I wasn't going to leave without them.

"Okay, John. When do we leave?" asked Sarah.

Those were the words I had wanted to hear. I was just a little surprised and disappointed it had taken so long for her to decide.

"What about me?" came Taylor's voice from outside the entrance where he'd been listening to every word.

I went to the entrance and pulled back the flap, where Grey was looking back at me, obviously agitated.

"How much did you hear?" I asked.

"Everything."

"That's going to be a problem," I said as I grabbed him by the arm and pulled him inside, throwing him to the ground.

Grey crawled straight to Sarah. "You can't go. It'll ruin our arrangement."

"I'm not so crazy about your 'arrangement' anyway," I replied.

"They'll want to know why I didn't stop you and where you've gone," continued Taylor.

"We have to go," she answered. "I'm sorry it's going to cause you problems, but it can't be helped. Maybe they'll find you another family."

"It's more likely they'll remove my head from my shoulders."

"I'm afraid Grey's eavesdropping has created another problem," I said. "Now that Mr. Grey knows about the valley, we can't leave him here. The valley must remain a secret, and leaving him here is too much of a risk."

"I won't say anything. Just that you left in the middle of the night, I didn't see anything, and I don't know where you went."

"I can't take the chance. You're coming with us," I said.

"And what if I don't want to go?"

"You don't have a choice," I said. "But why wouldn't you want to go? One day, they're going to haul you off too, just like they did me. Is that what you want? Then, there is the more imminent matter. After we leave, the Guard is going to pay you a visit, just like you said, and they're going to want answers. I expect it will be a very unpleasant visit."

Grey didn't answer, turning his back on us, mumbling to himself.

"Do you have family here?" I asked.

"No," he answered. "I have no one."

"Is there some other reason why you want to stay?"

"As long as I do as I'm told, I'm safe and taken care of here."

PARADISE

The only reason for me to attempt to convince him to go along was to make it easier and safer for the rest of us. A willing travel companion wouldn't attract nearly as much attention as an unwilling one. He was going, regardless. I couldn't take the risk of leaving him behind to report what he'd heard as soon as we'd left. If Governor Davis ever found out about Paradise existing in the middle of the wasteland, I knew it wouldn't take long for him to send troops to swoop down and exploit its resources and its people. Freedom there would cease to exist.

It was time to be blunt. "You know you're not really safe here, don't you? They're not going to find you another family as Sarah suggested. If you think that, you're dreaming. Ask her if she really believes it."

Taylor looked at her as her eyes shifted away, not wanting to make eye contact. I could tell she knew I was right. I hated to put her on the spot, but this situation needed to be resolved, and quickly.

"I think once it's discovered my family is gone, you're the first person the Guard is going to come looking for," I continued.

"The governor has spies everywhere. It'll be too dangerous trying to get them out," argued Grey.

"More dangerous than staying here? I don't think so. I can't make you any promises, but I believe you'll find the valley much better than anything you have here. And if we retrace my steps, we should be able to get away without a problem."

I wasn't leaving Taylor with much of a choice. Then something occurred to me. If he hadn't been listening to our family conversation, he wouldn't have known anything about us leaving. And after we were gone, he would without a doubt have been taken into custody and punished. How severely, I had no idea. But now, aware of the circumstances, he was being given a simple choice. Stay and most likely die or go and live. The choice couldn't have been any clearer.

"When do we leave?" asked Taylor.

"I think the best time would be in the morning when the streets are crowded with everyone going to work. We'll be able to move with the flow. I'm afraid if we tried to leave tonight, with fewer people on the streets, we'd be too visible and the chances of being stopped would be too high. Agreed?"

Sarah nodded. Taylor nodded agreement as well when I looked directly at him. "Good," I said. "Tonight, we need to pack the bare essentials to take along. We don't want to look like we're carrying any more than we normally would be for work. Don't worry about food or water. We have plenty."

"We?" asked Sarah.

"Yes. One of the men from the valley came with me. He's waiting with a horse and wagon south of town."

"What will he think when he sees me?" asked Taylor. "I assume he's only expecting you and your family."

"I guess you'll have to be Uncle Taylor," I replied in a semi-joking way.

I had no way of knowing what Levi's reaction would be or Samuel's when we reached Paradise. That wasn't my immediate concern. First, we would have to make it to the wagon.

"Cindy, why don't you help your mother pack.

PARADISE

Christopher, if you could gather our guns, especially the pistols. The rifles will probably have to stay behind."

"But Dad, those were Grandpa's," objected Christopher.

"I know, but I don't think we can conceal them well enough to try. We'll have to wait and see."

I turned my attention to Taylor. "What's your usual routine in the evening after my family goes to bed?"

"I keep watch outside the entrance all night and then in the morning, when they go to work, I go back to my tent to sleep." I could see Sarah's point. It probably had been a good thing to have him around. At night, when they were asleep, would have been a very vulnerable time. And for that reason alone, I was glad he had been around.

"Then, I suppose you should go back outside to avoid any suspicions, especially if it's where people are used to seeing you. I'm sorry, but you won't be able to go back to your tent before we leave."

"Just so you know, this is only the second time I've ever been in here," he informed me.

I guess he could read between the lines. I had been curious about the arrangement.

"Thanks," I said.

"I need to collect a few items from my tent in the morning. I can meet you somewhere," said Taylor.

"Sorry, can't let you do that," I said. "Too risky."

"Still don't trust me?" he asked. "Even after I've been watching over your family? You know nothing about me."

I didn't reply.

"I guess I'll be outside then," Taylor said, getting up. "See all of you in the morning."

MICHAEL R. WATSON

It made me uncomfortable to have him out of my sight. He could run off and report us to the Guard before I would even know he was gone. Periodically, through the rest of the night, I looked outside to make sure he was there. Each time I was surprised to find him still sitting by the fire. My family was busy during the night, not being able to decide on what to take. Or deciding, then changing their minds, then changing them again. I didn't have that problem. I had left everything behind two months ago. They were only things. Right now, my family was all I cared anything about.

* * *

I lay down in a corner of the tent out of everyone's way so I could relax and rest. It could be a while before I had another chance.

"Dad," said Christopher as he shook me. "I think we're about ready to go."

I hadn't intended to, but I had fallen asleep. As I sat up, Sarah brought me a cup of weak hot tea. It reminded me that coffee was a premium commodity here, another one of those items reserved for the privileged. Somehow, Samuel had been able to obtain an abundant supply, which he made available to everyone and I had taken full advantage of it. Chances were, thanks to his son, Ryder, it had come from the governor's own stockpile.

"This is the last of the tea, so I decided we might as well use it," said Sarah.

"Thanks. It's just what I needed."

"Come see what we picked out."

PARADISE

I followed her to where they had laid out only a few items on blankets. I didn't see anything of much importance. Most were keepsakes. I was surprised. Earlier they seemed to be having a difficult time deciding. "Looks good," I said.

"We're wearing two and three layers of clothing too," said Cindy proudly.

"Good thinking."

"Dad," said Christopher. "Here are all the guns and ammo."

We had more than I had remembered. I reached down and grabbed a Colt .45 caliber 1911 and a Smith & Wesson .38 revolver, which I handed to Christopher.

"Is this all the ammo we have?" I asked. Lying on the blanket were only twelve rounds for the .45 and six for the .38

"It's all I could find," answered Christopher, apologetically.

I smiled. "They'll just have to do, won't they. Go ahead and load your gun and hide it," I instructed.

"And the rifles and shotguns?" he asked.

"Sorry, Son. They're just too large to conceal. It looks like there's no ammo for them anyway. They'd just be dead weight."

"I understand. At least we have Grandpa's pistols," said Christopher.

"That's right. Now, get your backpack. We'll be leaving very soon."

"We've already eaten," said Cindy, "but there's some oatmeal still out over the fire if you're hungry."

"Thanks honey, but I think I'd just like to get out of

here. Has Mr. Grey eaten yet?"

Cindy and her mother exchanged sheepish looks.

"I don't think so," answered Sarah. "He was already gone when we got up."

I cursed to myself as I jumped up and ran over to the entrance to see for myself. He was gone. Now, it was time to panic. If he had gone to the authorities, they could show up at any minute. Grey had probably figured out there was another option open to him, other than the ones I had given him. And that was to turn all of us in for a reward.

"We've got to go right now!" I said.

"Aren't we going to wait for Mr. Grey, Daddy?" asked Cindy. It saddened me slightly, appearing that even she had become attached to him.

"We can't. If we stay here one more second, he'll probably bring the Guard here to arrest every one of us," I explained.

"John, I can't believe he'd do that," said Sarah.

"Are you willing to gamble on it?" I asked.

She thought briefly. "Kids, we have got to go," as she picked up a bundle and headed for the entrance.

* * *

Chapter 8

Just as expected, the dirt streets were filled with people on their way to work, some to the prison and some to the fields. We were given a few glances from our neighbors as we stood together outside the tent. If they realized who I was, most didn't show any recognition. One of our neighbors and a friend hesitated long enough to catch my eye and smiled, then went on his way.

"C'mon," I said as I stepped out into the flow of people, leading the way south. I kept my head down, avoiding eye contact with anyone. The governor had informants everywhere, those willing to provide information in return for rewards or favors. Desperate people did things they normally wouldn't have done before, for the sake of survival.

The further we distanced ourselves from our tent, there would be fewer who would recognize us. We were just going to work like everyone else. I had to force myself to slow down to a normal pace. No one rushed to get to work.

As we reached the south edge of town, the number of people began to thin out, most having already arrived at their work destinations. We no longer had the masses to shield our movement. Walking past the last row of tents, we were alone with no one else in sight. I showed them where I had come through the crude barrier of abandoned and useless vehicles and led them through to the other side. It looked as though we had pulled it off.

"Hey, you there!" came a shout.

Two of the governor's Guard stepped out, directly in front of us, from behind the dilapidated shell of a house. There was no use in running. Both men carried rifles, aimed at us and ready to be used. Maybe I could have made a run for it if I had been by myself, but not with Sarah and our children with me. And using my gun was out of the question. I'd have to try and talk our way out of this.

"Come here!" one of them shouted, motioning us over to him while the other one circled around behind, his rifle trained on us.

"Why aren't you at work?" he asked.

"We've been sent to one of the outlying farms to help out. We're on our way there now."

"Let me see your papers," he said, holding his hand out.

Sarah, Cindy, and Christopher produced theirs. I pretended to look for mine.

"I can't seem to find mine. It's probably back at the tent."

"And your work orders?" he asked, looking at us

PARADISE

suspiciously.

"I'm afraid it must be with my papers."

"You'll have to come with us. Someday, you people will have to learn responsibility."

I was instantly filled with dread. My plan was dead before it had had a chance. My mind raced to find an excuse that would change their minds. We followed one guard while the other one followed us. According to the direction they were taking us, we were either going to the governor's compound or to the Guard's satellite office outside the Tent City gate.

Suddenly, there was a grunt from behind. I turned around in time to see the trailing guard drop to the ground, Taylor standing over him holding one of my dad's rifles. I looked back to the front guard who quickly threw his hands into the air.

"Taylor?!" We exclaimed in unison. It surprised and bothered me when Cindy ran over and gave him a hug.

"Where did you come from?" I asked.

"I've been following you ever since you left the tent. I got there just as you were leaving. You should have waited."

"I thought ..."

"Yeah, I can imagine. You thought I had gone to report you, didn't you?"

"You're right. I did. But it seems things have worked out."

"I'm glad you caught up to us," said Sarah.

He seemed to have made quite an impression on my family, which I didn't understand or like at all.

"Don't you think we should be going before their

friends show up?" asked Taylor, moving toward the standing guard.

"What about him?" I asked.

When the guard turned toward me, Taylor cracked him over the head with the rifle butt, knocking him unconscious.

"Problem solved," said Taylor.

I led the way to what was left of the old barn where Levi said he would be waiting. In back, just as he had promised was the horse and wagon, but no Levi. He may not have expected us to show up this early since he had given us until sundown. We waited almost an hour before we saw him hurriedly coming toward us carrying a large bag.

Looking none too happy, he asked "Who's he?"

"A friend," I replied.

"Uncle Taylor," said Cindy.

"That's right. Uncle Taylor," echoed Christopher.

I smiled at them for wanting to stick up for him. But for the life of me, I couldn't see the attraction.

"I was only expecting your wife and children," said Levi.

"He's okay. We wouldn't be here without his help," I pointed out. I attempted to change the subject. "We should probably leave right away. There will be some mighty unhappy guards waking up any time now." I had to ask, "Did you get the supplies you needed?"

He ignored the question. "I'm ready to go. Get in," he instructed brusquely.

I decided not to push it right then. "By the way, this is my wife, Sarah, and our children, Cindy and Christopher.

PARADISE

And this you already know is Taylor."

"Ma'am," he said with a nod, giving Taylor a disapproving look.

"And family, this is Levi," I said.

"A pleasure," said Sarah, smiling.

After he had stashed what appeared to be a special bag into the side box, Levi climbed up into the buckboard and grabbed the reins. We climbed into the back seeing that Levi had evidently made more than one trip to meet his source. Several boxes of supplies were already stacked in back.

"Dad, can I ride up front with Levi?" asked Christopher.

"You'll have to ask him," I replied.

Levi had overheard, looking back and waving him up.

As Christopher stood to leave us, I whispered in his ear," He's not much of a talker."

"That's okay," he said. He didn't mind, he was doing something he'd never done before. It would be an adventure.

We pulled out immediately, heading south at a casual pace. One siren and then another began to wail loudly. The alarm had been sounded.

"You might want to pick up the pace a little," I advised Levi, but he had already decided that for himself, coaxing the horse to pick up the pace.

* * *

Governor Davis was sitting at his oversized mahogany desk when he heard the sirens go off. He stood and moved to the large window overlooking Tent City. Counselor Damon, who occupied the adjacent office, quickly entered the room after knocking at the door, stopping at the governor's side.

"What's all the commotion about?" asked the governor.

"It would seem we have had a family of workers leave our town without authorization, sir. It was the Thomas ..."

"I don't care anything about names. How many?" asked Davis.

"Three, sir. And we believe they were helped by one of the condemned. The family's father."

"And how did that happen?"

"I don't know, sir."

"How is it going to affect production?"

"Insignificant."

He thought for a moment.

"It doesn't matter. We can't have the workers walking off whenever they feel like it. I want them returned so we can make an example of them. Send the Guard to bring them back. Let me know as soon as you have them."

"Yes, sir," said Damon, turning and leaving the office.

"And stop those annoying sirens! They're giving me a headache!" ordered the governor.

*   *   *

Damon went directly to Gant, the Master of the Guard. He was already aware of the events that had taken place, receiving reports from the two guards who had been injured.

PARADISE

"I'd like you to send a squad of men to find these people and bring them back unharmed. They'll still need to be healthy enough to return to the fields. But once you find them, hold back and watch them. I'd like you to find out where they're going and then report back. They may lead us to others. Do you understand?"

"Yes, Counselor."

"Now, I'd like to see the two men who allowed their escape."

"That won't be possible, sir."

"Why not?"

"They can't be located, sir. I believe they may have also left, right after reporting to Gant."

Damon's face was turning red uncharacteristically. He normally remained in control of his emotions. He took a few moments before he spoke. "When your men bring back the workers, I want you to bring those two guards back too. Understand?"

"Perfectly, sir."

Gant knew what the guard's punishment would be. Incompetence wasn't tolerated. If caught, they would pay the ultimate price in the central courtyard for all the other guards to see. And there wouldn't be anything Gant would be able to do to stop it, not without his family suffering the consequences. The men were young, single, and he knew them well, having trained them from the beginning. That was why he had given each of them a horse and a chance.

* * *

We had been traveling almost two hours since leaving

the outskirts of town, each of us keeping a watchful eye. So far, there had been no sign of the guard.

"I haven't seen anyone yet," I informed Levi. He grunted without saying a word.

"Maybe we lost them," speculated Christopher.

"I don't see how," I commented. "Anyone should be able to follow these wagon tracks, and that's what has me worried. We should have seen someone by now or at least some evidence like a dust cloud from pursuers on horseback."

"Daddy, I see smoke," said Cindy, pointing behind us, off a little bit to the east.

I concentrated on the area where she was pointing. There *was* something off in the distance, barely visible on the horizon. Cindy had better eyes than I did. I would never have seen it if she hadn't pointed it out.

"Good eyes, Cindy. But it's not smoke. It's dust. We *do* have someone behind us."

Taylor perked up, looking for himself. "I don't see anything. Maybe it's just a dust devil or the heat waves playing a trick on our eyes."

"I don't think so. It'd be too much of a coincidence. And it's right where we came from. No, there's definitely someone back there," I said.

"What are we going to do now?" asked Sarah.

Levi was listening. "We're just going to keep on just as we have been. As long as we can stay a step ahead of them, you'll be safe."

"But we can't let them stay behind us the entire way. That would lead them to Paradise," I pointed out to Levi. Then something occurred to me, "What if they aren't

PARADISE

trying to catch up with us? What if they want to know where we're going? Maybe they already know about the valley."

Levi gave me a suspicious glance.

"But how could they know about it?" asked Sarah.

"There's only one way I know of," I said, turning to face Taylor.

"You can't be serious. You're accusing me? I'm the one who saved you this morning," Taylor attempted to reason.

"Pretty convenient, wasn't it?" I said, accusingly. "Maybe the reward was too good to pass up."

Levi looked back at Taylor, sizing him up.

"John!" said Sarah. "You're overreacting. We don't even know for certain there's someone back there."

"They're back there alright and there's an easy way to find out, by stopping right here. If they stop too, then we can be fairly confident they're keeping their distance for a reason, possibly to identify our destination. Did you hear that, Levi?"

I guess he was curious too, because we came to a stop. "It's a good time to water the horse anyway," he said.

Within a few minutes, the dust cloud had disappeared completely.

"It appears they *have* stopped," I said.

"That doesn't prove I told them anything. What do you have against me anyway?" Taylor asked, changing the subject.

"If the dust cloud reappears when we start moving again, that'll be proof enough for me," I said.

This time Sarah didn't say anything. She may have

finally begun to question his motives as I did.

After a short rest we started moving again. Everyone in the wagon was intently watching the trail behind, especially Taylor, focusing on the horizon. After an hour, there had been no reappearance of the dust cloud. We relaxed slightly. I glanced over at Taylor. He had a cocky look on his face.

"Well?"

"Well what?" I asked.

"I think you owe me an apology," he prodded.

"To use your own words, it doesn't prove anything. Maybe they're just being more cautious now, keeping a little further distance between us."

"What's it going to take for you to trust me? I didn't have time to tell anyone. I went directly to my tent, collected some of my belongings, and then came right back to your tent."

"So you say," I said, not convinced.

"I give up. Think what you want to. I don't know what else I can say to convince you. But you'll find out soon enough whether I'm telling the truth."

"That's what I'm afraid of."

* * *

We stopped as the sun was setting. It was too dangerous to travel at night with the possibility of falling off into a water-worn ravine or a quake-created fissure. Besides, we all needed a rest from riding in the wagon all day and we were hungry, having nibbled only on dried fruit and bread.

PARADISE

Levi took on the role of cook as he made a fire and prepared a pot of beans, handing out more of the dry, crusty bread to go with them. He then volunteered to keep watch while we tried to get some sleep.

"I'll take the second watch," said Taylor.

I didn't like the idea and started to say something, but seeing the look Sarah gave me, I decided not to. I would keep an eye on him anyway.

I had a hard time sleeping even though I was dog tired. I didn't trust Taylor and I was awake when Levi woke him for his turn at taking watch.

"If you hear or see anything out of the ordinary, come and get me," Levi told Taylor.

"Aye, aye, captain," Taylor whispered back, saluting with mock respect.

Levi didn't find him amusing in the least. He just turned his back to him and walked off to a spot away from the rest of us and laid out his bedroll. I watched in silence. Levi apparently wasn't sure about any of us, preferring to keep his distance as he slept. I had a feeling he wasn't going to get much sleep either.

Uneasy with Taylor supposedly watching over us, I drifted in and out of sleep, waking what seemed like every hour. The last time I woke, I looked around and didn't find Taylor where he had been only moments earlier. Sarah, Cindy, and Christopher were sound asleep near the fire. I stood and began to look for him. I saw his bedding was still laid out where he had left it.

I went over to where Levi had laid out his bedroll. He wasn't there either. "Levi!" I called out in a loud whisper. There was no reply. I tried again, a little louder, "Levi!"

I jumped, startled when a hand rested on my shoulder. I turned quickly to see Levi beside me.

"I want to show you something," he said, motioning for me to follow.

He climbed up onto the wagon and motioned me up.

Standing beside him he said, "Look."

My eyes followed to where he was pointing. Faintly, in the distance, was a glow, a fire. There was someone still directly behind us to the north. I looked at him and nodded.

"And there," he pointed to the east, "and there," as he pointed to the west.

"We're surrounded, "I said, stating the obvious. "I guess they want to make sure we don't get away."

"If it's the Guard," said Levi.

"Good point."

Then I remembered, "Have you seen Taylor?"

"No."

"He's not in camp. What do you think he's up to?" I asked, looking for agreement.

"I don't know."

"Well, we can't keep leading them in this direction or they're sure to find the valley."

"I know. I think we're going to have to leave the wagon. It's too slow and too easy to follow. I know another way where we can lose them. We should probably leave right now. Take only what you can carry. Keep it simple, we need to be able to travel fast."

"What about the supplies for Paradise?" I asked.

"We'll take what the horse can carry and leave the rest. It's more important to keep your family safe and Paradise's location a secret."

PARADISE

"Won't it be dangerous traveling in the dark?" I asked.

"Stay with me and you'll be fine," said Levi.

Out here, Levi showed a confidence I hadn't seen back in the valley. As we climbed down from the wagon, Taylor came strolling back into camp, fastening his belt. He seemed surprised to see both of us up.

"What's wrong?" he asked.

"Where have you been?" I asked. "Weren't you supposed to be on watch?"

"I was taking care of some personal business, if you must know," he replied, sounding offended. "I wasn't gone but a couple of minutes. ...Why? Did something happen?"

"We're leaving right now," I told him. "Take only what you can carry. We're leaving the wagon behind."

"We're leaving in the middle of the night?" he asked.

"Yeah. It seems we're surrounded by your friends," I accused, matter-of-factly.

"I said ... ," he started to say something, but I had already turned my back on him, walking away.

Levi was gathering food and water and a few other items to take, including the special bag, loading as much as he thought the horse could carry.

I walked over to Sarah and gently shook her shoulder.

"What's going on?" asked Sarah groggily, rising onto one elbow.

I knelt down beside her. "We have to go. The Guard seems to have us surrounded on three sides. Wake the kids. Take only what you can carry. We're leaving the wagon."

Still half asleep, Sarah and the kids gathered a few things and rolled them in their bedrolls. The rest they threw into the back of the wagon.

Taylor walked up to me. "Someday, you're going to apologize to me," he said, poking me in my chest with his finger.

I brushed his finger aside. "I'll be glad to, if I'm wrong."

*   *   *

We traveled all the next day on foot with only brief breaks, primarily for the horse and the children. This trail covered a much rougher terrain, making it harder on everyone. Levi had been right, it would be hard for anyone to follow us on this route, and the wagon never would have made it.

Frequently, either Levi or myself would fall back to look and listen for those following us. Neither of us trusted the task to Taylor, who acted frustrated at being excluded. Whether it was just an act for our benefit, or if he was being sincere, I didn't know and didn't care. Since leaving the main trail, there had been no indication our pursuers were still back there.

We entered an area that was too treacherous in the dark, even for Levi. He found us an out of the way spot where a campfire wouldn't be seen. We were grateful for a place where we could get a desperately needed good night's sleep before starting out again early the next morning. Levi had pushed us pretty hard all day, making sure we stayed well out in front of the Guard. He built a small fire in a shielded area and prepared another meal of beans. After eating and extinguishing the fire, Levi and I split the perimeter watch, letting Taylor watch over the

PARADISE

camp. It was obvious from his expression he wasn't happy about it. He pleaded for us to let him do his part, but we continued to have doubts about him, even though the kids apparently didn't. I could tell Sarah was beginning to have her doubts too by the way she seemed to be speaking to him less.

The sky was beginning to lighten when we all heard a noise just north of our camp. Levi motioned for us to be still and quiet.

"You there, in the camp!" came a man's voice. He was very close. Levi and I moved past the edge of the camp toward the voice. Lying on our bellies, we crawled up to the crest of a small rock outcrop where we attempted to see from behind a scraggly mesquite bush. Three men were on horseback, one out in front. From their dress, it was obvious these were not members of the Guard.

"Raiders," whispered Levi, shaking his head. "That's all we need."

I had heard warnings and stories about them. They were mostly men and some women who had either left the confines of Tent City to survive and live on their own terms, unwilling to let the governor dictate their future, or were those who had never gone to Sector 4, confident they could survive without anyone's help. In some ways I admired them for having the fortitude to do it, but the hardship to survive had changed many of them. Some were said to have become thieves and worse. We had received numerous warnings from the governor to avoid venturing too far from Tent City with there being too great a risk of being attacked by the criminals. I personally hadn't heard a single account of them attacking Tent City citizens, but there were plenty of stories about them attacking the Guard during collections, taking anything and everything that would help them survive.

The governor had reasoned that when the Raiders stole from his men, they were stealing from us. I didn't quite buy into his explanation since we only received token assistance from him on rare occasions anyway.

Taylor crawled in-between Levi and myself with my grandfather's rifle, pointing it in the direction of the riders.

"No!" whispered Levi forcefully, catching Taylor by surprise. "No shooting!" as he placed his hand on the rifle. He didn't remove his hand until Taylor nodded he would do as told.

Taylor looked at me in shock. I was as surprised as he was. If it took deadly force to protect my family, I would do it, whether I had Levi's permission or not.

"Shouldn't we at least let them know we're armed?" I asked. "It might make them think twice before trying something."

"No," answered Levi. "There's no way of knowing how many there actually are. What we need to do first is find out what they want."

He had a point. I nodded, but for reassurance I felt the .45 in my belt to make sure it was handy.

Levi shouted to the man, "What do you want?"

"We need to talk. Can I come in?"

"Come alone!" shouted Levi.

As the man approached, I ran back to camp.

"What's wrong?" asked Sarah, seeing concern on my face as I ran toward her.

"Sarah, you, Cindy and Christopher need to get out of

PARADISE

sight. Come with me."

I led them behind some brush in the shadows beyond the light of the campfire, not wanting the Raider to know about them. I told them to remain still and quiet and not to come out until I gave them the okay. I was sitting by the fire when Levi and Taylor escorted the man into the camp. He was younger than I had expected, perhaps mid-twenties and he didn't look like an immediate threat. He was about six foot, two-hundred pounds, give or take, appeared to be physically fit, had long dark hair, and a neatly trimmed beard. I suppose he could have been considered a handsome man. Levi asked him to join us at the campfire. Something was going on between the man and Levi. I must have missed something when I came back to camp. The man continued to stare at him, smiling, while Levi refused to make eye contact.

"We saw your campfires," I said, attempting to bait him into admitting the fires were theirs.

"Those aren't our fires," he corrected.

Levi, Taylor, and I exchanged glances.

"That's right," he said, "those are the Guard fires."

So, we had our answer, if we could believe him, we still had the Guard to contend with and now Raiders too.

"What did you want to talk about, taking everything we have or our surrender?" Taylor asked sarcastically.

I glared at him in a way he would notice and understand. We didn't want to start any trouble. We had no idea how many more Raiders were waiting in the dark.

"Not at all," the man said. "We've been watching you since you left the city and I'm here to offer our help. We don't have any more use for the Guard than you do."

"So, Levi was right, you *are* Raiders," I stated, looking for confirmation.

He looked at Levi, once again attempting to make eye contact. Levi remained silent. "I've heard some call us that," he said.

"What do you want in return for this help?" I asked, suspicious of his generous offer.

"Nothing, except maybe a new ally. We look forward to striking back at the Guard every chance we get. If helping you will do that, then we appreciate and look forward to the opportunity."

He didn't give me the impression of your typical thug, but more of an educated, reasonable, and rational man.

"As long as you know we're not going to help you fight them," proclaimed Levi.

"I understand. If there is any fighting to do, we will do it. Agreed?"

"How many men *do* you have?" I asked. "We only saw the three of you."

"Enough," he said, "but I didn't mean we would strike at them directly, it was more figurative than literal. An indirect approach seems to work best for us. Any kind of trouble or harassment we can cause them is a treat."

"What did you have in mind?" I asked. I could tell by the look Levi was giving me he didn't like associating with this Raider.

"We know a thousand places to hide from them. We're just offering to help you get away from them. By the way, where are you going?"

Exactly what I had been waiting for, the hidden agenda. They wanted to lose the Guard so they could

PARADISE

follow us instead. I didn't know if he knew about the valley or not and I wasn't going to mention it. Levi sat in silence slowly shaking his head. He finally looked up at the man, eye-to-eye. The Raider just smiled.

"Well, it doesn't matter," said the man.

"We're just trying to get as far away from Tent City as we can," I offered. "No place in particular."

He nodded and smiled a Cheshire cat type of smile. He obviously knew something I didn't and he seemed to understand our lack of trust. After all, he was a stranger, and a Raider.

"No strings attached. We'll help you get away and then if you like we'll part ways as friends. The satisfaction of helping you and making the Guard look like idiots is the only reward we need."

"Would you mind if we talked it over?" I asked.

"Please," he said, standing and walking away to the edge of the campfire light.

We huddled close together.

"Should we accept his offer?" I asked the others.

"We don't need him. We'll be fine without his help," commented Levi.

"I don't trust him," said Taylor, "but that's not the point. If he can protect us from the Guard and he's willing to deal with them, it could be worth the risk. We can worry about him later. Then we'll be eliminating one of our problems."

"I agree," I said. "Levi? What do you think?"

He remained silent for a moment. "Whatever you think, John. I guess a little temporary help couldn't hurt."

I turned to face the man. He was still smiling. His

disposition was a far cry from what I had expected from a Raider.

"We've decided to take you up on your offer," I said.

"Good! I'm so glad. Please start gathering your things together and break camp. I'll let my friends know you've accepted my offer and we'll be leaving soon."

"You should know there are more than just the three of us," I informed him.

"Yes, I know," he said, smiling, "a woman and two almost grown children."

As he began walking away, I asked, "What do we call you?"

"Ryder," answered Levi. Ryder showed a huge smile and gave us a wink. Obviously, I *had* missed something. Wait a second. I knew that name. This was Samuel's other son and Levi's brother.

* * *

Chapter 9

Days went by and Governor Davis became concerned when he hadn't received any news about the escaped family. He was afraid the workers would see him as weak or his Guard as incompetent. If the family of workers had been able to escape and evade capture so easily, he was sure others would attempt it. And he couldn't have that. The family needed to be brought back to serve as an example and a deterrent, especially the mother. And if the aid of the father was confirmed, he would experience a worse death than one of hunger and thirst in the wasteland. The children would go unharmed, but would be forced to witness the punishment of both parents. After all, they were still a valuable asset and would provide many years of service.

By now, the entire city knew what had happened and that the Guard had been sent to bring them back. Silently, the residents of Tent City were rooting for the Thomas family, but were also curious as to what would happen if they were returned. The governor was quick to announce a warning, if anyone else attempted to leave, punishment would be swift and extreme. Davis summoned Damon to his office.

"Counselor, what news do you have to report about the search?" asked Davis.

"I'm sorry, Governor. It would seem they've disappeared. I have sent word to the men to keep looking. I'm confident they will be successful."

"It's been three days! The Guard should have found them by now."

"I know, sir. We think they may have received help."

"Help? Help from whom?"

"The Raiders."

Governor Davis swore loudly as he picked up a polished stone paperweight and threw it at the concrete wall, shattering into hundreds of pieces. The prison, containing the governor's residence, had been overdesigned and built to withstand the test of time and any of nature's destructive forces, including earthquakes.

"I thought you had the Raiders under control?" asked Davis.

"Governor, the only times we see them is when they ambush our men while they're making collections. They strike without any warning."

"Do you think these recent workers have joined with them?"

"I don't know, sir." He paused. "I have learned something else you should be aware of. It has been

PARADISE

confirmed the father of the escaped family did help them to get away. He returned after being sent to the wasteland during the last culling two months ago."

"How is that possible? The only way he could have survived for that long out there is if he had help. Do you think he was rescued by the Raiders?"

"It's a possibility, sir."

"Who else could it be? He couldn't have survived on his own."

"If that's true, then it brings up another question. Have any of the others taken to the wasteland joined the Raiders too?"

"If so, their numbers would be growing along with our problems," determined Davis. "It would explain why the raids have become more frequent. These people were taken to the wasteland because they were obsolete and food was too precious to waste on them. Now, they are stealing the food they were once denied. We can't let this continue. I want you to send more of the Guard to help in the search for those workers. Their orders now include eliminating any Raiders encountered, but I still want the workers returned here alive, if at all possible. We must make an example out of them."

*　　*　　*

Ryder led us through an area of rocky terrain, making it extremely difficult for anyone to pick up our trail. Very few words were exchanged between him and his brother. Something had happened in the past, but neither was willing to talk about it.

I was still wary of Ryder, not fully believing he was doing this out of the kindness of his heart. Now that I knew he was Samuel's son, I could see similar mannerisms, especially their disposition, but he was also a Raider. Perhaps that was what Levi had a problem with.

After two days with Ryder and his men, we hadn't seen any signs of anyone behind us or anywhere else. Without any sign of danger, Levi came to me and suggested it was time to go our own way and let Ryder go his. I'd say we discussed it, but that wasn't easy to do with him. I kind of liked having Ryder around, just in case, but Levi wanted him gone. Whatever had happened between them seemed to have stuck with Levi more than his brother. Ryder didn't appear to hold any animosity against Levi.

At camp that evening we approached Ryder and told him we appreciated his help, but since it appeared we were out of danger, perhaps it was time to go our own ways. He didn't seem surprised or offended, just giving us a pleasant all-knowing smile.

"If that's what you want. We can give you some supplies in the morning for your journey. Are you sure you wouldn't like an escort a little further?"

"Thanks for the offer," I said, "but I think we'll be alright."

"Okay. Then I hope you have a safe journey."

The next morning we said our goodbyes and thanked them once again for all their help. Levi remained silent, standing at the edge of the camp, waiting impatiently for us. Ryder smiled and waved. The six of us set out on our own, Sarah and Cindy riding the horse together.

PARADISE

After we were out of earshot, I asked Levi, "Do you know where we are?"

"Yeah."

"Then, you know where Paradise is from here?"

"Yeah."

I looked at Sarah and the others and shrugged. Sarah found Levi's reluctance or inability to carry on a conversation amusing. I just found it frustrating. We'd just have to trust that he did know. However, I couldn't help having second thoughts and wondering if we should have asked Ryder to stay with us. Evidently, there wasn't any reason now to keep our destination a secret. It was where he had been raised.

Regardless, we were back on our own. And over the next few days, I continued to check behind us, unable to shake a feeling of uneasiness as though someone was watching. First watch tonight was my turn. Christopher joined me on a hilltop where I had a good vantage point. The sky was clear and the stars were bright. It was a beautiful night. Whether it was his or his mother's idea to join me, I didn't know and it didn't matter. I was just glad he was there with me.

I watched as Levi disappeared into the brush every so often, always coming back after only a few minutes. I suppose he was checking things out on his own. Taylor though, seemed perfectly at ease, sitting by the campfire chatting with Sarah and Cindy. Even though he had initially complained, it seemed he had become comfortable with doing nothing and having no responsibilities. I couldn't shake a feeling of uneasiness about him. My children, on the other hand, seemed to have accepted him fully. But they had an excuse; they were young and naive, easily swayed by a kind word and a friendly smile. I think Sarah was still trying to make up her mind. My gut told me he shouldn't be trusted. I couldn't understand why they refused to see it.

Christopher stayed with me all night, and even though he was asleep most of the time, it was nice to have him with me. The night passed without incident, all remaining quiet. Levi joined us at dawn, wanting to leave early, telling us we could be at Paradise by the end of the day if we pushed through. I hadn't realized we were so close, but it put me a bit more at ease. I was anxious for my family to see our new home. I had attempted to describe the valley, but I knew my words had been inadequate. No words could do it justice. Only when they saw it first hand would they fully understand.

After a long hard day, stopping only long enough to tend to the horse, the sun began to set. It was appearing as though we weren't going to make it there today after all. Then we heard a church bell begin to ring repeatedly. I let out a sigh of relief, explaining to Sarah, Christopher, and Cindy what it meant. We were almost there. Smiles immediately appeared on their faces. Cindy squealed with delight. The sound of the bell was loud, letting me know we were close. I still couldn't see anything other than the same arid and desolate wasteland we had been traveling through. Then a man appeared on the horizon on the trail directly in front of us. When we were close enough I recognized it was Samuel. The sentries had probably seen us coming when we were still a ways off. As we walked toward him, the valley began to open up. Levi was the first

PARADISE

to reach Samuel, handing him the special bag from Sector 4. Samuel patted him on the back as Levi continued down the sloping trail into town, never saying a word.

"John, I'm glad to see you made it back," said Samuel, shaking my hand, "and this must be your family."

"Samuel, I'd like you to meet my wife, Sarah, and our two children, Christopher and Cindy."

Taking Sarah's hand, "It's very nice to meet all of you." He then looked at Taylor. "John, who's this?"

"This is Taylor Grey. He heard us talking about Paradise, so, we didn't have much choice except to bring him along. Sorry."

"Thanks for the great introduction," said Taylor sarcastically.

"It's not a problem," said Samuel. "We're glad to have you here, Taylor."

"Thanks," said Taylor. "It's not like I had somewhere else to go."

"Did you explain the conditions, John?" asked Samuel.

"No, it never came up."

"That's okay. I'll explain everything tomorrow. Right now there is a group at Town Hall ready to welcome you all here."

"We met your other son, Ryder, on the trail," I mentioned. "He traveled part of the way with us after helping us get away from the Guard."

"Really? How is he? Is he coming?" asked Samuel. "His mother will want to know."

"He looked fine, but I don't think he's coming," I said.

"That's too bad. I mean about the not coming."

We walked over to where Sarah, the children, and

Taylor were already standing near the rim, staring out over the valley.

The dimming sky was still light enough to see the valley clearly. It appeared to be even more beautiful and peaceful than I remembered. Sarah had her hands on both sides of her face, as though she were holding her head steady from the staggering view.

"John, it's beautiful. It's everything you said it was and more," said Sarah.

"Yeah, Dad, this is great," echoed Christopher. "This is a lot better than Tent City."

"Very nice," said Taylor. "It's amazing it's been a secret for so long."

I didn't like the way Taylor said it or the smirk on his face. His expression wasn't just the joy of finally arriving here. There was something else, something sinister behind his eyes.

"Yes, and we expect to keep it that way," said Samuel. "We've been very blessed and I'm afraid it wouldn't last very long like this if the governor of Sector 4 found out about it."

We followed Samuel down the switchback trail as it sloped toward town. A small group of familiar faces was waiting for us at Town Hall with Jill, Paul, and Gary in the foreground. It was good to see them again. They must have come when they heard the church bell begin to ring. Jill rushed past Sarah and gave me a hug that lasted a bit too long. I looked at Sarah who raised an eyebrow and gave me a knowing smile. When Jill had set me free, I introduced Sarah to my former travel companions and friends.

PARADISE

Even though a potluck dinner had been prepared, we were more tired than hungry, exhausted from the long day and ready for a good nights sleep. Since arriving and being back with friends, I had let down my guard, realizing how tired I really was. The people who had come to welcome me back and to meet my family had started to leave, one and two at a time. Sarah helped a couple of the ladies clean up before they left. Soon we were alone with Samuel and my former traveling companions. We gathered at one end of the long community table.

"Did anything exciting happen while I was away?" I asked the group.

"Nothing here. We're more interested in what happened with you," said Paul.

"Can we talk about it tomorrow?" I asked.

"We'll make sure you don't forget," said Jill.

"And tomorrow we don't want you to leave out any of the details," said Gary, as the three got up from the table to leave.

"We'll walk with you," I said.

"I think we're going to turn in now," I told Samuel. "It's been a long day. I really appreciate everyone coming to welcome my family." I began to direct my family toward the door behind Jill, Gary, and Paul.

My cozy cabin had been fine for one person, but it was going to be a tight fit for four.

"You may want to sleep upstairs tonight," Samuel suggested. "We've been preparing you and your family more suitable quarters, a larger cabin. Unfortunately, it's not quite ready yet."

I saw an expression of uncertainty cross my previous

traveling companion's faces. I was sure they were recalling our first night in the upstairs room, behind locked doors.

"With real walls?" asked Sarah, her expression of surprise and joy was priceless. We'd all been living in a tent for five years now. Real walls would be a welcome change.

Samuel smiled at her excitement.

"I suppose we could stay up there a couple of nights," I said, hesitantly. "Without a locked door?" I asked for clarification.

"No locked door. And then Taylor can move into your old cabin tomorrow."

"A place of my own. That sounds good to me," said Taylor.

From their change of expressions, Jill, Paul, and Gary had relaxed when Samuel had said the door would remain unlocked. They each said "Good night" and moved to the door. Paul motioned me over. "Watch out for Taylor. All of us have a bad feeling about him."

"Me, too. Thanks. I'll keep an eye on him."

"Glad you made it back safely with your family. I'm anxious to hear all about the trip," he said as he turned and walked away with a smile and casual wave.

We hadn't really been together all that long on our trail of doom, but the ordeal we'd experienced together had bonded us together forever. I felt like I had known them all of my life and trusted each of them completely. We were family.

Samuel also left after telling us to have a good nights sleep and that he would stop by to see us in the morning.

We headed upstairs. It was just as I had remembered

PARADISE

with rows of cots along the walls.

Taylor turned around to go back downstairs.

"Where are you going?" I asked.

"I'm going outside for a while if it's okay with you," answered Taylor. "I'm not quite ready to turn in yet."

I was suspicious, but I nodded.

Shortly after Sarah, Christopher, and Cindy had settled in, they quickly fell fast asleep, exhausted from the long day. However, I wasn't quite ready to sleep. I was still uneasy with Taylor roaming around, so I went downstairs to check on him. Opening the front door, I found him sitting just outside on the stoop. He heard the creak of the door opening and turned around.

"Old habits die hard," he said.

I wasn't sure what he was talking about and I guess it showed on my face.

"I'm used to staying awake all night and sleeping in the daytime."

Even though I didn't trust him, I was grateful for him keeping my family safe while I was away. But I'd learned a long time ago to trust my instincts, and right now they told me he was no good.

"I think I may take a little walk and check this place out," he said, standing.

"I wouldn't wander off too far. You're still a stranger here. I'd hate for you to get shot."

He smiled. "You're not worried about me, are you?"

It couldn't have been further from the truth. "Come on up when you get ready," I mentioned, closing the door until only a crack remained. The room behind me was dark, not giving me away. I continued to watch him as he walked away until he disappeared down the street. I had a bad feeling about him having so much freedom. I had brought him here, which made him my responsibility.

During the last couple of months Taylor had spent a considerable amount of time with my family and they all seemed to trust him. After the short amount of time I'd spent with him on the trail, I didn't see it. What I saw was a snake in the grass waiting for his chance to strike. There was something about the look in his eyes and the feeling that everything coming out of his mouth was a lie. Even though I didn't have any proof, I couldn't help thinking he was up to no good.

Sarah came up behind me, peering over my shoulder. "Come on to bed, he'll be all right."

"That's not what I'm worried about." I forced a weak smile and closed the door.

* * *

I woke to the loud, repeated ringing of the church bell. It was clear something was wrong. I quickly slipped my boots on and headed for the door.

"John, what's the matter?" asked Sarah, just waking up.

"I don't know, but I'm going to find out. I'll be back as soon as I can."

Even though there weren't any windows in the upstairs room, a faint light filtered in through the doorway from a window at the top of the stairs. It was enough to take a head count before I left. Taylor was missing. Other than the cots where my family slept, there was no indication any

PARADISE

of the other ones had been slept on.

"Dad, can I come with you?" asked Christopher, now sitting up.

"No, you need to stay here and watch over your mom and sister. Can you do that?"

He nodded.

I don't think he was fully awake yet anyway. I ran down the stairs and out the door. With the sun beginning to peek above the horizon, a group had already gathered in front of Town Hall. From the yelling, it sounded as though they were upset. Someone continued to frantically ring the bell.

"What's the trouble?" I asked, joining them.

One of the men looked at me, anger in his face and eyes. "Your friend stole my horse and rode off."

I had been afraid something like this would happen. I shouldn't have let him walk off last night. "I'm sorry. Are you sure it was him?"

"It was him all right! That's how I got this!" he yelled, turning his head so I could clearly see a large red welt on the side of his face.

Samuel pushed his way through the crowd. "What's going on?" he asked.

The angry man went directly up to him, toe to toe. "This man's friend struck me and stole my horse! I knew we never should have allowed strangers here. What are you going to do about it?" The man's face appeared to be getting redder the more he vented.

"Joshua, you must calm down," said Samuel. "You are too quick to anger. Remember, you were a stranger here once too."

In an instant the man's attitude changed completely, becoming calm. It was as though Samuel somehow had control of him.

"I'm sorry, Samuel."

Samuel stepped back and addressed the rest of the crowd. "All of you, go on home."

The crowd was reluctant to go, but offered no argument. "Go on," he repeated, in a calm voice. "Get ready for work." They slowly dispersed and moved off. Obviously, his word was final. I had seen his words have this affect on people before.

Samuel turned to me. "John, I know it's not your fault, but some may not see it that way."

"There's only one reason I can think of for him to have stolen a horse. He's going to tell the governor about this place and lead the Guard back here for a reward. I won't let it happen, Samuel. I'll make this right."

"There's no reason to be concerned," said Samuel with his ever present smile, patting me on my shoulder. "The Good Lord will protect us." He turned and walked away, leaving me standing alone in the street. I couldn't believe his nonchalant attitude. I had never trusted in faith the way he did. I turned back toward Town Hall to see Jill, Paul, and Gary waiting for me.

"Did you hear?" I asked.

"Yes," said Jill. "I wish there was something we could do."

"I'd appreciate it if all of you could keep an eye on my family until I return."

"Then, you're going after him?" asked Gary.

"I have to. I'm afraid I don't have the same faith

PARADISE

Samuel does. I'm going to need a horse to catch him."

Levi stepped out of the shadows. "I'll have one here for you by the time you're ready to leave."

I nodded a 'thank you,' then went upstairs to tell my family what Taylor had done.

"I can't believe it," said Sarah. "He would never do anything to harm us."

"Well, he's done it now. If I don't stop him, I know he'll lead the Guard here. It'll change everything. They'll take over the valley and treat these people just like they do the ones at Tent City, like slaves."

Sarah sat on one end of a cot and began to cry. "I thought we could trust him," she said between sobs. "We treated him like a friend. How could he do this?"

"It's okay, Mom," said Cindy, sitting beside her and taking her hand. "He had all of us fooled."

"I have to go now," I said. "I'll be back as soon as I can." I gave Sarah a smile and walked out of the room.

"John!" yelled Sarah. I stuck my head back in. "Be careful."

I smiled again. "Always."

A horse was waiting just as Levi had promised, tied up in front of Town Hall. Jill was there too. She handed me a small bag and two canteens. "There's food in the bag," she said. I mounted up and gave her a nod. "Be careful," she said, the exact words my wife had used.

We needed to have a heart to heart when I got back. I nudged the horse into a trot. At the edge of town, Levi stood. He gave me a "Good Luck" as I rode by.

* * *

Chapter 10

I estimated Taylor had about a half-hour head start, potentially too far ahead for me to catch up. However, my chances would improve greatly if he pushed his horse to the point of collapse or if he had an accident. Either way, it would be to my advantage. There was another possibility. During the brief time I'd known him, he'd demonstrated an attitude of cockiness that annoyed me. If he believed he was far enough ahead to be safe, and slowed down, that too would give me a chance. I rode hard, determined to catch him, or until I knew I had failed.

Still dark, I had to assume he was staying on the main trail that he was familiar with. I couldn't see any evidence of him coming this way, but I had no choice but to keep going and hope I was right. Then the impossible happened. I came across his horse writhing in pain on the ground next to the trail with a badly broken leg. It appeared he had

PARADISE

stepped into a prairie dog hole. Taylor hadn't had the decency to put him out of his misery and I couldn't let it continue to suffer. I pulled out my pistol and dismounted. He was thrashing wildly, wanting the pain to end. As I stepped closer, a calmness came over him and he laid his head on the ground. Holding my reins tightly, I pointed the pistol behind his eye and pulled the trigger. It was quick and his suffering was over. Afterward, I didn't feel like continuing the chase, even though I knew Taylor was now on foot and near my grasp.

As the morning sky began to lighten, I could see where Taylor had hit the ground and rolled. As a result of the unfortunate accident, my chances of catching him had just greatly improved. I was sorry for his horse, but stopping him would be saving Paradise and everyone in it, not just a matter of getting even.

It appeared he had left the main trail and was heading toward the rocky area Ryder and Levi had led us through, making it harder for me to follow. But, with me on horseback and him on foot, I decided to gamble and stick to the main trail. I'd be able to move faster and potentially head him off.

With each of us on different trails, there was no way of knowing whether I was gaining on him or not. I stopped once, only briefly, to let my horse have a moment of rest and to have some water. There was a dead silence all around me, no sounds of insects, coyote, or birds. It was the same eerie absence of sound I had experienced when I was here before with the others. Then, the silence had only been broken with the occasional word uttered around the campfire and the crackling of the fire. Perhaps this silence was the new normal since nothing seemed to live here. I was feeling the same sensation as before, as though someone was watching. It was an unsettling feeling.

Then, I heard something familiar. I remained still, concentrating, as I tried to identify the sound and where it had come from. There were voices north of me. One good thing about the silence and these wide open spaces was that sound carried.

I walked toward the voices with my horse in tow. The voices were getting louder. They were excited. I tied the reins to a mesquite branch and moved closer, crawling on my hands and knees to the top of a small ridge. There was a fire with several men standing around it, all in Guard uniforms, one in a black officer's uniform. This had to be one unit sent to find us. I surveyed the campsite. There didn't appear to be any sentries. Then I saw him, Taylor, and he was excitedly talking to the officer. I cursed. I was too late. I had failed.

I couldn't make out what they were saying, but I could guess. Taylor undoubtedly was telling them everything about Paradise. He hadn't had to go all the way back to Sector 4 to report his discovery after all.

I guessed there were around thirty members of the Guard. The governor was taking our escape far too serious. Why should he care if one small family disappeared out of the thousands remaining in Tent City?

My gut had been right all along, Taylor was the snake I'd believed him to be ever since our first encounter when Sarah introduced us. He'd run to the Guard at his first opportunity, against us and for himself from the start. I had no doubt he intended to lead them to the valley and there

PARADISE

didn't appear to be any way of stopping them.

Even though it hadn't been mentioned specifically, I was under the impression Samuel and the others in the valley were against violence of any kind. And if that was the case, they wouldn't put up a fight, letting the Guard roll right over them. I knew Samuel wouldn't blame me, but it would be my fault. If it hadn't been for me going back to get my family, none of this would be happening. But I wasn't going to apologize for wanting a better life for them. The only way I could think of to stop them and protect the valley was to find Ryder before it was too late. I had my suspicions he was somewhere nearby. I doubted if the Guard did anything out here without someone from the Raiders knowing what they were up to. Perhaps they were watching me right now. Maybe it was the sensation I had felt earlier. I hoped I had time to find them.

The Guard didn't seem to be in any hurry to leave their campsite with night coming in only a few hours. It would probably be dawn before they moved out. If successful, there would probably be rewards and or promotions for every man in the group. A question that occurred to me was whether they had the authority to proceed to Paradise based solely on Taylor's word. It wasn't what they'd been sent out here to do.

I eased my way back to where I had tied up my horse. I untied the reins and began to mount. A hand rested on my shoulder. I jerked around, reaching for my pistol, expecting to see one of the Guard's sentries, but instead seeing Ryder with his hands up and a big smile.

"My, we're a bit jumpy, aren't we?" he commented, two of his men behind him, also smiling at my expense.

"You shouldn't sneak up on someone like that." I took a deep breath. "I was hoping you were close by. I need your help."

"I noticed. It seems one of your traveling companions isn't what he appeared to be."

"Oh, he turned out to be exactly what I thought he was. I just hoped I was wrong."

I didn't really know anything about Ryder either, other than him being Samuel's son. People can change according to their environment and he'd been living out in the wasteland for four years. If anything could change a person, that would do it. Granted, he had helped us get away from the Guard once already, but then so had Taylor, supposedly. Until I knew more about him, I was going to assume he was just the lesser of two evils. For now, I needed his help again, in stopping what I perceived to be the greater evil.

"Where's the rest of your group?" he asked.

I knew he already knew the answer to that. His brother had been taking us to Paradise even though the words hadn't been stated specifically.

"They're a little ways south of here in a safe place," I replied. "But you already knew that. I can't let the Guard get to Paradise or take my family back. Can you help?"

He continued to smile, but not in a suspicious or Cheshire cat way, not the way Taylor had. There was something familiar about it though and his whole relaxed demeanor. It reminded me of Samuel.

"I think we can help. Stay here and we'll be back in a little while." They tied up their horses to low-lying mesquite branches and took off together on foot, staying

PARADISE

low and strangely seeming to be enjoying themselves. I watched intently, anxious to see what good three men could do against a squad of guards.

Time passed slowly as I waited to see what would happen next. All of a sudden there was a commotion in the Guard's camp with men running and shouting with shots fired. I saw the images of horses running by their campfire and a growing dust cloud. The guards were running frantically in all directions. Ryder and his men must have cut loose and stampeded their horses. An act that would definitely disrupt the Guard's plans. The officer was yelling to his men, trying to restore order, telling them to retrieve the horses and find the intruders.

Shots randomly rang out. I heard the sound of movement in the brush as it came toward me. I ducked down and drew my pistol, prepared for whoever it was. Ryder and his men came running out of the brush, exhilarated, happy, and out of breath, as though they had just played a hilarious prank, which I guess they had.

"We should probably be leaving now," he said. "They're pretty ticked off, but it'll take them a while to round up their horses and regroup. Maybe it'll give us time to get away. They're going to want to get even with whoever they can get their hands on. All we did was slow them down temporarily. I think you can count on them to keep coming."

"Did you see Taylor?" I asked. "Without him, they won't know where to look for the valley."

"Sorry," said Ryder. "We did see one man ride off, probably sent for reinforcements. But, I can't say whether it was Taylor or not. It's probably best to forget about him for now."

"I can't. I've got a score to settle." I paused. "So, where do we go now?" I asked.

With a bright, wide smile, "Back to Paradise to join your family and friends, of course."

* * *

As we rode, the sounds of chaos from the Guard's camp faded away. We were headed south and Ryder was leading the way.

An hour later and the sun was above the horizon. I noticed we had merged with the main wagon trail again. I'd only been on this trail a couple of times before, but I felt like we were getting close to the valley. Then, I heard the distant ringing of the church bell, alerting the community of someone coming. It was good to be back.

As we approached the rim, the valley opened before us. The view was as breathtaking as the first time I had laid eyes on it.

I was glad to see Samuel and Levi waiting for us along the trail. Ryder continued toward them at the same leisurely pace. Samuel raised his hand for us to stop and Ryder dismounted. I didn't know what to expect. I became tense. I knew there was friction between Ryder and his brother, but I didn't know if whatever happened had also affected his relationship with his dad.

As Ryder approached him, Samuel broke into a huge smile and threw his arms around him in a bear hug.

"It's good to see you, Son!" he exclaimed. "You look good."

PARADISE

I was caught completely off guard, and relieved, letting out a sigh and beginning to breathe again. I hadn't been aware until that moment that I had been holding my breath.

Ryder returned the warm embrace. "It's good to see you too, Dad."

I learned later that Ryder stopped in every few months just to check in on his folks.

Their embrace continued for several seconds before Ryder pulled back and looked over at Levi.

"It's good to see you too, little brother." Ryder appeared to catch him off guard as he stepped over and picked him off the ground, giving him a huge hug, too. Though he tried to hide it, I saw a hint of a smile appear on Levi's face.

Samuel came to me and reached for my hand as I dismounted. "Thank you for bringing my boys home safely."

"Believe me, I didn't do anything. They brought me."

He smiled warmly. "Were you able to stop Taylor?"

"I'm sorry, I wasn't. When I caught up to him he had already met up with the Guard. I'm sure he'll be leading them here."

Neither his demeanor nor his expression changed at the news, only continuing to smile warmly.

Ryder stepped over, leaning toward my ear. "You'll find my dad is very difficult to surprise or upset." Then I saw that same knowing smile of Samuel's on his son's face.

"Don't worry, John. The Lord will watch over us," comforted Samuel.

Ryder gave me a smile and a slight nod as he mouthed the words, "I told you so."

Standing side by side, the similarities between father and son were obvious.

The other two men dismounted and were also greeted warmly all around, like a family reunion, which apparently it must have been.

"Is my family all right?" I asked Samuel.

"They're fine, waiting below for you. Go on," with a flip of his wrist he motioned for me to go.

"I'm worried," I stressed. "What are we going to do about Taylor and the Guard? They're coming. I'm sure of it."

"Don't worry about them. Go see your family."

"Just let me know what I can do to help. I'm willing to fight if it comes to that."

"I don't think that'll be necessary," said Samuel, attempting to reassure me, unsuccessfully.

"You don't have another son in the Guard, do you?"

He chuckled. "No, I don't. Now, go on."

"I'll take her," offered Levi, as he took my horse's reins.

I walked quickly ahead of the others down the trail into town, anxious to see my family again. The others were walking down leisurely, getting re-acquainted. I could have expected Samuel to react to danger this way, but Ryder seemed to be just as unconcerned. I couldn't help wondering if there was still something I didn't know.

Sarah, Cindy, and Christopher met me at the edge of town. We had a reunion of our own as we had a family hug.

PARADISE

"Did you get him, Dad?" asked Christopher, excitement in his voice.

"No, unfortunately," I answered. "I caught up to him, but just a little too late. I'm sure he told the Guard all about this place and plans to lead them here. We're all in danger now because of me. But, on the bright side, we do have some help. Ryder led me back here."

"Ryder?" asked Sarah, puzzled. "Samuel's son."

"Yeah. Strange, isn't it? He just seemed to show up right when I needed him."

"Well, I'm just glad you're back and safe," said Sarah, taking my hand and leading me away. "Let's go home. I've got a surprise for you. Our new place is ready."

* * *

The new cabin was a drastic improvement from the one-room cabin I'd been staying in previously. Much bigger, it was still a one-room structure. But, now that I was back I could work on furnishing it and making partitions for a little privacy. For now, we would be sleeping on bedrolls spread across the wooden floor near the wood stove, another surprise. It was a welcome change from our tent at Tent City. When I saw the look in Sarah's and the kid's eyes, I knew I'd made the right decision in bringing them here.

I lay wide awake and restless. How could Samuel be so calm? Trouble was on its way. If the Guard found their way here, it would change everything, ruining this community's way of life forever.

Sarah must have sensed my concern. After the children

had gone to sleep, she whispered, not wanting to wake them, "What's wrong?"

I didn't want to worry her. "I can't sleep. Too much excitement, I guess. I think I'll go for a walk," I said, as I sat up.

She placed her hand on my arm. "Don't get into any trouble." She smiled.

I walked to the small downtown area where all the lamps and candles in the storefront windows had been put out. I peered through the shop windows, not really looking at anything. Here, even windows were an anomaly. Everywhere else I knew of, windows had been the first to be destroyed, shattering from the earthquake activity. But somehow here they had survived, as did every structure in town. When asked how, Samuel repeated his only answer, God was watching over them. Since meeting him, his faith had been unwavering, which I admired. However, I believed the answer had more to do with the location, most likely far removed from any fault lines.

There was a light shining out the open stable doors at the end of the downtown area. I could see the occasional flicker of shadows cast out onto the road as I walked toward it. Crickets chirped and the cool breeze of the evening air touched my face. It was good to be back. I hadn't felt this safe in a long time. It felt like home.

I wasn't surprised to see Ryder and his two friends saddling their horses, apparently preparing to leave.

"You're leaving?" I asked.

"We have to. Danger is coming unless we can do something to stop it."

"But you seemed so unconcerned earlier."

PARADISE

"I didn't want to worry Dad or cause a panic with any of the others."

"Then I was right. We *are* in danger."

"Of course. But, I don't want anyone to destroy what this community has, and I'll do anything to prevent it."

For some reason, I felt better knowing I wasn't the only one concerned. I hadn't been over reacting after all.

"What do you intend to do?"

"Stop them."

"Just the three of you?"

"There are a few more of us than just us three," he said with his father's smile.

I hesitated before I asked, "I know it's none of my business, but why did you leave in the first place when you had everything you needed right here?"

"It just wasn't for me. It was too quiet, too sedentary a lifestyle. I had ambitions and I needed to see what else was out there. I would've continued to wonder "what if?" if I'd stayed."

"How did you know you could survive out there?"

"I didn't, but I had to try."

"Then, how did you become a guard?" I asked.

"I'd heard about the governor setting up the old prison for earthquake victims, so I headed straight there. I had seen the Guard in their uniforms from afar and was impressed. I was very impressionable when I was younger. I thought it would be an exciting improvement, a position of respect with room, board, and clothing provided. After making a few inquiries and going through a brief interview, I found myself recruited. I began to move up through the ranks, but I soon realized it wasn't what I had expected or wanted. You know the guys who brought you out to the wasteland in a wagon? I used to be one of those guys. That's how I ran into a group of Raiders, after dropping off my passengers. They actually stopped the wagon to rob me until I convinced them I had nothing for them to take. It didn't take much to convince me to quit the Guard then and there and to go with them. It's been four years since then and it was the best decision of my life."

"I got the impression your brother doesn't approve of what you do now," I commented.

"He's not very good at hiding it either, is he? But that's not the only reason. We got into it when I left. He thought I should stay to help Dad. After I left, he had to take over my duties, and he resented it, and I think he still does."

"How did your dad take you leaving?"

"He knew I'd never be happy if he forced me to stay. Of course he wanted me to, but he never tried to stop me."

"So, since you left, Levi's been making the trips to Sector 4 for supplies?"

"Yeah, and I don't think he's very happy about it."

"I'm sure he'll get over it one of these days," I said.

I was beginning to understand. Since Samuel had told Levi to take me to Sector 4, that may have been the reason for him being so quiet on our ride there; he was once again being told what to do and had been pouting about it. He had been forced to grow up before he was ready.

"Do you and Levi ever run into each other on his trips?"

"No, and I think that's the way he prefers it. But I make sure someone keeps an eye on him when he crosses

PARADISE

through the wasteland. He's still only eighteen and I don't want anything to happen to him."

Ryder noticed as his two companions mounted their horses. "I guess it's time for us to go. We need to find our scouts. They'll let us know what the Guard has been up to. You don't need to worry about them coming all the way here. We won't let it happen."

"How do you intend to stop them?" I asked.

"We'll think of something."

"If you see Taylor, please give him my regards."

With a nod, they rode away.

I turned to walk back to our cabin. I smelled smoke, which in itself wasn't strange, since everyone used firewood for heat and cooking. But, at this time of year and this time of night, it was peculiar. Ryder and his friends stopped.

"Do you smell that?" Ryder asked.

"Smoke," I confirmed.

There was a yellow glow on the edge of town. Ryder rode ahead of me as I ran toward it. One of the houses was on fire. I saw a dark figure running away from it. It was Taylor. He must have followed us back here from the Guard encampment.

Since the fire was in the valley, I hoped the Guard wouldn't be able to see its glow from their encampment. Even though it was many miles away, the glow could probably be seen against the night sky. I wondered if Taylor had intentionally set the fire as a signal.

The fire was growing rapidly. The wooden structure would soon be consumed. I became fearful when I heard screams coming from inside. Ryder heard them at the same time. He sent his friends after Taylor as he quickly rode to the back of the house. I ran to the front door. The heat was intense and the house was almost entirely engulfed. Entrance through the door was impossible with flames licking across its surface. Smoke boiled out of the front windows forming a thick, toxic cloud. I reached a side window at the same time as Ryder. The flames were spreading. Through the smoke we could barely make out the image of an older woman on her hands and knees next to the window, her hand pawing weakly at the glass. She was looking directly at us, coughing and begging for help with her watering smoke-filled eyes. The window was locked. I motioned for her to move back, but either she didn't understand, she was too afraid, or too disoriented to move. I still had my .45 in my waistband. I took it out and tapped progressively harder until one of the panes broke. Reaching in, I unlocked the window and forced it open. Smoke poured out. I took a deep breath and crawled inside, lifting her to her feet and helping her over into Ryder's waiting arms where we both helped her through the window. Outside, we helped her to a place a safe distance away as the fire continued to grow. She continued to cough deeply as she pointed back to the house, unable to speak.

"Is there someone else still in there?" I asked. She managed a slight nod.

Ryder ran back toward the house while I held her head in my lap. The house was now almost totally engulfed. Ryder disappeared through the same window. I knew the heat inside would be intense and the thick smoke pouring out of the window would make it hard to breathe and see. Seconds ticked by. What was taking him so long? Then

PARADISE

there was movement at the window. I laid the woman's head gently on the ground and ran to help. When I got to the window Ryder was trying to get out with the limp body of a little old man. I grabbed him from Ryder and pulled him out. He weighed almost nothing. Ryder stumbled out through the window, landing hard on the ground with his left shoulder, coughing deeply. I carried the old man over to the old woman's side, who I assumed was his wife.

A neighbor had arrived, cradling the old woman's head in her lap. She had almost stopped coughing, watching me and her husband closely. I checked the old man, patting out smoldering embers still burning on his left shirt sleeve. He wasn't breathing. I began CPR with Ryder helping with chest compressions. The company where I had worked, before the world had fallen apart, had made it mandatory for each employee to go through the training. I hadn't appreciated it until now. The old man wasn't responding. I glanced at Ryder. I went back to breathing air into his lungs. I wasn't going to give up. He had to come around. As the old woman realized her husband was gone, she began to cry. Tears, not related to the smoke, filled the old woman's eyes, rolling down her cheeks. I continued in an attempt to revive him. Ryder stopped the compressions and looked up behind me. I felt a hand rest on my shoulder. "He's gone, John. There's nothing else you can do," said Samuel softly, as he looked on.

It was so unnecessary. There was no sense in it. This man didn't deserve this. I looked at the old woman and mouthed the words "I'm sorry." She covered her face with both hands and began to sob uncontrollably, her entire body shaking, as her neighbor held her tight. Ryder had moved away, staring at the fire continue to consume the small house. A young lady offered him a drink of water. Soon, the house was beyond saving. The townspeople, who had come to help, realizing the futility of trying, were only able to watch.

Then, I remembered Taylor. He'd been the reason this had happened. I was sure he'd started the fire as a signal to the Guard. I clenched my fists and screamed to heaven in frustration and anger. It was all my fault. If I hadn't brought him, none of this would have happened.

"We have to put out the fire!" I yelled.

"It can't be saved," said Samuel.

"I know, but it's a signal fire. And soon the sun will be up and then they'll be able to see the smoke too," I said.

"He's right, Dad," said Ryder, now looking better after recuperating somewhat from inhaling so much smoke.

"Everyone, grab a bucket and form a line to the water trough," Samuel directed the crowd.

"Ryder, have you seen your two friends?"

Looking around, "No, I haven't."

"That's a bad sign. Taylor is on the loose, so we have to assume he may still be in town. And that means he could set another fire."

I was relieved when Sarah ran to my side, followed closely by Cindy and Christopher. Our cabin could have been the next one for Taylor to torch. With my family next to me, I had one less thing to worry about.

"What happened?" she asked, noticeably distressed.

"Taylor. He set fire to this house. We suspect it was a signal to the Guard. There was an old couple still inside. The old man is dead."

PARADISE

She couldn't believe her ears. This was a side of Taylor she'd never seen or could have imagined. There'd been no indications of trust issues before John had come for them. Then she had begun to see Taylor differently, but would never have guessed he was capable of this kind of violence.

"Mr. Grey did this?" asked Cindy, watching the fire being extinguished. She wondered if she had heard wrong.

"Yes."

"Sarah, I want you and the kids to stay here with Samuel. I don't want you to go back to the cabin, not until Taylor's been caught or until I let you know its okay. Samuel, it might be a good idea to have everyone gather at the church until its safe. I'll go door to door and warn any others to go to you while I'm searching for Taylor."

"You should stay with us," pleaded Sarah.

"No. I can't. He's my responsibility." I turned to leave.

"I'm going with you," said Ryder.

"Be careful," called out Sarah as Ryder and I split up, heading to opposite sides of the street.

We knocked on doors without waiting for a reply, yelling for anyone still at home to head for the church. The early morning air was still, filled with smoke hanging in the air like a floating shroud.

There was a woman's scream from the far end of the street. Ryder and I broke into a full run toward it. One of Ryder's men, Darby, waved to get our attention. He was kneeling down behind a tree a short distance from a small cabin.

"We have him cornered inside, but he has a hostage," said Darby. "Sims is watching the back."

We could see the front door, barely hanging by one hinge, probably kicked in by Taylor. It was impossible to see inside the dark interior.

"Taylor! Come on out! You can't get away," I yelled.

"I think I'll stay right here a while longer," he shouted back. "I'll come out once the Guard arrives. And it shouldn't be too long now."

He could be right. They could be on their way, if they had seen the fire to guide them. Since we didn't know if they had or not, Taylor needed to be dealt with so we could prepare.

I decided to try to coax him out. "They're not coming. We put the fire out. There isn't any signal for them to follow."

He didn't reply. That was good. Maybe he was thinking about his options.

"What do you suggest?" I asked Ryder. "We can't just sit here and wait and we can't rush the cabin, the person inside could be hurt."

"If they aren't already," Ryder pointed out.

"Let me talk to him," said Samuel as he came up behind us, continuing toward the cabin.

"Dad! Come back. He's too unpredictable and dangerous," said Ryder, standing up to go after him.

"Nonsense," said Samuel as he waved Ryder away and continued to walk toward the front door.

"Stop right there, Samuel," said Taylor forcefully. "Or I'll kill her."

Now we knew it was either a girl or woman he held captive.

"There's no sense in that," replied Samuel. "And it

wouldn't be in your best interest. You'd lose the only bargaining chip you have." Again, Taylor had no reply.

"What do you propose?" asked Taylor.

"Let the girl go and I'll give you my word you can ride out of here unharmed."

* * *

I couldn't believe my ears. After everything Taylor had done? There was an old woman mourning her dead husband at the other end of town at this very second. And he had betrayed every person in this valley by leading the Guard here.

"He can't do that," I said to Ryder. "Is he trying to trick him into coming out?"

"Not my dad. He's a man of his word and means exactly what he says. No tricks."

"I don't think I can let Taylor just ride away," I told Ryder.

* * *

"What guarantee do I have?" Taylor asked.

"My word," Samuel replied, still standing in front of the door.

"Why don't I just wait until the Guard gets here?"

"For one thing, as John pointed out, you don't even know whether or not they saw the fire. So, how long are you willing to wait and see? I'm giving you a free ticket to get out of here. Now, are you going to take it or not?"

There was another moment of silence. "Bring me my

horse!" shouted Taylor.

Samuel looked to Ryder and nodded. Ryder understood, running off for the horse.

"It's coming," said Samuel, clasping his hands together behind his back. "Now, send out the girl."

I heard a laugh within the cabin. "Nice try, old man. Not until the horse is here."

"I gave you my word," reminded Samuel.

"I know. It's John and Ryder I'm worried about."

"They won't do anything. Come on out."

The door slowly swung open awkwardly on the remaining hinge. A few moments later the hostage began to slowly appear, followed closely by Taylor with his arm around her waist. A pistol was held to her head. It looked like the one I had given Christopher. He had stolen it at some point on our journey together. In the bright moonlight I could see clearly. It was Jill. I hadn't considered until that moment the hostage might be someone I knew. It shouldn't have mattered who it was since an innocent person's life was in danger. But it did. His hostage was someone I personally knew, and a friend. Whether Taylor had specifically chosen Jill or if it had been just pure blind luck, I had no idea.

Ryder rode up on a horse and dismounted, holding out the reins to his dad. Ryder stepped back.

"Here's your horse, now let her go," said Samuel firmly, perhaps with a slight edge in his voice, appearing to grow tired of Taylor's games.

Taylor kept a firm grip on Jill as he retrieved the reins from Samuel and moved toward the horse.

"Jill, are you all right?" I asked. She gave me a slight

PARADISE

nod. Her face showed the terror she was feeling, her eyes wide with tears running down her cheeks.

Taylor smiled. "A friend of yours, John? Well, isn't this an unexpected coincidence."

"Let her go, Taylor. That was the deal," I said. I could feel the blood rushing to my face as I became more angry.

"Not here. At the edge of town," he said. He then forced Jill up into the saddle and he swung up behind her. He now held the pistol tightly against her side while he held the reins in the other hand.

"This isn't what you agreed to," I repeated.

"Deals were made to be broken," he said as he showed a toothy arrogant smile.

Ryder's two friends were now on the other side of Taylor with his back to them. They were slowly moving in. He glanced around and saw them just as they were getting near enough to strike. He shook his head at them and motioned for them to come around to where Ryder and myself were standing. As soon as they had joined us, Taylor turned back towards us. "It's been a real pleasure. I'll probably see you all again very soon, but next time I won't be alone." He let out a laugh and kicked the horse in the flanks, riding off in a gallop.

I ran after him, Ryder at my side.

"Let him go," said Samuel. "We're better off without him and we already have one of our brothers to bury."

But it wasn't him I was worried about, it was Jill. We cut through yards in an attempt to head him off before he started up the one lane road out of the valley.

We arrived just behind him. He was riding up the road alone. Surprisingly, he'd dropped off Jill just as he said he would. She was lying on the ground and Darby was checking to make sure she was alright. I pulled my .45 and took aim. Ryder grabbed my arm.

"Don't shoot!" he said. "Not here."

I looked at him without understanding.

"Why not? After everything he's done?"

"Dad gave his word no one would stop him from leaving the valley."

Taylor was too far away now anyway. I stuck the pistol back into my waistband.

"What do you suggest we do now?" I asked.

"We go after him before he gets too far ahead."

"But you said ..."

"Dad said no one would stop him from leaving. Well, he's left, so, now we go after him."

Ryder's companions had mounted and approached with two horses in tow.

"Expecting me to go with you?" I asked.

"Aren't you?"

"Of course. Just let me check on Jill first."

"She took a hard spill, but she's going to be okay," said Darby from his saddle.

I could see she was to her feet now and a small group was tending to her.

"Then, let's go."

"Don't you need to tell Sarah where you're going?" asked Ryder.

"She'll know."

* * *

Chapter 11

Counselor Damon anxiously entered the governor's office. The governor was standing at the window overlooking Tent City.

"I have great news, Governor. A member of the Guard search party has just entered through the gate. The escaped workers have been located, but unfortunately our men were ambushed before they could reach them. The courier relays a message that reinforcements are needed."

"Ambushed? By who? One family of workers? I doubt if reinforcements will make a difference if your Guard is that incompetent."

"It's as we suspected, sir. They're being aided by the Raiders, and there is something else."

"More good news, Counselor Damon?"

"Perhaps. The man who was in your service as a protector for the missing family left with them. It would appear he convinced them to take him along, but has remained in contact with the Guard incognito. According to his last report, there is a luscious green valley within the wasteland …"

The governor's eyes widened with interest.

"I wasn't aware anything of worth remained in the wasteland. "

"No one did, sir."

"Where is this man now?" asked Davis. "And can he be trusted?"

"The last we knew, he had joined the Guard detail and was leading them to the alleged valley when they were ambushed by the Raiders. The valley is supposedly where the family has taken up refuge. As far as being able to trust him? I feel sure he can be trusted as long as some sort of compensation is forthcoming." Counselor Damon handed a piece of paper to the governor. "The man, Taylor Grey, sent this with the rider."

Governor Davis read it silently, a smile growing on his face. "How long to reach them?"

"Two hard days to where they were ambushed."

"They'll have their reinforcements. This note says there are over one hundred people living there, young and old. We can use the younger ones as workers and eliminate the old ones. It also says they are farmers, growing grains and vegetables, and raising livestock. Those resources will make a nice addition to our food supply. He says they call it Paradise. Perfect."

The prospect of acquiring more supplies and more workers produced a hint of a disturbing smile. Then the smile disappeared as quickly as it had appeared. "If this

PARADISE

valley does indeed exist, I must have it. This will give us an advantage over the other Sectors. See to it Master Gant takes adequate troops and personally leads the attack."

"As you wish, Governor."

*   *   *

It was still dark when we rode after Taylor. We had to assume he was headed straight to the Guard's last known encampment. The advantage was on our side since Ryder knew the area better than most and Taylor had only been this way twice before. We wouldn't know how far ahead he was until we could physically see him or his dust trail by the light of day. When I asked, Ryder assured me there wasn't a shortcut. The hope of catching him before he reached them was slim. We could only try.

We didn't know if the Guard had continued toward the valley after our ambush of their encampment or if they had stayed put, regrouping until morning. There was also the possibility they had proceeded south if they had seen Taylor's signal fire. Even if we caught up with Taylor, it wouldn't necessarily remove the impending danger that was sure to come. The Guard now knew the general direction and even without Taylor as their guide, they would probably be able to eventually find the valley on their own, unless they were to be discouraged in a major way.

At sunrise and after riding for several hours, there had been no sign of Taylor. By noon we approached the location of the previous night's ambush. We dismounted and crawled across the sandy soil, snaking through the clumps of sagebrush to where we could see into the Guard camp, if it was still there. Both of us were somewhat surprised to see that it was. Ryder pulled out a small pair of binoculars, handing them to me. Their security was much tighter this time with sentries posted at regular intervals around the camp's perimeter.

"What do you suppose they're waiting for?" I asked.

"I don't know. Possibly reinforcements?" Ryder replied. "Remember, one man rode off in that direction."

"It looks like our boy is there," I said. "And he looks upset. He keeps pointing this way, but the apparent guard-in-charge continues to shake his head. Whoa! You should have seen that?" I handed the binoculars back to Ryder. "He just knocked Taylor to the ground. I wish I'd done that."

Ryder looked, still in time to see Taylor picking himself up off the ground and back away from the officer. "I guess he got tired of him too," said Ryder. We exchanged smiles at the unfortunate incident.

"Darby, Sims," whispered Ryder, motioning them over. They crawled over to us. "It looks like we're going to need some help. Can you go and round up some of the boys and let them know we need their help? Make sure they know it's just a request for volunteers. They don't have the same ties to Paradise as I do."

Darby smiled. "They'll all want to help. If not to protect the valley, then to strike back at the Guard and Davis. How many men do you think we're going to need?" asked Darby.

"As many as you can round up on short notice. We're going to make a stand right here."

PARADISE

"Okay, but it may be two or three days before we can get back."

"I know. Just come back as soon as possible. We'll hold them off as long as we can. If they're waiting for reinforcements, it'll probably be a few days before the guard can come back from Sector 4."

"What are you going to do if the reinforcements arrive before we can get back?" asked Darby.

"Let's just hope they don't."

"Do you want Sims to stay here with you?" asked Darby.

"No. We'll be alright. Come in quietly and slowly from the west on your return. I don't want to alert them with any unnecessary noise or dust clouds until we're all here. It would spoil the surprise."

"We'll see you soon. Stay out of trouble, will you guys?" said Darby.

"We'll try our best, and thanks."

They crawled away to where their horses were tied up.

Ryder was acting more as a leader than as just one of the group, and they were following his instructions without question. There was more to Ryder than I had originally thought. I was beginning to suspect he was more than just one of the boys.

Now, it was a waiting game, to keep an eye on the Guard encampment and hope they didn't advance, and if they did, to hope Ryder's Raider friends arrived in time to stop them. When I asked how many men would be coming, he'd just smiled and said, "I'm not sure, but I think you'll be surprised." His response didn't fill me with confidence. As before, he didn't seem to be concerned in the least, even with this encounter soon to unfold. On the second day, we decided to pull back to a safer distance where we could still see their camp without obstructions and where it would be less likely to be detected. If they decided to advance, we'd know about it just as easily from our new location. It was a boring wait. Not a sound came from their camp. As late afternoon turned to evening, it appeared they were settling in for another night, in no hurry to go anywhere, which suited us just fine. Ryder and I took turns catching up on the sleep we'd missed. Once things started to happen, who knew when we'd get another chance.

In the early morning hours of the fourth day just before sunrise the silence was suddenly broken. Drowsy only moments earlier, we were now both wide awake and alert. The reinforcements had arrived, even though it was still dark. They must have traveled straight through. I was overwhelmed by the number of torches that appeared in and around the camp. It appeared the governor had sent more than a hundred men. I looked at Ryder, wondering what was going through his head.

"This doesn't look good," I said. "And I'm guessing your men won't be here for another day or more. Have any bright ideas?"

"Nothing comes to mind," he replied.

"Look! We may be in luck, they're dismounting."

"They probably need to rest and water their horses after that long of a ride. If Taylor told them how treacherous the landscape is from here on, they're probably just being cautious, waiting for good light before proceeding south."

"Do you suppose we could try the same stunt you

PARADISE

pulled the other night by stampeding their horses?" I asked.

"No. I'm sure they're on high alert now and it appears there are too many sentries to slip by. We'd never pull it off."

"I just wish there was something we could do other than sitting around and waiting."

"When they move out you'll see plenty of action," said Ryder.

"Even though it's just the two of us, I'd rather do what we can now to disrupt their plans while they're not expecting it instead of waiting and meeting them head on. I'm not suicidal."

"Did you have something in mind?" asked Ryder.

"What if we built several fires between us and their camp?" I asked. "It might give the impression we have an army of our own. They might not be so anxious to proceed then."

"It would take a while to collect all the firewood and any noise might alert them that someone is out here."

"If we're careful and can stay quiet, they won't be alerted until we light them. We're just sitting around anyway. Are you game or not?"

He paused, staring into my eyes; I suppose he was trying to read my thoughts to see if I was genuinely serious, Then, he smiled. "Sure, why not?"

We spent the next couple of hours attempting to be as quiet as possible while collecting dead mesquite branches for the three wood pile locations, ready to light. With the mesquite brush being sparsely spread across the landscape, it was harder than I had thought to find enough branches for the fires. At every sound, we'd stop and drop down, anticipating trouble, not knowing whether the sentries were roaming outside the camp perimeter. It made both of us jumpy.

The coming dawn began to lighten the eastern sky just after we finished. Soon, it would be too bright for them to see the glow of the fires, but they'd be able to see the smoke easily, still serving the same purpose.

As the sky became brighter, we could see that the number of guards had grown considerably, and activity throughout the camp was frantic. Tents were coming down and horses were being saddled. It appeared they were getting ready to move out.

"How many men did you say you had?" I asked, concerned over the number they were up against.

"As my dad would say, "have a little faith.""

"I think this is going to take more than a little faith."

He just smiled in that annoying 'don't worry about it' way. It was his dad's smile again.

We heard the sound of hooves approaching rapidly behind us. We jerked around. In the hazy morning light it was still too hard to make out who it was at a distance. Had the Guard slipped in behind us? I aimed my pistol, ready to fire. The sound came closer. I relaxed and let out a deep breath as Darby came into view and dismounted a short distance away. He stooped low as he joined us.

"We didn't expect you until tomorrow," said Ryder.

"I passed the word around for help to come as soon as possible. I brought a few men with me and I know others will come as soon as they hear they're needed. Thought you might need some help sooner than later."

"How many men did you bring?" asked Ryder.

PARADISE

"Maybe fifty. They're back a little ways waiting for instructions. What do you want me to have them do?"

Ryder explained about the wood piles and where to find them, asking Darby to split up and spread out the men. We stayed near the central woodpile while he had Darby place two men at each of the two other piles. Lighting the center fire would be the signal to light the others. The intent was simple, the fires and the show of their numbers would hopefully discourage any further advance or aggression from the Guard. The rest of the men were to be spread out behind the bonfires. It probably wouldn't work. He knew Gant. He wasn't one to be intimidated. He had his orders and carrying them out would be the only thing that mattered. But, perhaps their numbers would cause Gant and his men to hesitate their advance long enough for more of the Raiders to arrive and provide assistance. Not wanting to tip our hand too soon, Ryder would wait until the very last moment before lighting the center fire, watching for when the Guard appeared to be moving out.

We didn't have long to wait. The sun was up now and we could see the encampment even clearer. It seemed the number had magically increased yet again from only moments earlier. It appeared daylight had been what they had been waiting for. They were mounting, preparing to advance. Taylor was easy to spot. He was the only one not in uniform, following Gant around like a yapping puppy.

Darby came back to us, the word had been spread as directed. Ryder gave the okay to light the center fire. As the fire grew and engulfed the wood pile, gray smoke began to rise, forming a vertical column into the still morning air. Soon, the other two fires flickered to life, both growing into spectacular bonfires. The rising smoke was spotted almost immediately from the Guard encampment with all activity momentarily coming to a stop. The fires had done their job. Then obvious confusion had overcome the camp. Master Gant was pointing. Three pairs of men mounted their horses, each pair riding toward a fire, apparently sent to scout them out.

"We can't let them report back," I told Ryder.

"I know," he answered, motioning for Darby to come over.

"Darby, I need you and Sims to split up and go to the other fires and intercept those riders. We can't let them report our true numbers back to Gant."

"Do you want them taken alive?" he asked.

"If possible. But, if they resist, do whatever you have to."

Darby nodded he understood and left, motioning for Sims to go with him.

"What about the two coming this way?" I asked.

"I'll take care of them," Ryder assured me.

I had lost sight of the riders to our east and west, but the two coming toward us were clearly visible from our position behind a small mesquite tree. They had slowed their horses to a walk, cautiously moving toward the fire, alert and ready for trouble. Their weapons were drawn. They stood tall in the stirrups for a better vantage point. Two shots rang out from the west. The riders in front of us stopped, looking in that direction, exchanging words. I couldn't make out what they were saying, but from their reaction and the tone of their voices it was obvious they were concerned. Two more shots rang out from the east.

PARADISE

An instant later I was startled by two quick explosions near my head, jerking my hands up to cover my already painful and ringing ears. Two shots had been fired and two dead riders had fallen with their horses running off. I looked at Ryder in shock. He was holding a rifle, still aimed toward the riders, smoke rolling from the end of its barrel.

"I thought you were going to try to take them alive," I asked.

He just shrugged. I don't know what I had expected. Ryder, from the short time I'd known him, had never shown any signs of violence. As Samuel's son, I didn't think he could really do it, rather leaving it to someone else. I was wrong. It appeared living in the wasteland had hardened him. I was sure his father wouldn't have approved.

There was a sudden increase of activity in the Guard's camp, no doubt a result of the shots heard and the riderless horses returning. It resembled an ant hill just stepped on. Everyone in camp was running around frantically, except one, Master Gant. He stood in the center of the encampment, near the main campfire, silently staring in our direction. It seemed as though he was looking directly at me. Taylor stood beside him, pointing in our direction, and from his antics he was obviously yelling at him. Gant looked away from us, seemingly becoming aware of Taylor for the first time. Words were exchanged and Taylor backed away to a safe distance after being poked in the chest. Gant began to shout orders, regaining control of his men.

* * *

"What are you waiting for?" Taylor yelled at Gant, frustration in his voice, and a bit too edgy, loud, and disrespectful. "It's just the people from the valley. They're right out there. Your scouts are probably dead, but you have them outnumbered."

Gant had been trying to ignore Taylor, but now turned toward him, looking at him with contempt. "How do you know how many men they have? Have you seen them? It's my understanding there could be Raiders with them. And I'm not rushing blindly into an ambush."

"I was in their town. They're sheep. Religious fanatics. They wouldn't hurt anyone. And so what if there are a few Raiders with them?"

Gant had to bend over to be nose-to-nose with Taylor, poking his finger forcefully into his chest. "Those sheep, or whoever they are, probably just killed six of my men."

Taylor opened his mouth to speak, but the intense look in Gant's eyes made him think twice about it. He rubbed his cheek as he remembered the backhand the other officer had given him.

* * *

Chapter 12

Master Gant tripled the sentries around the perimeter of the camp during the night. He realized they were still vulnerable in the dawn's dim light and in a region to which they were unfamiliar. It didn't appear there was anything else to do until the sky became bright enough to see what they were up against. It was already clear to Gant that Taylor had no idea of what these people were capable of or how many were actually involved.

Gant kept his eyes focused to the south. He had ordered the sentries to check in on a regular basis and if they didn't, he'd know why. He didn't want any more surprises. As the sky continued to lighten to the east, the landscape surrounding the camp became illuminated, giving Gant his first real look at their surroundings and their opposition. What he saw was not what he wanted to see, but at the same time he wasn't surprised. Spread out in a semi-circle to the south was a line of two hundred or more men on horseback. He was outnumbered by two to three times. And these men weren't the gentle sheep-like men Taylor had described. These men were ready to make a stand. And his loss of six men earlier was proof.

Gant yelled out, "Get me Taylor!"

He had been nearby and had heard the summons, running to Gant's side. Taylor followed Gant's gaze to the south. His jaw dropped as he too saw the resistance.

"Are those the men you were talking about? The men we outnumbered and who would be so easily defeated?"

Taylor swallowed hard. Their opposition was close enough he recognized two of the riders, Ryder and John. "No, Master Gant, those are the Raiders. I had no idea there were so many of them. They must have called for their own reinforcements. And I can see the father of the escaped family with them too."

"It's obviously clear you have no idea what's actually going on out here. Do you have any other great insights or suggestions?" asked Gant rhetorically with disgust.

"No," answered Taylor without elaborating for once.

"Well, I have a suggestion for you. Stay away from me, out of my sight, and keep your mouth shut."

Gant returned his attention to the situation at hand. "Someone, bring me something I can use for a white flag and my horse."

Taylor's jaw dropped open once again. "You're not going to surrender, are you?"

"I told you to keep your mouth shut. But, no, I'm not going to surrender. I just want to talk with them."

"I should go with you then. I know these people," said

PARADISE

Taylor.

"Obviously, you don't know them at all. But, it might not be a bad idea for you to come along. If you can't be quiet though, I'll give you to them to get you out of my hair."

Taylor didn't believe Gant was being serious. They still needed him to find the valley. But, he was glad he was being allowed to go along, eager to see John's face when he rode up next to and under the protection of Master Gant.

* * *

"Someone's coming!" shouted one of Ryder's men.

Ryder and I looked to see two riders coming toward us, one much larger than the other and carrying a white flag.

"It looks like they want to parlay," I commented.

"I guess I should see what they have to say. Want to come along?" asked Ryder.

I didn't have to answer, he already knew what I would say.

We rode forward a short distance, breaking from the line, forcing the two riders to come to us.

As they approached, Ryder and I recognized the larger of the two, a huge hulk of a man, Master Gant. It was then I realized how determined the governor was. He would only have sent his best if he wanted to guarantee success. Gant had a reputation for never giving up, always accomplishing what he set out to do, regardless of the odds. Then I recognized the smaller rider, Taylor. My jaw tightened and my teeth clinched together as I was filled with rage. He had to be the reason Gant was here. Gant would never have been sent away from Sector 4 just to bring back runaway workers. One of his subordinates could do that, which was exactly who the governor had initially sent. Gant had to have been sent to take over the valley, based on Taylor's word. That meant he wouldn't be going back until he'd accomplished his mission.

"Gant!" blurted Ryder under his breath. "Why did it have to be him?"

His reaction seemed to be an expression of both respect and fear. I had briefly forgotten he worked under Gant during his time in the Guard.

Gant's 'all business' expression never changed as they rode up. Neither did Taylor's, however his was more of a sneer that said 'things were going exactly as he wanted.' He sat tall in the saddle, cocky and arrogant. Gant and Taylor stopped ten feet from us.

Taylor couldn't contain himself. "You might as well give up. You don't stand a chance against the Guard." He looked at Gant to back him up.

"Shut up, Taylor!" said Gant. "Remember what I told you."

Taylor's smile faded away, but only temporarily.

"Ryder," said Gant.

"Gant," acknowledged Ryder.

"We want Taylor," I blurted out. "He's responsible for the death of an elderly man."

"Take him. And you're welcome to him," replied Gant.

Nervously, Taylor's smug grin returned at what he hoped was a joke, not fully knowing whether Gant was being serious or not.

"Let us pass and a lot of bloodshed can be avoided," said Gant.

"We can't do that. We know what you're after and we won't allow it, but I would like to avoid bloodshed too. So, I suggest you go back to Sector 4 and tell the governor you couldn't find what you were looking for."

Gant's expression never changed as he continued to stare at Ryder for several seconds, then stated, "Have it your own way. Their blood will be on your hands." He quickly reined his horse around and galloped back toward the camp. The sudden exit left Taylor alone, facing us. The smirk that had been on his face moments earlier was now replaced with a fear for his life.

"How could you turn on the people in Paradise after they took you in, treating you like family," I asked.

Taylor screamed through gritted teeth, "Those people aren't my family. My family is Sector 4." I knew he had said it out of spite rather than conviction. I could tell even he didn't believe it. "And once we've taken over the valley, the governor will reward me, and then I'll be important at Sector 4 and you'll be dead."

"There's two problems with that," said Ryder.

"Yeah. What's that?" asked Taylor.

"He'll never get control and that means your reward will most likely be a noose."

Anger flashed from Taylor's eyes, knowing there was truth in what he said. Without another word he turned toward the Guard camp, whipping his horse into a full gallop. "We'll see about that!" he yelled over his shoulder.

I heard the sound of a horse quickly coming up behind

us. I turned to see Darby approaching, coming to a sliding stop, and dismounting.

"More of the men just showed up, Ryder," he announced. "They've been filtering in all night long. Where would you like them?"

"For now, just have them spread out and join the others as a show of numbers."

Darby remained motionless. Ryder saw concern on his friend's face, seemingly hesitant to tell him something. He gave Darby a questioning look.

"There's something else," Darby said. "Someone else has come too. It's your dad."

Ryder was noticeably disturbed by the news, cursing under his breath. He didn't have time for this."Take me to him."

I decided to rejoin the front line and give Ryder and his dad some private time together.

Ryder stopped when he saw I wasn't following. "I want you there with me when I talk to Dad. You seem to be able to talk to him better than I can. We need to get him to go back before he gets hurt. Maybe he'll listen to you."

I wasn't going to argue with him. I actually agreed with him that his dad shouldn't be here. It was too dangerous and I knew he wouldn't defend himself if it became necessary. We found Samuel sitting at a small campfire in good spirits, calmly chatting with a few of the other recent arrivals. He showed no signs of concern at the battle that was about to take place.

Samuel's face lit up when he saw us approaching.

"Come on over, Son." He threw his arms around him in a hug like they hadn't seen each other in ages, even

PARADISE

though they had been together just a few days earlier.

"Dad, you shouldn't be here. Please go on home."

"But I think I can stop all this and keep anyone from getting hurt, on either side."

"I'm not so concerned about them."

"I'm surprised you'd say that. It's not how I raised you, Ryder. They have families just like we do. Just give me a chance to talk to them and see if I can stop this. Please, Son. You know I've got to try."

Ryder couldn't help smiling just a little. He knew his dad and knew his mind was made up. He would try, somehow, even without his blessing.

In the brief time I'd known father and son, I continued to see how alike they were, one as stubborn as the other. I knew Samuel meant well, but I also knew he had unrealistic expectations. His sunny disposition would mean absolutely nothing to the Guard.

"It won't do any good, Dad. I'm not going to let you risk your life. You need to go back to Paradise where every one there counts on you."

"Doesn't this encounter affect me and everyone else in the valley too?"

"Of course it does."

"Then let me try." He waited without saying another word, letting Ryder mull it over.

"Okay. But only if we do it my way."

Samuel smiled. "Whatever you say."

*   *   *

"Master Gant! Two riders coming this way!"

Gant, who had been sitting near the campfire, stood and walked out to the edge of the encampment, watching as the riders approached. He could see two men on horseback coming their way carrying a white flag. His expression never changed, rarely showing any emotions. He knew they weren't giving up, understanding their position. From what he'd heard, they had something wonderful and wouldn't let Governor Davis get his hands on it. However, he had his orders. This was his place in this new society, whether he agreed with it or not. He had his family to think of. He sent one of his men to ask what they wanted. The riders stopped and waited for him to come to them. One of them he recognized to be Ryder, a former member of the Guard. The other one was older and had a familiar look about him, but he couldn't quite place him. The rider came back in short order with a message.

"They want to talk to you, Master Gant" he said, and looking at Taylor, "and only you."

Gant had his horse brought to him and slung himself effortlessly into the saddle.

"I'm going with you," declared Taylor.

"No, you're not."

"You can't go out there alone. You'll be a sitting duck."

"Watch me." Gant turned to one of the Guard, "If he tries to follow me, shoot him."

He rode toward the riders at a casual pace. When he was close enough to recognize them a slight seldom-seen grin appeared briefly, then disappeared. He pulled his horse to a stop when he reached them.

"Hello, Daniel. It's been awhile," greeted Samuel.

PARADISE

"How have you been?"

Ryder was confused by his dad's familiarity with Gant. He had never heard anything from either of the men about knowing the other.

"What are you doing out here, Samuel? You shouldn't be here," said Gant, appearing to be genuinely concerned.

"That's what I tried to tell him," interjected Ryder.

The comment went ignored by both Gant and his dad.

"I could say the same thing to you, Daniel," replied Samuel. "I know you don't want bloodshed here any more than I do, so from one old friend to another, why don't you go back to Sector 4 and we'll go home? What do you say?"

"You're right, I would prefer there wasn't any bloodshed, but I have my orders."

"You can't win," interjected Ryder again. "Your orders won't mean very much when you and your men are dead."

There was a moment of silence between the three.

Samuel continued, "You're welcome to come and live with us and leave that world behind."

Ryder couldn't believe what he was hearing. What could his dad be thinking by inviting the enemy to the very place they were fighting to protect?"

"It's too late to change."

"Then do me another favor. Take your men back to Sector 4. Tell the governor you came up against insurmountable odds and you didn't want to lose the governor's men. He may not like it, but he'll understand and bloodshed will be prevented."

"What do you mean 'another' favor?" asked Ryder.

"Daniel agreed to keep an eye on you while you were

in the Guard," explained his dad.

"What? You knew each other before the quakes?" This was all news to him.

"Quite a while actually. We were good friends once, and I hope we still are," said Samuel, smiling.

"We are," confirmed Gant.

*　　*　　*

News had spread through the Guard encampment that Master Gant was meeting with two of the Raiders. Most had gathered to watch, anxious to know the outcome. After seeing the line of men on horseback, they knew the odds were against them. Most of the men just wanted to go home. They weren't soldiers. They had only taken positions with the Guard for the food and shelter.

Taylor still wanted the Guard to attack. The meeting was taking too long. He paced back and forth in front of them, attempting to work the troops into a frenzy by questioning their courage as men and to provoke them into taking action. A few, as disillusioned as Taylor, were falling for it. A few battle cries began to rise, and the mood of the crowd began to change, with the chants spreading rapidly.

A shot rang out from the Guard camp. Taylor swung around to see Samuel fall to the ground. A hint of a smile crept onto his face.

*　　*　　*

Chapter 13

Ryder and Gant quickly dismounted. The initial shot was followed by a volley of others. Staying low, Ryder crawled to his dad, relieved to see he was still alive and conscious, bleeding freely from a wound through his upper arm. Gant grabbed the white flag lying on the ground and wrapped it tightly around the wound.

"It was still a good idea," moaned Samuel, wincing from the pain as he tried to get up.

"Shut up and lie still!" demanded Gant.

The Raiders, witnessing the shooting, came to high alert, ready to launch an assault, just waiting for Ryder to give the order.

"We need to stop this right now!" said Ryder. Gant nodded agreement. "Dad, I need to leave you for a minute. Are you going to be okay?"

"I'm fine. Go ahead."

Ryder stayed low as he worked his way over to Gant's horse. Gant had been able to keep a firm grip on the reins. The other two had been spooked away by the gunfire. Ryder stood up, the horse between himself and the Guard encampment, facing his own men and waving his arms. Gant did likewise, facing his men.

"Hold your fire!" they both yelled.

They were each recognized by their own men. "Hold your fire!" they repeated. Weapons were hesitantly lowered on both sides.

"Help me," Ryder urged Gant. "Please." Both helped Samuel to his feet.

"Take my horse," offered Gant.

Ryder didn't argue. He just wanted to get his dad to safety and it was the least Gant could do since his men had been responsible.

In the saddle, Samuel placed a hand on Gant's shoulder, "Thanks."

"Thanks?" asked Ryder sarcastically.

"I'm taking my troops back to Sector 4," Gant told Samuel. "I was looking for an excuse not to lead these men against you or the valley. From what I hear, you have a good thing there. I wouldn't do anything to ruin it. If my punishment for failure isn't too severe, maybe we'll see each other again under more favorable conditions."

"I'd like that," said Samuel. "I'll see you again old friend."

They began the walk back to their own lines, Ryder leading the horse and supporting his dad. "Stay down, Dad."

"Mission accomplished," said Samuel, slumped over

and holding tightly to the saddle horn with his good hand. Ryder could only shake his head in disbelief.

* * *

Taylor made no effort to hide his anger, cursing loudly, when Gant returned and announced they would be returning to Sector 4, but fell silent and backed away as Gant strode quickly toward him.

Gant was fed up with his antics, pointing a finger at Taylor. "I'm going to give you a choice, either return with us where I'll report you for the death you caused or you can stay here with the Raiders and answer for it."

Taylor didn't reply, biting his tongue, as his face turned red with anger.

"Well?" asked Gant.

"Governor Davis will hear about this and you'll be the one who pays!" blurted Taylor.

Gant didn't have a chance to respond as Taylor had already stormed off. One of the Guard looked to Gant, wanting to know if he should go after him. Gant shook his head. They all watched as Taylor mounted a horse and sped away, whipping it into a full gallop. Gant was curious, but not concerned, about what Taylor would tell the governor, certain Taylor wouldn't mention his actions had resulted in an old man's death. But, even if he did, he was fairly certain Governor Davis wouldn't care since the old man would have been one of the first eliminated after the valley was taken anyway.

"Who fired that shot?" Gant asked his troops.

The men looked around at each other, exhibiting

innocence, with no one willing to speak up. Gant had no doubt they knew who had done it, but he decided not to push the issue.

"Gather your gear and break camp. We're going back home." There was an audible sigh of relief, without one complaint. The Guard was made up of men from a huge variety of backgrounds, some had come from law enforcement or the military, but most were from backgrounds not familiar with confrontation or battle. And none were anxious to be thrown into a fight with overwhelming odds against them. Especially Raiders, rumored to be a seasoned and deadly bunch. Gant knew their hearts weren't in it.

He regretted that Samuel had been shot and he hoped it had been an accident, the result of fear and nervous energy. Fortunately, he knew Samuel was going to be alright.

The men were ready in a matter of minutes, eager to go home.

* * *

Ryder returned to us leading a horse with one hand on the bridle and the other stabilizing his father in the saddle. When I saw them coming, I couldn't tell how bad Samuel had been injured. I ran out and took up a position on the other side of the horse, helping to support Samuel.

"How is he?" I asked Ryder.

"I'm fine," answered Samuel, forcing a weak smile. Until then, I wasn't even sure he was still alive.

"Did you see who did it?" I asked. "Was it Taylor?"

PARADISE

"It doesn't matter," mumbled Samuel, still leaning over the saddle horn.

Back at camp, I helped Ryder get his dad down. We had some of the men make a bed of blankets in the back of Samuel's wagon, and set him gently inside. Ryder checked the makeshift bandage. The wound had stopped bleeding for the moment, but he'd already lost a good deal of blood. He looked pale.

"Do any of you have medical training?" Ryder asked the men who'd gathered nearby.

"Sorry," came the response.

Samuel cracked his eyes open and winced as he forced himself up on one elbow. "I'll be fine, just get me back to Paradise where Emma can take care of me."

Ryder stared into his dad's eyes for a few seconds. "Okay, Dad."

Samuel grinned as he lay back down, closing his eyes. "Thanks, Son," he mumbled.

"John, are you coming with me?" asked Ryder.

"I might as well, I missed my chance at Taylor, and it looks like the Guard is moving out, so the danger is over."

Our horses were brought to us, which we tied to the back of the wagon.

"Do you need anything, Dad? It's going to be a rough ride back," asked Ryder.

"Don't worry about me. Let's get going."

Ryder and I climbed up onto the buckboard.

Darby walked up to the wagon, asking Ryder, "What do you want us to do?"

"Stick around until they've gone, then tell everyone thanks and send them home. I'll see all of you back at

Haven in a few days."

"Should we leave someone here on guard just in case they decide to come back?" asked Darby.

"I don't think they'll be back anytime soon, but that would probably be a good idea. See if you can find a couple volunteers."

"No need. Sims and I will stick around a couple of days."

"Thanks, Darby," said Ryder, reaching down to shake his hand.

Darby never addressed me directly, either in a friendly or unfriendly manner. I guessed it would take a bit longer to gain his trust, even though Ryder and I had already become friends.

Ryder released the brake and flipped the reins while giving the horse a 'giddy up.' I found I was finally able to relax. There was no apparent danger behind us and by tomorrow I'd be back with my family.

Then I remembered something Ryder had said to Darby. "Where is this 'Haven'?" I asked.

"It's where a large group of us live, but that's not important. Let me tell you something that *is* and you're not going to believe it. I just learned my dad and Gant are old friends!"

*   *   *

Taylor rode past Tent City, directly to the prison gates. The guard on duty refused to allow him to enter until Taylor pulled up his sleeve to show a tattoo signifying him to be a protector in the governor's service. The guard

PARADISE

waved him through after patting him down for weapons.

A skeleton crew of the Guard was all that remained at Sector 4, just enough to maintain order, protect the governor, and to make sure the workers stayed productive. Taylor was patted down again at the doorway into the governor's office. Announced and given permission to enter, Taylor burst into the governor's office with Counselor Damon protectively stepping in front of the governor.

"Master Gant has failed," he blurted over Damon's shoulder. "He's bringing the entire Guard back."

Governor Davis looked up from the paperwork on his desk. He leaned back in his chair, noticeably disturbed by the abrupt interruption.

"What happened?" asked Damon. "I thought you were going to lead Gant and the Guard to the valley."

Davis, silently, was giving his full attention, waiting for an explanation.

Unexpectedly, Taylor immediately felt an air of animosity turn on him because he hadn't done what he had promised.

"I would have," Taylor began to explain, "but the Raiders blocked our way and Gant refused to fight."

"And you just had to rush back here and tell us about it?" asked Damon.

"It was my duty, Counselor. I thought you should know."

Both Damon and Governor Davis recognized a brown-noser when they saw one. Past experience with people like him told them he couldn't be trusted, but a snake might still have uses.

"Master Gant must have had a good reason," stated Davis. "He's always been a loyal follower. How many Raiders were there?"

"More than I had expected," confessed Taylor. "But I'm confident the Guard could easily have defeated them if only they'd tried." Gant had humiliated him in front of the other guards and Taylor was determined to pay him back by making him look incompetent or even cowardly. But he would have to do it carefully because he also knew Gant was favored by the governor, preventing him from embellishing the situation too much. A misplaced word could potentially backfire, losing any chance of credibility with the governor.

"I'm sure you'll understand if we wait to hear Master Gant's report before taking any kind of action," said Counselor Damon.

Governor Davis remained silent, turning his attention away from Taylor, back to shuffling through the paperwork on his desk. He didn't like communicating directly with the lower classes and avoided contact whenever possible. Just being in Taylor's presence made him feel dirty, wiping his palms on his pants legs repeatedly. The only reason he had made an exception this time was because of his extreme interest in the valley. Based on what Taylor had reported to the first Guard unit, the resources there would be extremely valuable and allow him to expand his territory considerably. Since hearing about it, he hadn't been able to think about anything else. It had crossed his mind briefly that the valley was only hearsay, yet to be confirmed. And now, Taylor's credibility was in question, but it was worth the effort to find out.

PARADISE

Taylor stood uncomfortably in silence waiting to answer any further questions. He opened his mouth to speak, but was cut off by Damon, "That will be all. Stay available in case we have further questions after Master Gant's return."

Taylor was puzzled by the dismissal. He had tried to do everything asked of him.

"Guard," Damon called, "please escort Mr. Grey to his quarters."

Dumbfounded, he was led away, the guard shutting the large office door behind them.

"What do you think?" asked Damon.

"I think he's one of those people who'll do anything to get ahead," answered Davis. "Including stretching the truth."

"No. I mean about Gant."

"Gant is no coward. Whatever he did, it was for a good reason. I trust him completely."

After the governor's statement, Damon was hesitant to bring up an all important question, but knew it had to be asked.

"Governor, I'm going to play the role of devil's advocate, if you don't mind. What if there is some measure of truth to what Tyler said? Suppose Master Gant didn't attack for some other reason?"

Davis' posture became rigid at the audacity of Damon to even mention such a thing. "Devil's advocate or not, I don't like what you're implying. I suggest you withhold your comments and judgment until we've heard from Gant himself."

"Yes, sir," answered Damon. He had raised the

question. It was his obligation. Now, no matter what happened, he couldn't be blamed if it turned out to be true. "There is another question needing to be addressed."

Davis sighed but remained silent. After Damon's last comment, he wasn't particularly looking forward to the next one. He waited impatiently for Damon to continue.

"We may have acted in haste earlier when we sent the Guard to claim the valley. In hindsight, we only had the word of Taylor the valley existed at all."

"And your point being," stated the governor.

"Well then," continued Damon, "I recommend we verify its existence before any further action is taken." To make sure it didn't seem as though he was placing blame, he made sure to use the inclusive 'we.'

The governor nodded in agreement. "That's a very good idea, Counselor. And how do you propose we do that?" asked Davis.

"We need to send someone we can trust to check it out first-hand."

"I agree completely. When can you leave?"

"Me? That's not what I do. What about my duties here?"

"I trust you, Damon. I'd really appreciate your help if you'd do this as a favor to me. And I think your duties can wait until you return."

Damon recognized the familiar look in the governor's eyes and the tone of his voice. Even though it would have sounded like a request to anyone else, it wasn't. He wasn't being given a choice.

"But I don't know where to go," Damon pleaded.

"That's why you'll need to take Taylor with you."

PARADISE

Damon didn't like Taylor or trust him. The idea of spending several days alone with him on the trail wasn't his worst nightmare, but could turn into one.

"I doubt if he'll be willing to go."

"I'm going to leave it to you to convince him." Davis gave him a knowing smile.

* * *

Upon arriving at Paradise, we passed the small cemetery at the edge of town. It was hard to miss the fresh grave with wildflowers covering it. I had forgotten temporarily about Taylor until that moment. Somehow, he would pay for what he'd done. Then I remembered Jill had been injured the same terrible night and wondered how bad her injuries had been, also a result of Taylor's spree of violence.

I didn't have long to find out. The church bells had been sounded to signal our approach, and many of the town's people had come out to meet us. Jill was one of the first to reach the wagon. She looked as though she would be alright with only a small bruise on the left side of her forehead. Ryder stopped in front of Town Hall. As I climbed down, Jill caught me off guard, throwing her arms around my neck. I gave her a friendly but brief hug in return.

I noticed Sarah standing nearby, smiling. I wasn't quite sure whether it was because she was glad to see me or because she was amused at Jill's apparent infatuation. Maybe it was both. Either way, she appeared to be in good spirits and I was glad to be home. I stepped back, gently removing Jill's arms.

"How are you feeling?" I asked.

"A few bruises, but I'll be alright. Thanks for asking," she said.

I immediately felt as though I may have fueled the fire by asking.

She now spotted Sarah, placing her arm around my waist for effect. Once again I removed her arm, receiving a sympathetic and understanding look from Sarah, who was now joined by Cindy and Christopher. From the looks of their clothes, they must have come straight from the fields to meet us.

I moved to the back of the wagon where Ryder was helping his dad from the wagon. His mom, concerned to see Samuel injured, asked what had happened.

"I'm afraid he's been shot," I answered.

She looked at Ryder, looking for an explanation.

"I'll explain later, Mom."

Emma began to check her husband out, pulling the bandage back to look at the wounds, front and back.

"Don't fuss. I'll be alright," insisted Samuel.

"Shush," she said. Satisfied he would be alright, she leaned over and gave him a kiss on his forehead.

"Let's get him to our cabin," she said.

One of the men stepped forward to help Ryder with his dad.

I turned to find Sarah right behind me with the kids. We all shared a welcome home hug.

"Is Samuel going to be alright?" she asked.

"I think so. He'll just have to take it easy for awhile."

"What happened out there? Did you stop them, Dad?"

PARADISE

asked Christopher excitedly.

"We sure did! The Guard came but Ryder called for assistance from other Raiders. You should have seen how many there were. Even Master Gant was there. And it turns out he's a friend of Samuel."

"Then how did Samuel get shot?" asked Sarah.

"We're not sure who did it, but we think it was an accident."

"Are we safe here, Daddy?" asked Cindy.

I smiled as I looked down at her concerned innocent face. "I think we're going to be just fine. Let's go home."

*   *   *

Chapter 14

Damon came to Taylor's tent alone to assure a discreet face to face meeting without prying eyes or ears. It was to prevent a scene at headquarters, should things get out of hand. Taylor was both surprised and worried when he opened the tent flap to be greeted by Damon. The reason for the personal encounter couldn't be good.

"May I come in?" asked Damon.

Taylor peeked outside, past Damon in both directions. It looked as though he had come alone and there didn't appear to be any one watching. He found it curious Damon was without his usual escorts.

"Of course. Hurry."

Damon was slightly amused. It seemed Taylor didn't want to be seen talking to him any more than he wanted anyone to see him there. Damon insisted Taylor take a seat and then proceeded to tell him why he was there.

PARADISE

"Go back to the valley? Just the two of us? Not on your life!" shouted Taylor. "I won't do it! Do you know what they'll do to me if we're caught?"

"It's my understanding you are the only one who can lead me there."

Taylor stood up and began to nervously pace back and forth, kicking up a slight dust cloud off the dirt floor.

"Isn't that right?" prodded Damon.

"Yeah. That's right! But I already did my part. I tried to show the Guard the way there, but you already know how that turned out. I'm not going there again, especially not with just you." Taylor's attitude began to take on a change, less intimidated by Damon, with a touch of arrogance beginning to surface. After all, he was the only one who knew the way to the valley. They needed him and that made him valuable.

Damon detected the change, and didn't like it. His demeanor took an immediate turn to the dark side at Taylor's lack of respect. Physically, Damon wasn't an imposing figure, but Taylor knew what he was capable of. The look he saw in Damon's eyes brought him back to reality, his brief moment of rebellion squelched.

"We'd never be able to get through anyway," reasoned Taylor. "Don't you think they'll be on their guard now for anyone coming that way?"

"And that'll be to our advantage. It'll be much easier to find concealment and slip through their lines with just the two of us."

"How about if I draw you a map?" asked Taylor, trying anything to keep from going.

The trip would be easier with an agreeable person than

with one he had to coerce or physically force. With the governor's blessing, he had been given the green light to do whatever was necessary to obtain Taylor's cooperation. Just asking for himself wasn't working. It was time to pull out his ace.

"The governor would like you to go with me," said Damon.

Taylor didn't need him to say anything else. He thought Damon could have led with that. He gave a sigh of surrender. Even though he had gone through the motions of refusing to go, he knew it was hopeless. He'd never had a choice. He liked living in Tent City, working indirectly for the governor. And he was far better off than many who lived there, being allowed to avoid all forms of physical labor in exchange for certain tasks.

Regardless, he tried one more argument. "Now the Guard knows the general direction. They'd be able to find the valley on their own if they just kept going in the same direction."

Damon was losing his patience. "The governor insists you go," he clarified.

To remain a citizen of Sector 4, he had to do what he was told. No questions. Governor Davis had the last word. Taylor sat, placing his head in his hands. "I'm not going to get out of this, am I?" He looked up.

Damon shook his head. "Be ready to leave at first light tomorrow. Meet me at the compounds main gate. A horse and supplies will be waiting." He stepped through the tent flap, then stuck his head back inside. "Don't make me come looking for you. It'll make me and the governor very unhappy."

PARADISE

*   *   *

As instructed, Taylor was at the gate when Damon arrived. At first, Taylor didn't recognize him. Usually, Damon was impeccably dressed for his position, with never a hair out of place. But today, he was dressed simply, appearing as one of the field workers, with dirty and torn clothes, and an unshaven shadow. It occurred to Taylor that Damon, wisely, was attempting to be inconspicuous during their journey. It would be far less likely for him to be recognized by any Raider scouts, allowing them to move freely across the countryside essentially undetected. The only thing to possibly raise questions was the fact they would be on horseback. It meant they were either Raiders or thieves, either way to be left alone.

A member of the Guard brought out two horses by the reins, each with a bedroll, a bag of supplies, and two canteens each. Without saying a word, Damon mounted his horse and nodded to Taylor he was ready to go, tapping his horse in the flanks with his heels and trotting away. Taylor quickly grabbed the reins from the guard and mounted, galloping to catch up, but remained behind Damon.

Damon was confident he knew the general direction for the first part of the journey. Taylor's input wouldn't be needed until later. He wasn't looking forward to the time when he'd have to rely on Taylor or have to look at his backside.

As mid-day approached, Damon brought his horse to a halt, Taylor stopping beside him.

"What's wrong?" asked Taylor.

"Someone's coming. See the dust cloud?"

Taylor hadn't been paying attention, but after Damon had pointed it out, it was obvious.

"Should we hide?" asked Taylor. "It could be Raiders patrolling the area."

"Or it could be the Guard returning." He paused to think about it. "Let's duck behind what's left of the old farm house over there and watch."

They moved off the trail toward the collapsed blackened skeleton of a farm house to use as cover. Dismounted, they patted the neck of their horses to keep them calm and quiet. Hidden from sight, they waited. The sound of pounding hooves came closer. Taylor extended his neck to get a better look.

"Stay back!" hissed Damon.

Taylor wasn't a child and didn't like being treated like one. However, he wasn't in a position to argue. Mumbling obscenities under his breath, he dropped back out of sight.

"What was that?" asked Damon, more as a warning than actually expecting a response.

* * *

"Master Gant!" shouted his second in command. He had spotted two riders quickly leaving the trail.

Gant continued as if nothing had happened. "I saw them," he said with a sigh. "Keep moving."

"But we should check them out. They could be Raider scouts."

Gant would just as soon let them be. Two riders weren't worth the trouble. Recently, he had become far less interested in pursuing such matters. Soon he would be

PARADISE

turning forty, and his time too would be up. Neither the governor nor the counselor had brought the subject up. So, he didn't know if there was the chance of an exception in his case or not. Though not confirmed, the common belief was that the governor himself was well past the age of termination.

He assumed his second, Travis, would be replacing him as leader of the Guard. A brief trace of a grin came to his face as he thought 'Master Travis.' It didn't have quite the same ring to it as Master Gant and Travis wasn't exactly an imposing figure. He wondered how the men would follow him. But Travis did have the character only the governor and counselor could appreciate, a loyal brown-noser to the end. Gant had seen a dark side emerge more than once. If Travis was allowed to lead the assault, the people in the valley would be forced into slavery or killed without a second thought.

Travis was right about this though. As long as he was still in charge, it was his duty to check them out. He realized he'd been less motivated recently than when he had first fallen into the position. In the beginning, he had been less resistant to do whatever was required of him. He had his family to take care of. It was security, providing both food and shelter inside the walls. Now, he couldn't afford to give the governor reason to replace him, especially if there was the slightest chance of becoming an exception.

Gant held up his hand for the column to stop. He gave Travis a nod, sending two men, one to each side, to surround the debris and flush out the riders.

* * *

After hearing the hooves come to a stop, Damon risked a quick look. It *was* the Guard, led by Gant, and two of the men were coming their way, weapons drawn.

"They spotted us," said Damon, "and are coming this way. We need to show ourselves before they open fire."

Fear spread over Taylor's face as he pulled his gun.

"Put that away," demanded Damon. "Do you want to be shot?"

"They may shoot us as Raiders anyway," argued Taylor.

Damon stepped out, one hand in the air, the other leading his horse. Taylor hesitated, cursed, and followed. Damon's stealth skills hadn't been as good as he'd thought. They would have to do better as they proceeded south. One of the Guard dismounted as the other trained his rifle on the two. The reins were grabbed from their hands, roughly guiding them back to Gant.

Master Gant remained in the saddle as the two were brought to him. They were told to stop ten feet from Gant, forced to drop to their knees by a rifle butt to their lower backs. Damon, angry and wincing in pain, slowly raised his head to look into Gant's eyes. Gant had to do a double-take. He quickly dismounted and rushed to help him to his feet.

"Counselor Damon?" asked Gant, not knowing whether to trust his eyes.

Damon smiled through his pain, still unable to stand erect.

"I'm sorry, Counselor. I didn't recognize you dressed

like that. What are you doing out here?" He lifted the chin of the other man, still on his knees. "Taylor?"

"We're doing a little recon of our own. I'm impressed you spotted us. You're to be commended for your alertness," said Damon.

The two guards, who had been so rough with them, now realizing who they had manhandled, lowered their rifles and stepped back, fearing the consequences.

"Thank you, Counselor. You really shouldn't be out here alone, especially with him," said Gant, with a glance to Taylor. "I imagine he's already told you about the opposition we met."

"Yes, he did. That's why we're here, to penetrate their line of defense, and to confirm the existence of the alleged valley."

Taylor didn't know whether to be offended because they didn't fully believe him or feel justified because the governor had believed him enough to check it out. A smirk appeared on Taylor's face specifically for Gant's benefit, emphasizing the point that he had been asked to personally show the counselor the way. To Damon, as a jab at Gant, "They could have broken through the Raider lines if Gant had tried." Then he turned to Gant, "I told you you'd pay."

"Shut up, Taylor!" ordered Damon, the smirk disappearing from Taylor's face.

"The fact is, Counselor, we were outnumbered and after "someone" shot one of the leaders from the other side under a flag of truce, I decided it was not the time for a full-on confrontation."

"There's no need to explain, Master Gant. Both the governor and I trust your judgment."

Taylor's mouth dropped open with surprise.

"Why do you think the Raiders are so intent on keeping us out of the valley?" asked Damon. "Why would they care?"

"Alleged valley," corrected Gant.

"Right. Alleged valley."

"I'm sure I don't know, sir," Gant replied. He paused. "If you would allow me, Counselor, I strongly urge you to reconsider continuing on your quest. The Raiders will be on high alert now. It would be a miracle if you got through. At least let me send someone reliable with you."

Gant glanced at Taylor.

"What do you mean by "alleged" valley? I've been there," Taylor blurted out defensively at Gant. "It's more than you can say."

Damon stepped up to Gant. "I just follow orders like you," he said calmly. "The governor wants to know for sure."

"I can understand why he'd have doubts," said Gant.

"The two of us should be able to get in and out without any trouble," continued Damon.

"No offense, Counselor, but today could have ended very differently if it had been someone else who spotted you."

"I appreciate your concern," said Damon, "but this is something I have to do. If we could have our horses returned, we'll be on our way."

Gant motioned to the two apprehensive guards to return Damon and Taylor's horses to them.

One of the men handed Damon his reins. He began to plead, "I'm sorry, Counselor. I didn't know it was you."

PARADISE

Damon smiled. "You were just doing your job." Damon pulled his pistol and shot him dead center of his forehead and then without another word carefully lifted himself into his saddle, his lower back still tender. The other guard stood paralyzed, his eyes wide with terror, knowing he was next. Damon gave him a sideways glance, then holstered his weapon.

Gant wasn't surprised at Damon's action, having seen him perform similar acts before. He ordered the man to be tied across his horse's saddle.

With a nod to Gant, Damon nudged his horse into a trot down the trail, followed closely by Taylor.

* * *

Governor Davis was excited at the prospect of adding a new resource like the valley to his little empire. He was almost to the point of being giddy, having to fight back the urge to scream for joy. He still didn't know whether he believed Taylor Grey's story, but if it was true and could take it for his own, he would have a huge advantage over his fellow governors. It would indeed give him bragging rights with the increase of manpower and resources. He was finding it increasingly difficult to contain himself from telling the other governors. He was on the verge of exploding. He smiled as he thought of the praise he would receive from the Chief Governor. Then it occurred to him, there was one major problem with sharing the news after the valley had been acquired. Once Chief Governor Charles Grayson knew about it, he was afraid he would claim the territory as his own. Perhaps, it would be best to keep the valley a secret resource for now. But if the Chief Governor was to find out about it second hand, then there could be hell to pay. The more Davis thought about it, the more he began to realize the valley could become a curse instead of a resource, if it wasn't handled properly.

* * *

A few days after their return, Samuel was back to sitting on his front porch in his favorite rocking chair, his right arm in a sling. He rocked slowly, taking in the beautiful sunny and warm day, enjoying the light breeze. Ryder and Darby walked up from the stable where they had spent the night. They had been offered cots in the room above Town Hall, but they had declined, feeling it was too confining. Darby had arrived at Paradise just the night before, after a couple of uneventful days of watching for returning guards.

"Dad, how are you feeling today?" asked Ryder.

"I'll be fine. Your mom won't let me do anything, so here I sit."

She heard them through the open front door, stuck her head out and smiled, "Good morning, boys. Would you two like some breakfast?"

"That'd be great, Mrs. Yoder," replied Darby as he wasted no time in hopping up on the porch and entering the house. With their current arrangement in Haven, a good home-cooked meal was a real treat and not to be passed up. Ryder was right behind his friend, but Samuel caught his arm as he went by, pulling him close.

"You know, Son, you don't have to hang around. I'm

PARADISE

going to be fine and I think the trouble is over for now."

"I know, but I think we'll stick around just a little longer, just to make sure. I don't know if I can get Darby away from Mom's cooking anyway."

*   *   *

Chapter 15

"It's good to be home," I said, smiling and taking in a deep breath of the sweet air in the valley.

"I like the sound of that," said Sarah. "Home. I never dreamed there could still be a place like this."

"We were very fortunate. It's like someone was watching over us. And I don't mean Samuel, even though it's true we wouldn't be here without him."

As happy as I was at this moment, I knew our troubles weren't over yet. The Guard had supposedly returned to Sector 4 for the moment, but Taylor was still out there and the governor wasn't likely to give up so easily. It was a certainty he would send the Guard back at some point to try again, this time with even more men. If he was willing to share the resources, there was the chance he could seek help from one or more of the other Sectors.

For the time being, all was peaceful and calm, routines

returned to some degree of normality. I would enjoy it as long as it lasted.

*   *   *

    Damon, refusing to follow Taylor until he had no other choice, retained the lead while following Taylor's directions. Since being spotted early on, they avoided riding on any of the main trails, but maintained a parallel course nearby. At night, as another precaution, Damon insisted they not have a campfire, nothing to draw attention to themselves. Over the next two days they came close to several other parties of one to three people without incident. None of them paid them any attention. They looked like everyone else now and that was how they were treated. Most minded their own business in the wasteland, unless you came too close, had something they wanted, or you wore a uniform.

*   *   *

    Most of those who had been successful at surviving in the wasteland were roaming scavengers, living off what they could scrounge or steal. Some, finding it difficult to survive on their own, had joined with others like themselves to form small groups for survival's sake. There was strength in numbers. Ryder, after leaving the Guard, had been taken in by one of these groups. In a short time his leadership ability became obvious, convincing many of the small groups to join forces to form an organized group.
    After several raids on Guard transports, they earned

the name Raiders, so named by the governor. In time, under Ryder's leadership, the members of the Raiders grew into a brotherhood of sorts, the closest thing to family some would ever know again. Ryder discovered some were former guards like him, and some, he guessed, had questionable backgrounds since they refused to talk about their former lives, preferring to leave it all behind. Everyone had a story, but nobody asked and nobody cared.

Some of the quake survivors chose to remain on their own. These were the die-hard survivalists and scavengers who would never trust anyone else, preferring to die rather than depend on someone else.

Preppers belonged to that group, but were different and few in numbers. In general, these individuals had made preparations before the earthquake devastation, readying themselves for any large scale survival event, whether natural or economic. Some fortified their housing so their location could be defendable against attacks from those who were unprepared and who would eventually become aggressive out of desperation. Inside the walls, food had been stored or food plots made for long term survival, a water source established, and weapons and ammunition readied.

One thing the scavengers, survivalists, and preppers had in common was that if someone came too close and threatened their domain, they would do whatever it took to defend it. The aggressors would get what they deserved. Ryder and his men quickly learned where not to go, honoring these people's rights to be left alone, giving them a wide berth.

The Raiders never took from other survivors, only

PARADISE

from the Guard collection patrols who had scavenged items from the abandoned remains of homesteads and small towns. They didn't suffer from any guilt, knowing the residents of Tent City would never see these goods anyway. Ryder knew from his time with the Guard that the items stored in the lower level of the compound were only used for the governor, his staff, and his privileged friends.

Ryder, determined to help his new friends survive, shared a few of the skills he'd learned from his dad, converting some of the Raiders into farmers by creating food plots. The citizens in the sector, whether from inside the compound or from Tent City, all were equally unaware of how the Raiders were surviving, believing it was strictly from stealing from others. They feared them the same as any other roaming criminals, a result of the governor's warnings and propaganda. It was another way of keeping the citizens from wandering too far from Tent City and Sector 4, or sanctuary as the governor liked to call it.

*   *   *

Taylor informed Damon as they approached the area where the confrontation had taken place.

"Lead us around," instructed Damon, for the first time relinquishing the lead. "There could still be sentries posted here."

Taylor gladly jumped out in front. "The valley's only one long day's ride from here," informed Taylor.

"It'll be sunset in a few hours," observed Damon. "We should stop and talk about what we're going to do when we get there. You can draw me a map." Past the would-be battlefield they found a grove of mesquite that would give them cover while they planned ahead.

After dismounting, Taylor began to collect dead limbs.

"We won't be needing those," said Damon. "We're not going to have a fire tonight either. It's too dangerous here. Come sit over here and let's talk."

Taylor threw down the armload of limbs, showing his annoyance. Damon could have said something five minutes sooner. He then kneeled next to Damon.

"How many ways are there into the valley?" asked Damon.

"Just one by horse or wagon. But you should be able to see the town and valley from anywhere along the rim."

"That's good. I just want to see for myself that it's everything you said it was and then get out of there without any contact with the locals. Tomorrow afternoon we'll stop a little ways out and wait until the sun sets. It should make it easier to get close without being seen. Can you find your way in the dark?"

"No problem. It was night when I left there the last time."

There wasn't much else to say. Neither was interested in making small talk with the other. The sun set and they each rolled up in their bedrolls. Taylor wondered why they hadn't eaten, but he remained silent, deciding he could last as long as Damon. Angry and with a growling stomach he eventually fell asleep. Early the next morning, before the sun came up, Damon woke Taylor with a kick. "Let's go!"

"What about breakfast?" asked Taylor. "I'm starving. We didn't even have supper."

Damon dug into his pocket and pulled out a piece of

PARADISE

jerky, throwing it at him. "Satisfied?"

It was amazing how good an old dried out piece of meat could be. Taylor couldn't wait for this trip to be over and to get back to his normal life.

They rode in silence most of the day with Damon once again in the lead. Taylor continually had to correct Damon's direction when he ventured off course. As Damon had planned, they stopped to make camp that evening a safe distance from Paradise, according to Taylor. They waited for the sun to set, again in silence, time dragging on slowly. Neither man cared anything about the other. They were only together because they'd both been forced into it. After the sun had disappeared, Damon had them wait another hour past dusk before moving out.

During the wait, they had only spotted one wagon with one lone man at the reins as he casually rolled by on the well-worn trail toward the valley. Cautiously, they came out from the trees and proceeded south. The near darkness helped to give them cover but also made it harder for them to see any dangers ahead. When they were about a quarter-mile from where Taylor believed the valley rim to be, Damon had them dismount and tie up their horses and proceed on foot.

At fifty yards they could barely make out the rims edge, visible only as a gaping black hole in the ground. Crawling on their hands and knees to the edge, Damon finally saw it. From what he could see at first glance, it appeared to be surprisingly just as Taylor had said. Smiling, Damon silently took in as much as he could under the dim light of the partly cloudy moon-lit sky. The windows in the homes stood out, glowing from the lights inside. Trees were scattered throughout and he thought he saw the reflection of the moonlight off the still water of a small lake. This is what he had hoped to find, but wouldn't have been surprised if Taylor had exaggerated. He was becoming convinced. The governor would be very pleased.

"I need to see more," said Damon. "I need to determine if it's actually worth fighting for."

Taylor couldn't believe it. "I already reported everything I saw. You can see I was telling the truth about the valley. Why would I lie about what's in it?"

"I want to see for myself and we're already here. Stay here and wait for me if you want. It shouldn't take long for me to check it out."

Taylor had no intention of arguing about staying put. He couldn't risk being spotted and identified by anyone there anyway. Most of the community had met him and would know him on sight. The chances of escaping again would be slim to impossible. He was glad to let Damon take the risk. Even if Damon was spotted, Taylor wasn't sure anyone would recognize him with his current appearance. The only possibility would be if citizens who had come from Sector 4 recognized him, and if so, he would have the same slim chance to get away as Taylor did.

However, from their encounter with Gant, it had been proven even people who knew Damon well wouldn't necessarily recognize him. With his current garb and unshaven stubble, the odds were in his favor. If seen, he would most likely be only seen as a stranger, because in a community this small, everyone knew everyone else. A stranger would stick out. But then again, these people were

PARADISE

so naïve, they'd probably greet him warmly as a new arrival.

"It'll be better for both of us if no one sees you at all," commented Taylor, "so no one will ever know we were here." In reality, he didn't care if Damon was captured, he knew the way back to Sector 4.

Then a terrible thought occurred to him, in returning to Sector 4 without Damon the valley would remain unverified. The governor could blame him for Damon's absence, whether captured or dead. This had just taken a nasty twist he hadn't previously considered. He was going to have to make sure they both returned.

"I'm coming too," declared Taylor.

"No. You stay here. We can't risk someone recognizing you."

"The same goes for you. If anything happens to you, the governor's going to blame me."

"So, you want to save your own hide. Very touching."

"You got it."

Damon thought a moment and then agreed, "You're probably right. You know the lay of the land better than I do anyway." He paused. "But if you do anything to bring attention to us, I'll shoot you myself. Understand?"

"Yeah, I understand perfectly."

Damon had Taylor go back to the horses and fetch a rope. He tied one end to a sturdy mesquite tree and threw the rest of the coil over the edge into the darkness below.

Damon went first, rappelling to the valley floor, approximately thirty feet below. Taylor came next. Halfway down, while attempting to get a good foothold, several large fragments of sandstone broke free, noisily falling to the valley floor. "Look out!" Taylor whispered loudly.

Damon jumped to the side just before the fragments hit the ground and rolled away. Taylor reached the bottom without another incident.

"You almost got me!" said Damon angrily.

Taylor began to reply, but decided against it.

"Now, watch what you're doing," said Damon. "Someone may have heard the noise." They stood motionless a few moments, listening for any sound of someone coming.

"It was just rocks falling. Nothing suspicious," whispered Taylor.

"Take me on a tour around the perimeter. Remember, we don't want to be seen by anyone," said Damon. "In and out as quick as possible."

Taylor nodded. "Follow me."

Staying behind cover whenever possible and moving within the shadows, Taylor led him past the downtown area, skirting the residential, livestock and farming areas. They had only seen a couple of men, one closing up the blacksmith shop and one sitting and rocking on his front porch. Taylor recognized Samuel, but didn't bother to point him out to Damon.

Returning to where they had left the rope, they had to cross the one road leading into town. A sentry sat under a nearby tree. They saw no evidence of a weapon.

"He's not even armed," whispered Damon.

"They don't believe in it," replied Taylor. "If he sees something suspicious, he's supposed to run to the church and ring the bell."

"You were right about one thing. If we could get past

the Raiders, we could take this place easily."

"That's what I've been saying," said Taylor, exasperated.

* * *

Gant and his men returned to Sector 4. Most were relieved when the encounter with the Raiders had not escalated. Only a couple had voiced their disappointment. Gant hadn't been surprised. These men were always ready to fight just for the sake of fighting, no matter what the reason. In the beginning, it had been easy to fill positions in the Guard with the requirements set extremely low. A warm body who could follow orders was essentially all it took. Volunteers had been plentiful since recruitment included a place to live within the prison walls for themselves and their families along with regular meals, something not always possible on the outside. As the ranks were filled, the standards became stiffer, with many turned away.

Many of the families had come to the 'safe haven' in response to circulars delivered to their dying communities, claiming to provide a place of safety with plenty of food and water. In the beginning, it was an enticement most couldn't ignore. At the time, the only other option had been to make due on your own and pray you could survive. Contrary to the governor's promise food and water became harder to come by every day. Conditions had quickly deteriorated at Tent City as the truth became evident. Their safe haven had turned into a work camp with no way of escape. Trapped, they were forced to do whatever they were told or suffer the consequences. Family welfare was a powerful means of leverage.

Gant was summoned to Governor Davis' office as soon as he had passed through the gates and before he had time to dismount. He sighed heavily. On the long ride back he had continued to think about Samuel's invitation to come to the valley with his family. He had told Samuel it was too late. He had made his choice. But, was there still time to make a change? Didn't his family deserve a better life? When he'd taken this position, there hadn't been any options. Now, there was a choice. But, perhaps the other people at the valley wouldn't welcome him as openly as Samuel would. His options ran through his mind once again as he walked to the governor's office.

He also thought about what he would say to the governor. Yes, there had been a chance they could have defeated the Raiders and advanced to the valley, but his heart hadn't been in it and knowing his men, neither was theirs. These men weren't soldiers. Besides, his long-time friend, Samuel, had been there and he couldn't let anything happen to him. Gant had never seen his friend's valley, but he knew it existed and from what he had heard it was a beautiful place, a paradise in an otherwise damaged and hostile world. He had already made up his mind, he wouldn't be a willing aid in the governor's plan, knowing it would destroy such a place.

Gant knocked on the open door, waiting for permission to enter. Governor Davis, sitting at his desk, looked up and smiled.

"Ah, Master Gant, please come in and have a seat," said Davis, motioning him to the chair facing his desk.

PARADISE

Gant straightened his uniform and removed his cap as he sat down, expecting a reprimand for his failed mission.

Davis looked at him for a few moments before speaking, collecting his thoughts, and then realized he was making Gant uncomfortable. He needed to be tactful. Gant had been with him since Sector 4's inception and had been an integral part of his success. Even though he was the governor and what he said was final, he didn't want to say anything that Gant might take exception to. Granted, the mission had been a failure, but that could only have happened if the situation had been out of Gant's control. A direct accusation of failure wouldn't do. Gant was a great leader and all of his men liked and respected him. He was the key to his continued success.

"Master Gant, I understand you encountered resistance in the search for the valley."

"Yes, sir." Gant kept it short, feeling he didn't need to explain, knowing Taylor had already told his side of the story.

"You know, we need that valley. Not just for me, but for all of us. According to Taylor, the valley has all the resources we need to make things better for our life here. Wouldn't you like for your family to receive better and more plentiful rations? And at the same time surely you can see how it would go a long way in improving morale around here. We have to have it."

"Then you're sending us back?" Gant asked.

"As soon as Taylor's story has been verified. I sent Damon with Taylor to be my eyes to check it out."

"We met them on the trail."

"If Damon comes back with a positive report, you will

be sent to claim the valley for us."

"Respectfully, Governor, I'm afraid the price may be too high. There were significantly more Raiders than we had men. And those were just the ones we saw."

"That may be, Master Gant, but they are scavengers, society rejects. Your men have been trained by you. I'm confident you've taught them well and they'll be more than ready to meet any challenge."

"You honor me, sir, but we could lose many of your men," pleaded Gant.

Davis didn't like having his orders questioned and he was losing his patience. But he took a deep breath and forced a smile. "Be prepared to go when I give the word. Now, go and get ready. And no excuses this time. Understand? And don't worry about the men. We can always find replacements."

"Yes, Governor."

*   *   *

Gant entered his family's living quarters within the prison walls. His wife, Donna, could tell immediately something was wrong. She had already received word through the grapevine that the men were back and had been waiting patiently to welcome him home. Their twin sons, fifteen years old, too young for the Guard but too old for school, were somewhere inside the walls on a maintenance and stocking detail. Those living inside the walls didn't work in the fields with the Tent City people. Early on, jealousy had become an issue between the two groups, the haves and the have not's. So, the governor had segregated

PARADISE

the two groups to eliminate future problems and the exchange of information.

"What's wrong, Daniel?" she asked with concern.

"Have you ever thought about leaving this place?"

*　　*　　*

Chapter 16

"How do we get past him?" whispered Taylor.

"We'll backtrack and work ourselves around him," answered Damon.

"It's too dangerous," replied Taylor, taking off toward the man on guard.

"No!" yelled Damon in a loud whisper. The last thing he wanted was to make their presence known. He stayed where he was, helplessly watching Taylor dart from tree to tree, working his way to the unsuspecting guard, using the shadows for cover whenever possible.

Taylor made it to the opposite side of the tree where the sentry sat. He looked back to Damon who tried to wave him off, shaking his head no. Taylor pulled a knife, its blade glistening in the moonlight. There was nothing Damon could do, except watch. Taylor acted quickly, reaching around and thrusting the blade into the man's

PARADISE

chest. The man, sleeping, hadn't had a chance, dying instantly, his head slumping forward. Taylor waved the furious Damon over. Now, the townspeople would know someone had been there. Exactly what Damon and the governor hadn't wanted, and Taylor knew it. Damon looked at the dead sentry. He appeared to still be sleeping.

"You idiot!" shouted Damon in a loud whisper, backhanding him. "What were you thinking?"

Taylor took a step back, wiping the blood from his lip and holding the knife up. "Don't ever do that again, or I'll kill you!"

Damon had had it with Taylor. He had served his purpose, was out of control, and had become a liability.

"Get going," said Damon, ignoring Taylor's threat.

"They'll just think someone from inside the community did it," Taylor tried to explain.

"From what you've told me about them, it's not likely."

When they reached the rope, Damon told Taylor to climb first. Taylor grabbed the rope and placed his first step on the cliff wall, beginning to pull himself up. Damon pulled his own knife and stepped toward Taylor, quickly placing one hand over Taylor's mouth and thrusting the blade upward into the small of Taylor's back. Taylor gasped as his grip tightened on the rope momentarily then released, dropping heavily to the ground. Still conscious, he looked up at Damon. "Why?" he uttered.

"You couldn't be trusted," Damon stated matter-of-factly.

Spitting blood, a brief laugh escaped Taylor's lips at the irony. Then he was dead.

Damon grabbed his arms and began to drag him. At first he was just going to find a place in the heavy brush to leave him. Then he began to think. Since the sentry had been killed, it would be difficult to keep their intrusion a secret. Or would it? Maybe Taylor had a workable explanation after all. Perhaps he could change how it was perceived. Not too far away they had passed a cemetery. He smiled as a plan began to form. He drug Taylor's body to the cemetery and not seeing anyone around, placed him on the fence near the gate, his arms spread apart, his chest out. He would be easy for the townspeople to find. With the tip of his knife he carved "A GIFT" into Taylor's chest. Now, he hoped, whoever saw him would assume Taylor killed the sentry, and someone from their own community had then taken matters into their own hands as retaliation. Then, there wouldn't be any reason for them to believe he hadn't acted alone. Damon stood back and admired his handiwork. Hearing voices, he scrambled back into the brush. Cutting a limb off a bush, he quickly swept the drag marks, returning to the rope and beginning the climb.

With Taylor dead he was sure they'd consider the danger to be over. There was no reason to believe they would come looking for him. Back on top he recovered the rope and worked his way silently back to where they had left the horses tied up. He untied the reins of Taylor's horse and set him free, slapping it on its hind quarters. Finding a single horse would support the idea of one intruder, contributing to the deception. Damon began the long ride back to Sector 4. The governor would be pleased to learn the valley *did* exist and had all the resources he had hoped for.

PARADISE

* * *

We woke to the repeated clanging of the church bell. I quickly pulled on my jeans and boots, grabbing my pistol as I rushed outside. The sky was just beginning to lighten. Several people ran by, including Levi.

"What's going on?" I asked him.

"It's your friend Taylor. He's at the cemetery and he's been killed. And the man we had on watch is dead too."

Levi was one of the few people in the community who openly blamed me for bringing Taylor there.

I couldn't believe my ears. Taylor had come back? Again? Alone? Why? Sarah came to my side, taking my arm, followed by Christopher and Cindy.

"Did he say something about Taylor?" asked Sarah.

I started not to tell her, knowing they had become friends of sorts while I'd been away. Even after everything Taylor had done, I knew she still had a connection with him and didn't think of him in the same way I did. Reluctantly, I said, "Taylor's dead."

Sarah became weak in the knees, cupped her hands over her mouth, and sunk to the ground as she began to cry. Cindy placed an arm around her shoulder, but showed no emotion. She had come to accept what Taylor actually was.

"Stay with your mother," I told Christopher and Cindy. "I'll be back in a little while."

"Dad, can I come?" asked Christopher.

I hesitated. Christopher was almost a man now. I nodded. "Okay, come on, but stay close." We both rushed toward the cemetery. When we arrived there was a large crowd already gathered. I made my way through the crowd to see what everyone was staring at. Taylor was hanging spread-eagle on the fence with the words "A GIFT" carved into his chest. The body of the community's sentry had been laid nearby. Samuel was examining both bodies. He slowly turned to face the crowd.

"Does anyone know anything about what happened here?" asked Samuel, and then, looking from face to face, waited patiently for anyone to speak up.

The crowd remained silent, a few looking around for some kind of response, and a few weakly shaking their heads.

"They were both killed with a knife," stated Samuel.

He looked in my direction. I had an idea of what he was thinking.

After a few additional moments of silence, Samuel concluded no one was going to speak up.

"Could a couple of you men help me get him off the fence?" asked Samuel. "He shouldn't be left up there as a public exhibit. And Mark's body needs to go to the stables."

Ryder and Darby, standing nearby, stepped forward and began to untangle Taylor from the fence and ease him onto the ground.

"Mark!" yelled a woman from the back of the crowd. Everyone turned to look, stepping back to clear a path for her. "Mark!" she repeated in panic.

"Someone, stop her!" shouted Samuel.

But it was too late. She stopped and glanced at the man being removed from the fence, then saw her husband, stumbling and falling onto his body, crying uncontrollably.

PARADISE

"Could some of you help Mrs. Newman home?" suggested Samuel.

A couple women came forward, trying to console her and to lift her to her feet, but she fought to stay with her husband. Only with help, she was helped home.

"Go on home, folks. We'll let you know when we figure out what happened here. Right now, I'm going to guess Mr. Grey killed Mark Newman while he was on guard duty last night and then someone killed Mr. Grey in retaliation."

Paradise didn't have a town marshal and they'd never needed one. If anyone had a dispute, they came to Samuel who acted as mediator. Crime of any kind had never been an issue. Without an official title, he was their marshal, counselor, and on Sundays, their preacher.

The crowd slowly began to disperse after taking one last look at Taylor's remains. Mark's body had already been removed to the stable where it could be prepared for burial.

"John," asked Samuel, "could you stick around for a bit?"

I nodded and turned to my son. "Christopher, go on back and check on your mom. I'll be along soon."

"It was like he was two different people," commented Christopher, staring at the body for a few more moments before turning and slowly walking away.

"What do you want us to do with him?" asked Ryder.

"We'll bury him here with Mark and everyone else," replied Samuel.

"He doesn't belong in the cemetery with the good people of Paradise!" yelled Ryder.

"Everyone deserves a decent burial, Son."

"He doesn't and I won't help dig his grave!" shouted Ryder as he stormed off. Darby shrugged his shoulders to Samuel and followed after his friend.

"Would you give me a hand, John?" asked Samuel. "Let's move him to the back of the cemetery."

They carried him through the gate and set him along the back fence where Samuel took off his jacket and laid it across Taylor's face and chest.

Now alone, Samuel stepped up to me, looking into my eyes, "Did you do this?"

I was taken aback. "Of course not. Why would you think such a thing?"

"You *are* one of the few people who wanted to see him dead."

"I think there were more people than you think," I countered.

"Well, anyway, I know you felt responsible for bringing him here. And the only other person who immediately comes to mind is the Widow Wilkins, since Taylor was responsible for her husband's death. But since she's eighty years old and not physically able, I don't think she's a very likely candidate. So, that leaves you at the top of the list."

"I'm not sorry he's gone, but I give you my word I didn't have anything to do with it. Maybe whoever was responsible is afraid to come forward, even though he did us all a favor."

"There just aren't many men here who are capable of doing something like this," said Samuel.

"Except for me, you mean." I thought about Ryder and

PARADISE

Darby. They were just as capable, probably more so from what I had witnessed, but I wasn't going to mention them. "I'm not sure it's much of an issue anyway. He killed Mark while he was on duty, not a threat to anyone, and in return someone killed Taylor. I, for one, am relieved we don't have to worry about him anymore."

"If you didn't do it," continued Samuel, "then there's still a killer among us, whether they were justified or not. I have to think about the community. Do you think there's still a reason for these people to be afraid? I can't reassure them until we know for certain who did it and why."

I didn't have an answer for him. I only knew that I was innocent, but someone had done the community a favor by giving them "A GIFT" and I for one was grateful. I had spent many sleepless nights remembering the things Taylor had done and stressing over what he might do next.

Sarah was no longer crying when I returned to our cabin. She was busy at the stove preparing a breakfast for us. Our family sat together at the table, blessed the food, prayed for Mark's wife, and ate together in silence. Taylor's name was never mentioned.

That evening, at dusk, the entire community gathered for the gravesite services. Mark Newman's service was first. Samuel said some wonderful words over the young man followed by two songs. Mark's newlywed wife, seated near the gravesite, was inconsolable. After the service, the young widow was escorted away. The members of my family were the only ones who remained behind with Samuel for Taylor's service, receiving disapproving stares from the others as they wandered away. I was only there at Sarah's request. Ryder and Darby leaned against a tree in the distance, watching. As Samuel began to speak, Sarah began to cry once again. The words he said over Taylor were brief and I was thankful.

Afterwards, Samuel, Sarah and the children headed to the Town Hall where the community had already gathered for a potluck dinner. I stayed behind, motioning for Ryder to join me. He came over accompanied by Darby.

"Did you do it?" whispered Ryder. "It's okay if you did. I would have done it myself if given the chance."

"No, I didn't," I said. "And that's the same thing your dad asked. So, are you saying *you* didn't do it?"

"Sorry to say, but no, I didn't do it either."

I looked at Darby, Ryder's constant companion.

"Don't look at me."

"Well, someone did," I said, speaking the obvious. "Have any ideas who could have?"

"None. But someone brought a horse into the stable today. It could have been his. It had the Guard's markings on it. Levi said it was found roaming free above the rim."

"A Guard's horse? It probably *was* Taylor's then. Maybe we should take a look around up there. Does Levi know exactly where it was found?" I asked.

"If he doesn't, I'm sure he can find out," answered Ryder.

"It's too dark to do anything now. Let's meet at the stable at first light," I suggested.

"What are we going to be looking for?" asked Darby.

"I'm not sure. Just a hunch. If you were Taylor, would you have come back here alone?"

* * *

PARADISE

Levi led me, Ryder, and Darby to where the horse had been found grazing.

"Ryder, why don't you come with me," I said. "We'll go west along the rim from here. And Darby, you and Levi check it out to the east. Keep your eyes open for anything suggesting Taylor wasn't alone. If you find something, signal us with a single shot into the air and we'll do likewise."

Darby looked at Ryder. It didn't occur to me until then he probably didn't like the idea of me telling him what to do. Ryder nodded and Darby and Levi rode off.

Ryder and I rode side by side watching the ground for hoof prints.

"I'm not seeing anything," said Ryder.

"This may not be the way he came to the valley. Maybe Darby and Levi will have better luck."

"Stop! Look here!" Ryder said excitedly, as he dismounted.

"Did you find hoof prints?" I asked.

"I found something better. Footprints."

I dismounted and joined him to get a closer look.

"You're right. No mistake about it," I agreed. "And there are two sets headed toward the rim." I began to look around further. "Here's another set! From one person, leading away from the valley." I looked in the direction they led and saw nothing but scrub brush and sand.

"This is what we were looking for, wasn't it?" asked Ryder.

"Exactly what we were looking for. There were two people."

Ryder pulled his pistol. "Want me to signal the

others?"

"Sure, go ahead," I answered.

Ryder pulled his gun and fired a single shot into the air. He had fallen into the position of leader of the Raiders partly just by chance, being in the right place at the right time. The men liked him and gladly followed him. Another reason was he had grown up in the area and knew it well, occasionally accompanying his dad when looking for supplies, and frequently sneaking off as a boy to explore the surrounding area. He was a natural leader, and smart, and it came easily to him.

It was comforting to know Ryder was willing to let me take the lead on this without any hesitation. Perhaps it was our age difference, me as a middle-aged elder, or because I seemed to have some of the same values his father did.

At about one hundred yards from the rim the vegetation became dense, making it harder to follow the meandering footprints through the tall grasses and heavy brush.

We saw Darby and Levi approaching. Ryder explained what we'd found.

"You know, John, we don't know whether either set of these footprints belonged to Taylor," mentioned Ryder. "It could have just been someone from the valley."

"I know, but who else would have a reason to be up here, and on foot. If I'm right, these footprints should lead back to where they tied up their horses. Levi, could you check it out?" I asked.

He smiled at being given the responsibility. Still young, he liked being given the opportunity to prove himself.

PARADISE

"I'll go with him," offered Darby.

Levi's smile faded away. "I don't need any help!" snapped Levi.

"I'd feel better if we stayed paired up," I suggested. "There could still be a killer on the loose. Okay?"

Levi thought about it as he looked around. Knowing I was right, he nodded agreement. He and Darby led their horses back to the north, away from Paradise and the rim. Ryder and I followed the footprints back toward the rim's edge.

"Look here," said Ryder. He pointed to the trunk of a mesquite tree. "See where the bark has been worn away recently? I'll bet this is where they tied a rope so they could get down." At the rim, the area had been trampled by activity. I looked over the edge. It was a vertical drop of twenty-five to thirty feet to the valley floor. I could see where the sandstone cliff face had been scuffed up as someone rappelled down.

"This is definitely where someone went down," I said. "If you'll bring a rope, I'll go down and take a look around."

Ryder quickly returned with the rope and tied it to the same tree the intruders had used and threw the coil of rope over the edge.

I grabbed the rope and turned my back toward the valley, pulling the rope taut and setting both feet on the edge of the rim. Then, with one small step at a time, I lowered myself down the cliff face.

Ryder watched from above to know when I'd reached bottom.

"See anything?" shouted Ryder.

I didn't answer right away, looking closely around the immediate area. "It would be easy to stay concealed from the town down here." I paused while continuing to search the area. "I see drag marks. It looks like a person was drug away from the cliff." Then I noticed my boots were coated in sand. I scraped away the top layer of sand with my hand. Underneath, my boot was covered with blood. Someone had kicked clean sand over the blood-stained earth in an attempt to hide it.

"I think we just found where Taylor was killed," I announced, looking up at Ryder.

"Do you want me to come down?" asked Ryder.

"No. I'm going to follow these drag marks. I think we both know where they'll lead. I'd appreciate it if you'd take my horse and meet me at the cemetery. Would you have Darby and Levi join us?"

"See you there," agreed Ryder as the rope was pulled up and out of sight.

The trail of drag marks was easy to follow, even though someone had haphazardly tried to brush over them in the dark, probably in a hurry. As I suspected, they led to the cemetery. In a matter of minutes, Ryder, Levi and Darby rode up.

"It was just like you thought," said Levi excitedly. "We found where two horses had been tied up. One of the riders appears to have ridden back north."

"You were right about the drag marks too," said Ryder.

"Just a gut feeling," I said. Praise from Ryder was appreciated, but not necessary. I knew if he had been the one to rappel down, he would have uncovered the same

PARADISE

evidence as I had. "That suggests Taylor was not alone and that his killer's no longer here, apparently having gone back to Sector 4. I think that'll relieve a lot of people's minds. Samuel needs to be told."

"Have any idea who it could have been?" asked Ryder.

"None, whatsoever, and we may never know," I answered. "But whoever it was, they now know the way to Paradise. That means we're still in danger and there's a good chance they'll be back and with more men this time. We won't be able to let our guard down for a second."

"I'll spread the word to the rest of the Raiders and mention it to dad," said Ryder.

"I know why *you* want to keep this place safe," I said, "but why would the rest of your men care or want to put their lives on the line for this valley?"

"Because, this is one of the few places where good still exists in this world. We have to protect it at all cost. Without a place like this, there's no hope of things ever going back to some form of normalcy."

"For a no-good Raider, you're very philosophical," I observed with a smile.

* * *

Ryder, Levi, Darby and I went directly to Samuel's house. It was late morning now and Samuel was once again on his front porch, rocking gently. He smiled on seeing our group approaching. I noticed he was no longer wearing the sling on his arm.

"It looks like you boys have something on your mind," commented Samuel.

As the self-appointed spokesman, I got right to the point, "We don't think Taylor was killed by anyone from the valley. We think it was someone from Sector 4. Someone who came here with Taylor."

"And that someone placed Taylor on the fence to make it look like one of us did it," added Ryder.

"We saw where two individuals entered the valley by rope from the rim and we found where Taylor was killed. Whoever did it tried to cover their tracks unsuccessfully and then rode back north on horseback," I continued.

They waited for a response while Samuel sat silently, considering all he had just been told. "Then, we don't have to worry about one of our own being a killer. I was having a hard time believing any of them could have done anything like that. Everyone will be glad to hear things can return to normal."

"No, I'm sorry to say, we won't see normal for a while," I insisted. "Now, whoever was with Taylor knows where the valley is and that person is a killer. And I wouldn't be at all surprised if he had been sent by Governor Davis. They're bound to be back, and with others."

Samuel's warm smile never waivered, always the optimist. "God will take care of us."

Even though I admired Samuel, there were times when he infuriated me. Ryder could see how his father's comments and attitude were affecting me. Understanding completely, he leaned close and whispered, "This is one of the reasons why I left."

I wasn't ready to give up. "Doesn't the bible say 'God helps those who help themselves'?

PARADISE

Samuel's expression never changed. "Actually, no, it doesn't. That quote comes from one of Aesop's Fables when Hercules was asked for help and he replied 'The gods help those who help themselves."

I have to say I was impressed. Samuel was a surprising fellow. "Would you at least agree to increase the number of guards on watch? Every person here is still in danger."

Samuel could see I wasn't going to let this go. He didn't believe it was necessary, but it wouldn't hurt anything either, and since Taylor's death was still fresh in everyone's minds, it might provide better peace of mind for the community. "Okay, I'll see to it."

* * *

Chapter 17

Donna was caught completely by surprise when her husband asked if she'd ever thought about leaving their home of the last five years.

"Why would we leave," she asked. "It may not be ideal, but we have everything we need right here. You know how hard it would be to survive out there on our own."

"I know. But are you really happy here?"

"Why are you asking? Is there something wrong?"

"What if I knew of a safe place, a valley, that had grass, trees and flowers, with plenty of food and water, and freedom?"

She looked at him with concern. She'd never heard him talk like this before. "The valley?"

He looked at her with surprise.

"Secrets are hard to keep around here," she said. "But,

PARADISE

it can't be real. I don't think places like that exist anymore. And you know as well as anyone we're better off in here than anywhere on the outside, that's why we're here."

He took hold of her by both shoulders and looked directly into her eyes. "There is a place," insisted Gant with a whisper.

She was beginning to worry. Maybe he had been working too hard. She knew how serious he took his position as Master of the Guard. Was the stress finally getting to him? Something had brought this on and she wanted to know what it was. "Are *you* wanting to leave?" she asked.

"I don't know. I just wanted to know what you thought about it." He paused. "Donna, I'm not crazy. There is a place, the valley, where there are other people living normal lives. Good people."

"How do you know this?"

"I talked to a man who lives there. An old friend from before."

"Did you see the valley when you were out there?" she asked.

"No, but I know it exists. I trust him."

She looked into his eyes. They had been married for twenty years and she knew him well. His eyes told her he was being sincere. He was telling the truth or at least he believed he was. "Where is this place?" she asked.

"South, deep within the wasteland," he answered as he sat in a chair along the wall and sighed heavily. It was a relief to get the load off his chest. He had been hesitant to mention anything about it at all, but after the fact, he was glad he had.

She moved over and sat next to him. "I don't know what brought this on, but if it's something you want to do, then we should do it."

"I don't want to do it for me. I want it for all of us, a chance to get away from this place and be normal again. Before you know it, we'll both be forty and be forced to leave our boys alone to fend for themselves. But if we leave together, all of us, maybe we'll be able to see our grandchildren someday."

"Don't you think Governor Davis would make an exception in your case? You've done everything he's asked of you and you've been a great leader of the Guard. We know he's done it before."

"We can't count on it and there's something else. Governor Davis has sent Counselor Damon to personally verify the valleys existence. And if he comes back with confirmation, I'll be ordered to lead an attack against my friend and his people, just so the governor can have it for his own use."

"It sounds like you've already made up your mind," said Donna.

"Just tell me you're happy here and I'll drop it," offered Gant.

"Governor Davis won't like it," she warned.

"I know," replied Gant.

She sighed. "When would we leave?" she asked.

"Soon. Within the week."

"That's awfully quick. What about our sons? What if they don't want to leave?" she asked.

"I'll talk to them, but I can't imagine why they'd want to stay."

PARADISE

He could tell he hadn't convinced her entirely by the continued look of concern on her face. He leaned over and gave her a kiss. "Don't worry. It's the right thing to do."

* * *

Gant knew he didn't have much time to make plans. If successful, Damon and Taylor would return with confirmation of the valley, just as Taylor had reported. Then he would be summoned again by the governor, and he knew what he would be ordered to do. Knowing Davis as he did, he'd be ordered to leave immediately. At the moment, the question was when would they return. He guessed four days, maybe a week at the most. They needed to leave before that happened. There was no time to waste.

As Master of the Guard, he was given free reign anywhere inside or outside the compound walls. That freedom would be essential in getting his entire family out, but it still wouldn't be easy.

He found the head of maintenance, his sons' boss, and asked where he could find them. Gant could have waited until the boys came home at the end of the day, but he was anxious to know how they felt about leaving, a necessary element in his planning. As directed, Gant found them in the woodshop. They smiled when they saw their dad standing in the doorway. They hadn't heard he was back from the wasteland.

Even though he hadn't told his wife where he had been sent or why, somehow word had gotten out, and she knew. Almost everyone inside the compound had heard about the valley and they were all anxious to hear about it. What they didn't know was that his friend and an entire community already lived there and it would probably have to be taken by force. Regardless of whether Samuel and his people put up a fight or not, an attack would result in the loss of many lives.

There were two other workers in the shop. Gant waved for Aaron and Adam to follow him outside where they could have some privacy.

"Hey, Dad, it's great to see you made it back alright," said Adam.

"Yeah, Dad. Did you find the valley?" asked Aaron.

"You know about the … ?" Gant began.

They saw the surprise on his face. "It's okay, everyone in here knows," said Aaron.

"I've got to tell you boys something and I'm not sure how you're going to take it. So, I'm just going to come right out with it." He paused, looked around, and then in a softer voice, "Your mother and I have been talking about leaving this place." He waited for a response.

The boys looked at each other and smiled.

"Great, Dad," said Aaron with Adam nodding agreement. "When do we leave?"

It was Gant's turn to smile. "I was hoping you'd feel that way, but I didn't want to make any assumptions. You're both fifteen and almost grown men, capable of making your own decision." They had been forced to grow up fast inside the compound walls with little to no chance of just being boys, not being able to do the things boys should have been able to do.

"If you and Mom go, we're going too," said Adam. "We wouldn't want to stay here without you."

PARADISE

"What about your friends?" their dad asked.

"What friends?" answered Adam.

"I'm ready to go right now," said Aaron excitedly.

"Slow down. First, I have to figure out a way to leave and give us a decent lead without drawing attention to ourselves."

The boys exchanged a look. Aaron, the oldest by a few minutes, spoke up. "We know a way. There's a passageway leading from the lower level of the compound to a concealed hatch outside the fence. Both ends of the passage are hidden and locked. And guess who has access to the key."

"Are any of the doors guarded?" asked their dad.

"No," answered Adam. "There's no reason to. Hardly anyone goes down there. The main room is just used to stockpile supplies. We're usually the only ones sent down there to either bring items out or to place more items in storage. No one else likes to go down there. They think it's kind of creepy and it smells funny. We shouldn't run into anyone."

"Let's talk more about it later tonight. I just wanted to let you boys know what we were thinking about and see how you felt about it. Now, go on back to work and don't mention this to anyone."

The boys rolled their eyes. "We know, Dad," they said in unison.

Gant couldn't have been happier after talking with his twin sons. He began to think of things he hadn't thought of in years, five years to be exact. Days when he had taken his sons fishing or hunting. They had been ten when they'd come there, old enough to immediately be put into training and to perform light-duty work.

When they had initially arrived, they had been placed in Tent City with everyone else. But, it didn't take long for Gant, an imposing presence, to be noticed. His credentials as a former sheriff had made him a shoe-in. Once he had been made Master of the Guard, life had been made easier on all of them. His family had been moved inside the prison walls into two adjacent cells and Donna no longer had to work in the fields. It was cramped, but it had been worth it to have a permanent roof over their heads, real walls, and to be given regular meals. It was a drastic improvement from what the remaining poor souls of Tent City had to endure.

Gant began to think about how blessed he and his family were. Was he being ungrateful for considering leaving? Perhaps he shouldn't have even mentioned it to his wife and sons, risking what they had and possibly even their lives. Once they left, there would be no coming back without some sort of retribution. Gant wasn't worried about himself. If his intuition was right, he'd be forced to leave within the next year anyway, when he turned forty.

* * *

That evening after they had eaten in the dining hall, Aaron and Adam joined their mom and dad in their living quarters. With hushed voices, they began to make plans. However, there was too much noise and too little privacy in the tight conditions of the cell. Eavesdropping was a concern. It had been rumored that Davis had eyes and ears everywhere. Not wanting their plans to be halted before

PARADISE

they had a chance, they decided to venture outside into the central courtyard where they found a vacant picnic table in the corner with no one around. Before the facility had been abandoned for a newer and upgraded facility, the yard's original purpose had been as the exercise yard for the prisoners.

Gant started by warning his sons. "There are no guarantees our attempting to leave will work out. We could be caught and punished. And if we are able to get away, there is plenty of danger outside these walls. You boys will soon be on your own, so you need to think about yourselves."

"Are we going to the valley?" asked Adam.

"That is our hope," answered their father.

"As long as we can stay together," said Adam, "I believe it's worth the risk".

"You're stuck with us, Dad," Aaron pointed out.

Daniel and Donna smiled, Donna holding onto her husband's arm and squeezing.

"I think the best time to leave is around two hours after curfew. I'll make my usual rounds to make sure the guards are at their posts, then go back to our room and wait for the others around us to settle in and go to sleep. Leaving then should give us the widest window of opportunity before discovery. You boys said you had access to the key for the doors?"

"Yes. It hangs on a nail in the maintenance shop," answered Aaron.

"Can you make a copy? Once we've left and they discover our absence, we don't want to give away our avenue of escape by a missing key."

"We can do it," said Adam, with a nod of agreement from Aaron. "How long do we have?"

"I don't know yet. It could be anywhere from four to seven days. I'd say to do it as soon as the opportunity arises." He paused. "And start choosing what you want to take. Keep it simple and light. We want to be able to move quickly when we do go. Any questions?"

Aaron and Adam shook their heads.

"Then, why don't you boys go back to your room. Try to get some sleep and we'll see you at breakfast," instructed Gant. "Maybe by tomorrow I'll know more. I'm going to sit here with your mother for a bit longer."

Their sons got up and each gave their mother a kiss before heading back inside.

"Have you had a change of heart?" he asked, seeing the concern on Donna's face. "It's not too late to change our minds."

"No, we're ready. I just hope nothing goes wrong. I'd hate for our boys to have to pay for our mistake."

"Don't worry. I won't let anything happen to them," said Daniel, in an attempt to comfort her. He would do everything in his power to make sure they stayed safe, but at the same time he knew he had made an empty promise. One he had no way of controlling."

*   *   *

The next morning, Gant was once again summoned to the governor's office. Damon couldn't be back already, it was too soon. Knocking on the open door, he was warmly welcomed by Davis as was the usual case.

PARADISE

"Please have a seat, Daniel."

Gant couldn't recall the governor ever calling him by his first name, which immediately raised a red flag. He took a seat facing the governor's desk and waited. He'd seen the governor more in the last two days than he had in the previous month. There couldn't be any way for Davis to know about his family's plans.

"It has come to my attention, Daniel, you are approaching the age of forty. And as you know, we have established a well thought out plan to sustain our survival."

Gant sat in silence with no change of expression.

"And as you also know, exceptions have been made in the past."

Continuing to show no emotion outwardly, Gant was giving his full attention.

"I'd like to offer you a deal of sorts. A reward is probably a better word." He paused. "Assuming Damon comes back with favorable news about the valley, I'd like you to take it for me. And if you're successful, which I'm sure you will be, I'm prepared to offer you an incentive, to extend your service time to the age of forty-five." Governor Davis showed a huge, toothy smile, sure Gant would be overwhelmed with his very generous offer.

Surprising to Davis, Gant remained seated and unmoved. Davis' smile faded and then quickly returned as he extended his hand over the desk. "Do we have a deal?"

Gant didn't reach for the governor's hand, a blatant and obvious act of rejection. Davis lowered his hand. "It's a very generous offer, Governor, but if I'm ordered to take the valley, no incentive is necessary."

Davis was baffled and becoming angry, his face

beginning to turn red. "Then you're refusing my offer?"

"It's not my intention to upset you, Governor. I just want to assure you that as long as I am here, you can count on me to do my duty."

"I appreciate your candor and your loyalty, Master Gant," said Davis, baffled and upset at Gant's unenthusiastic reaction to his well intentioned offer. "I'll let you know when Damon returns and what he found." Davis pretended to go back to paperwork on his desk, which Gant took to be his dismissal. The office had taken on a chilly quality, a distinct contrast to when he had first entered.

* * *

Each day, Gant anticipated Damon's return. And he could see the stress affecting each member of his family. If they waited until he returned to make their escape, it would most likely be too late. Having never seen it personally, Gant was convinced the valley existed and knew that once Damon returned he would be ordered to take it for the governor. So, they had to leave before Damon got back, but not before they were ready.

Unfortunately, things weren't going as planned. Adam and Aaron had been reassigned to work in another area of the compound and hadn't had the opportunity to copy the all-important key. Without access to the underground passageways, he began to contemplate option B. He had free reign outside the walls, but for his family to accompany him the reasoning would have to be plausible and not out of the ordinary. He concluded the most

PARADISE

reasonable way would be to have the appearance of a family outing. Sunday was two days away. It was the one day of the week when most of the Guard were given free time. It would be the perfect time to take such a ride. He told Donna and his sons of the new plan. They wouldn't be able to take much with them, only the bare essentials. But at the same time, they needed to bring enough food and water, inconspicuously, for a long journey. He asked his family to start saving things like bread from their meals. They'd have to conceal it in their clothing.

Saturday evening, after the evening meal in the dining hall, the family joined together at the familiar picnic table in the central courtyard. Gant had noticed a change in the attitudes of his family over the last few day, an excitement and anticipation in their voices. It reminded him of a time years ago when getting ready for a vacation. But now, a serious question needed to be asked one last time.

"Since tomorrow is the day we've been waiting for, I need to know if any of you has changed your mind about leaving and I need you to be completely honest. I won't ask again. I promise."

Each of them exchanged looks. Donna spoke up, "We're all ready to go, Daniel." Gant received a nod of agreement from both boys who for once seemed to be taking the decision seriously.

"Okay then, we'll leave tomorrow morning as planned. We'll meet for breakfast at 8:00 like we always do, then casually make our way to a buggy I'll have waiting near the gate." Seeing concern in their faces, Gant attempted to reassure them again, "It's going to be alright. We've taken these kinds of outings before. There's no reason for anyone to be suspicious." He saw Adam and Aaron force a weak, but unconvincing smile. "After breakfast you'll have time to go to your living quarters and gather up your food and water. Hide it as best as you can and we'll meet you at the gate. Now, try to get a good night's rest. You're going to need it."

* * *

In the dining hall they all sat together at one of the long community tables. There was chatter all around from the other diners, but the Gant's were silent. Gant noticed Adam and Aaron were just picking at their food.

"Better eat up, boys," said their dad. He could have explained why, but he didn't trust prying ears around them.

"I don't feel so good," explained Adam.

"Me either," said Aaron.

"You'll be alright. It's just nerves," said Gant.

One of the other diners turned around to see who was talking. Gant wasn't surprised. Another case of prying ears. "Turn around and mind your own business!" he voiced loudly for all the surrounding diners to hear. Several, including the nosy one, got up with their trays and moved to other seats. Gant's identity, out of uniform and on his day off, was unmistakable and an imposing figure anyway.

"Donna, you feeling okay?" he asked.

She nodded her head as she stood and grabbed her tray. "Let's do this," she announced matter-of-factly with determination.

* * *

PARADISE

The buggy was waiting at the gate as Gant had instructed. As was the case on every Sunday, he allowed skeleton crews to rotate on and off duty, giving his men more time with their families. He had already informed the guard at the gate of his intention for the day, just in case someone, like the governor, asked. Gant was proud of his family, behaving just as though it was any other outing.

A mile from the compound Adam let out a "Yeah!" His brother echoed the sentiment.

"Feeling better?" asked their dad, both he and Donna smiling at the reaction. "You might want to hold onto your excitement for a little longer, at least until we're out of sight. We're not out of danger just yet."

It was good to get away from the confines of the compound, but Donna always felt sad too when she saw the destroyed remains of homes and abandoned cars on both sides of the trail, only a reminder of what once had been. Sadly, some of the cars showed evidence of once being lived in.

Five miles from the Sector 4 compound Gant stopped the buggy in the middle of the trail and turned to face his sons and wife.

"I said I'd never ask again, but I'm going to mention it." He paused. "We still have time to go back. As far as anyone back there knows, we are just on another Sunday outing. We can turn around and go back and no one will be the wiser. Any second thoughts?"

"How many more times are you going to ask us, Dad?" asked Aaron.

"Yeah, Dad, we said we wanted to go, so, let's go," said Adam, exasperated.

MICHAEL R. WATSON

Donna smiled and pointed down the trail. Gant flicked the reins and they continued on their journey to Paradise.

*   *   *

Chapter 18

It was just past midday when Gant pulled back hard on the reins, bringing the buggy to an abrupt stop.

"What's wrong?" asked Donna.

Gant kept his eyes on the trail ahead. "I'm not sure. There appears to be a rider coming this way." He squinted, straining his eyes to see through the heat waves.

"I see him, too," announced Adam.

Gant flicked the reins and they began to move forward again, now at a somewhat slower pace than before. The rider was getting closer.

He cursed under his breath. "I was afraid this might happen," said Gant.

"What?" asked Donna.

"I think it's Damon, on his way back to make his report. Nothing's changed. We're still just on a Sunday outing. Just act normal. He'll notice if anything seems out of the ordinary."

As the rider came close, Gant stopped the buggy. Damon smiled as he rode up beside them and stopped.

"Lovely day for a ride," commented Damon. "Hope you're enjoying your Sunday. This *is* Sunday, isn't it? I've lost track of time." He looked directly at Donna. "Good to see you ma'am." Then looking at their sons. "And your boys have really grown." He and Gant had been under the governor's direction since the beginning, but they'd never been close, and they'd never be friends. Suspicious by nature, he kept it cordial, all the time wondering why Gant and his family were so far out.

"It *is* a nice day. How was your trip?" asked Gant, already knowing the answer.

"Very good," answered Damon. "You'll be happy to know everything Taylor said was true. You'll probably be sent back there very soon."

It was then that Gant realized Taylor wasn't with him.

"I'm glad to hear it. By the way, where is Taylor?"

"I'm afraid he had an unfortunate accident and didn't make it."

Gant suspected what had happened and wasn't surprised. Taylor had served his purpose and hadn't been needed any more. Taylor had been a thorn in Gant's side, but he hadn't necessarily wanted him dead, just for him to go away. "Sorry to hear that."

"You're kind of a long way out aren't you?" asked Damon.

"Not really. We'll probably be turning back soon though," replied Gant.

"Maybe we could ride back together?" proposed

PARADISE

Damon.

"Thanks, but I think we'll go a little further before we turn back. We still have the rest of the day and like you said, "It's a lovely day for a ride."

Damon looked over each one individually and suspiciously. He smiled slyly. "Well, then I guess I'll see you back there later."

"Sounds good," said Gant, as he flicked the horse into motion.

Damon sat stationary in the saddle as he watched them ride away.

"Do you think he suspected anything?" asked Donna when they were out of earshot.

"I don't know," answered Daniel. "Maybe we should pick up the pace just a little."

*   *   *

Damon arrived at the front gate around suppertime. Tired and sore from all the time in the saddle, he opted to go to his living quarters first, before reporting to the governor. He knew how anxious Davis was to hear from him, but he needed to clean up first and relax just a moment. He washed away the dust and grime from his face and neck. The cool water on the back of his neck felt so good. He stared into the polished metal mirror, pleased at what he saw. His eyes closed momentarily as he braced himself against the basin.

There were three loud knocks on his door. "Counselor! Are you in there?" Someone yelled from the hallway.

Damon snapped awake, evidently having nodded off

on his feet. It took only an instant for him to gather his senses.

"Yes. What do you want?"

"The governor would like to see you!" the person shouted.

Irritated by the interruption, Damon walked to the door and flung it open. A young guard was standing nervously in front of him.

"I'm sorry, sir," he apologized. "The governor received word you were back."

Damon could see the young man was in distress. "I'll be right there."

"Yes, sir." Then he saluted, even though it wasn't necessary, and waited.

Damon could tell there was something else on his mind. "Yes, what is it?"

"May I accompany you, sir?"

Damon couldn't resist a hint of a smile. The young man was obviously following orders. "Sure. Wait out here." He changed into clothes more appropriate to his position, approving once again of his slightly distorted image in the mirror. He took a deep breath and walked out the door. "Let's go," he said to the young guard.

The governor was pacing in his office when Damon arrived.

"I've got it from here," Damon told the guard, who nodded and then turned and left.

Damon knocked and waited for permission to enter. He had worked under the governor since the beginning, but such acts of decorum were still expected. Davis stopped pacing when he saw it was his long-time counselor.

PARADISE

"Come in, come in," said Davis impatiently. "Where have you been? I heard you came through the gate an hour ago."

"I wanted to make myself presentable, sir."

"You know I've been waiting for your report."

"I'm sorry, Governor. I should have come directly to you. Would you like to hear my report now?"

The governor glared at him. "Of course I want to hear it!" yelled Davis. "What did you find? Was Taylor telling the truth?"

"It was everything he claimed it was with trees, crop fields, garden plots, a small lake, livestock, and people."

The governor's eyes gleamed, looking over Damon's head as though he was picturing it in his mind. A broad smile spread across his face. After several moments had passed he realized Damon was staring at him.

"Was it heavily fortified? Were you discovered?" asked Davis.

"There was only one sentry and he never saw us."

"Then Taylor was telling the truth about that, too. Where *is* Taylor?"

"I'm afraid he won't be coming back." He made no attempt to explain.

Davis detected a smirk on Damon's face, dropping the subject. Taylor had already served his purpose.

"As far as I can tell, Governor, our only resistance will be from the Raiders, if they should interfere again."

"This time it'll be different," said Davis. "This time we'll be expecting them. Would you ask Master Gant to join us?"

"I don't believe he's here right now. I met him and his

family on the trail today on my way back."

The governor's face showed concern. "Where were they going?"

"Just out for a Sunday ride is what they said," Damon said, implying it may not have been the truth.

"Don't you believe them?" asked the governor.

"I don't guess I have any reason not to."

Davis looked at Damon with a puzzled expression, but decided not to pursue it. He trusted Master Gant.

"Well, let me know when he gets back. I'd like to talk to both of you. We have plans to make."

"Yes, sir."

The governor, initially upset at Damon for not coming to him immediately, became cordial once again. He had received the good news he had been hoping for. All was forgiven. Things were about to change in a major way.

"Have you eaten yet?" he asked.

"Not yet, sir."

"Tell the kitchen I said to prepare you a nice thick, juicy steak. You deserve it for doing such a fine job."

"Thank you, sir. And I'll bring Gant with me as soon as he returns." Inside, Damon was fuming from being rewarded like an obedient dog by the condescending oaf. He didn't need his permission to have anything he wanted from the kitchen.

*   *   *

Damon had sent word to the guard at the front gate to notify him immediately on Master Gant's return. The sun had set some two hours earlier and there still hadn't been any sign of Gant or his family. He expected to be summoned by a displeased governor at any moment, sure the governor was growing impatient.

Damon went to Gant's living quarters, calling past the privacy curtain, and after receiving no reply, went in. No one was there and nothing looked out of the ordinary, nothing to indicate anything suspicious. He went to the front gate where a different guard from earlier stood watch. The guard had been made aware of the order left with the previous guard. Gant and his family had not returned. Damon cursed. It was time to report Gant's absence to Governor Davis before being summoned. He hoped Davis would appreciate the gesture.

The governor was at his desk, as he almost always was, when Damon entered his doorway. Davis immediately jumped up and shot around his desk. "It's about time you two showed up!" Then as Damon entered his office, Davis noticed that he was alone. "Where's Master Gant?"

"He hasn't returned yet."

The governor's jaw dropped as he pulled out his father's wind-up pocket watch and checked the time. Master Gant played a major role in Davis' plans, from keeping order to motivating the workers to handing out the governor's justice. And now, more than ever, his abilities were necessary to claim the valley. Without Gant, his entire scheme and future plans were in jeopardy.

"Something must have gone wrong. Send the Guard to search for him. They could have broken down or been attacked by Raiders. Gant should have known better."

"It's dark, sir. It'll be almost impossible to see anything until morning."

"They could be in trouble. So, do as I said and send a squad of the Guard to search for them now. Understand?"

"Yes, sir."

As Damon left, Governor Davis plopped back down into his large leather over-stuffed chair, tired and dejected. He opened the lower right-hand drawer of his desk and removed a never-opened bottle of scotch. He'd been saving the rare treat for a very different occasion, one of celebration, but at this moment it seemed appropriate.

* * *

Gant drove the buggy through the night. He was amused and amazed at how easily his boys had been able to sleep sitting up in the back as they bounced along the rough trail. Donna had stayed awake and alert, watching for anything out of the ordinary while keeping her husband company. They stopped briefly a couple of times to water the horse and let it rest. He had found a couple of windmills not far off the trail by following the sound of ungreased squeaky bearings. Only one was pumping water, the other one was either dry or something was wrong inside the well. Perhaps another victim of the earthquakes. Animal tracks surrounded the working well. It appeared there were still some cattle around, along with deer and an assortment of smaller animals. It was an oasis worth remembering in the wasteland.

Most landowners were long gone, leaving when their homes had been destroyed by the quakes. A few, however, had stuck it out, living in one-room shacks or tents, trying to survive by living off the land. Without gasoline or

PARADISE

diesel, their tractors were no more than eerie metal sculptures in the over-grown fields. However, some had planted small gardens near some of the windmills. These survivors were a sturdy bunch, the ones you had to watch out for. They were naturally suspicious of strangers, liked to be left alone, and were very protective of what little they had left. Gant had been cautious when approaching these places. Any owners still around would likely play it safe and shoot first at anyone they considered to be a threat, whether they were or not.

Mid morning of the second day he stopped along the edge of the trail so everyone could stretch their legs. For breakfast they nibbled at what they had brought. There was nothing that needed to be cooked, a fire being a bad idea anyway. A twig snapped and Gant spun around to see what had caused it. He held up his hand for everyone to remain quiet. He didn't see anything and only silence followed. After several seconds he told his family to get back in the buggy. The place was making him feel uneasy.

They all loaded into the buggy and as Gant flicked the reins four horses rushed out from the brush, surrounding them.

"We don't have anything of value," declared Gant.

"We'll see about that," said the front rider facing them. "Get down!"

"We can take them," whispered Adam, leaning forward behind his dad.

"No. Just do what they say," said his dad firmly. He was the first to stand up and step to the ground, offering his hand to Donna to help her down. The boys slowly followed suit.

One of the riders dismounted while the others kept their guns trained on the family. When he got close, he quickly realized how big and imposing a figure Gant was.

"Put your hands up so he can frisk you," ordered the leader, still on horseback.

The family followed Daniel's lead and did as they were told. The man on the ground moved in and patted each of them down, finding only bottles of water and bread rolls. Checking Gant, he became excited when he found a 9 mm pistol in his waistband, grabbing it and backing away quickly. He handed the gun up to the leader who looked it over and then shook his finger back and forth while making a "tsk, tsk" sound with his mouth. He slipped the gun into his own waistband.

"Check to see if there's anything of value in the buggy," instructed the leader.

It didn't take long for the man to see Gant had told the truth. The man shook his head to the leader.

"You have less than we do. You didn't come out here very well prepared." Confused, he asked, "Why are you out here?"

Gant didn't see any reason to hide anything from them, openly answering, "We're looking for someone."

"And who might that be?"

"Samuel Yoder."

The riders exchanged looks. "What do you want with this Samuel Yoder?" asked the leader.

"He's a friend."

The leader smiled. "Oh, really?" Then he paused a moment, considering whether it might be true. "You better come with us."

PARADISE

Until then, Gant had tried to be cooperative for the sake of his family. "Unless you're taking us to Samuel, we're not going anywhere." Gant knew better. He had no means of negotiating or fighting back. He was curious how they would respond, and he found out.

"You don't have a choice." The leader pointed his gun at Gant, which didn't faze him in the least. But then the man swung it until it pointed directly at Donna. "Understand?"

Now, he had to assume how far they would go, or it could have been a bluff, but he wasn't about to gamble with Donna's life.

"Everyone, get back into the buggy," instructed Gant, helpless, with a growing anger and frustration. Alone, he had other options, but now he had only one responsibility and that was to keep his family safe, even if only for this moment. There was no way to know whether the riders knew Samuel or not, but their reaction to his name suggested they did. And if so, were they taking them to him?

The leader and one of the other riders had a brief conversation in hushed voices, then the rider rode off in a gallop. The leader waved for Gant to follow while the other remaining riders followed.

"Dad," whispered Adam as he leaned forward, "what do we do?"

"Nothing for now."

"Daniel, I don't like this," said Donna, her face showing her obvious concern.

He looked at her, trying to smile, "It's going to be alright." He wished he believed it himself.

Gant questioned his decision to bring his family out here into this hostile environment. He knew from experience it could be dangerous. But, in his heart, he knew it was worth the risk. It had all happened so quickly. There hadn't been enough time to properly plan and get ready. It was his fault they were in this predicament. He shook his head to remove the negative thoughts, refusing to second guess himself or think about it one more second. They were here and he had to deal with their current situation.

One chance occurred to him. His sons were only fifteen, but they were big for their age and they'd been trained in self-defense by him. Even though he didn't like the idea of placing his sons in harm's way, the three of them might just be able to overtake their captors, given the right opportunity.

"Boys," whispered their dad, "I may need your help. Can you do it?"

"No!" whispered Donna forcefully.

"There may not be another way," replied Gant.

"It's okay, Mom. We can help," assured Aaron.

"Be ready to step in when I make my move," said Gant. "It won't work if either of you hesitate. So, just watch me." He looked back. "Okay?" They both nodded.

They rode in silence the rest of the day. Their escort was extra cautious, preventing an opportunity of escape. Donna was inwardly grateful.

The leader led them off the main trail onto a less traveled one. Donna looked at her husband with a worried face. He had run out of reassurances. They passed two armed men along the edge of the trail, weapons at the

PARADISE

ready. A few minutes later they entered a clearing containing an encampment. There was a group of men congregated around a campfire. They turned to look, but didn't seem surprised or concerned. A few tents surrounded the campfire, appearing to be a long-term arrangement.

They came to a stop with the leader dismounting and motioning for them to get down.

"Hungry?" he asked.

Gant looked around at his family, surprised by the question. They hadn't eaten since their light breakfast. He nodded.

"There's usually something hot over at the fire. Help yourself," he offered as he walked off, entering one of the tents.

Gant was confused as was his family. At their first encounter, they had been forced at gunpoint to go with them and now they were apparently being given their freedom, in the camp anyway. As they approached the fire, the men stepped away to give them easy access.

Filling tin plates they found near the fire, Adam whispered, "What do you think, Dad? Should we make a run for it?"

"No!" said Gant and Donna in unison. Gant continued, "This isn't the time or place. We don't know how many men are here. So, just eat. We don't know when we'll get another chance."

While eating a bit of what resembled some sort of vegetarian soup, the rider who had ridden ahead entered the camp. Gant watched as he traded words with the camp leader who then came over to them.

"Someone is coming to see you. He should be here sometime tomorrow morning to ask you about Samuel. So, if you'd like to share any information with us, now would be the time."

Gant remained silent.

"Well, then, you'll have free reign, as long as you stay out of trouble. Okay?"

"Sure," replied Gant. "Is Samuel coming?"

"I very much doubt it," said the leader as he turned and walked away.

During the evening, the men in camp left them alone as long as they didn't wander too far away from the buggy and campfire. Gant tested their security once by moving past the light of the campfire with the men springing into action, herding him back where he belonged.

The day had started with Daniel and Donna in high alert mode and had stayed that way after their midday encounter. The stress, along with riding in the buggy all day had made everyone in the family bone tired and it was evident when Gant looked into their faces. A tent wasn't offered, so they laid on the ground while Donna slept on one of the buggy seats. Gant sat on the ground with his back against one of the buggy's wheels. He had no intention of sleeping. Two of their captors, undoubtedly told to keep an eye on them, appeared prepared to stay awake too. During the middle of the night, two others swapped out with them and re-kindled the fire. Otherwise, the night was quiet and peaceful, without incident. Gant still didn't get it. The attitude had changed completely since their first encounter. Initially, they had been kidnapped and now they didn't appear to be in any

PARADISE

immediate danger. It just didn't make any sense, but he refused to let his guard down with a false sense of security.

Just before sunrise, Gant heard the sound of pounding hooves approaching the camp. There was more than one horse. He jumped quickly to his feet. One of the men on guard let out a distinct whistle, which caused a frenzy of activity in the camp. Seconds later the camp leader came out of his tent. He went over and stood next to Gant who towered over the man.

"It's who we were waiting for. This should be interesting. We're about to find out if you're a friend of Samuel's after all. I hope you were telling the truth."

With the flurry of new activity, Adam, Aaron, and Donna were now wide awake. The boys took up a protective stance next to their mom.

The riders were getting closer. When they entered the light of the camp's fire, Gant was surprised when he recognized one of the riders. The rider seemed to be just as surprised to see him and smiled.

"Master Gant, it's so good to see you," said Ryder, with a bit of sarcasm. He had been under Gant's command until he had defected. He had never understood why the other guards had liked him. Perhaps he hadn't stayed long enough to find out. But, something about how easily he had carried out the governor's sometime inhumane and insane orders hadn't set well with him. At hearing Gant's name, the eyes of the surrounding men widened and their weapons were drawn, pointed at Gant. They had never seen him before but they knew him by reputation. Many of their friends had suffered at his hands. Fearing the worst, Gant backed toward his wife and sons, placing himself in front of them as a shield.

"There's no need for those. Put your weapons down," instructed Ryder to the men, as he and Darby dismounted.

Reluctantly, one by one, they obeyed.

"You know this man?" asked the camp leader.

"Of course. We're old comrades." Darby chuckled at the sarcasm.

"What should we do with them then? They say they're looking for your father."

Ryder walked over to Gant, standing toe to toe, having to look up, like everyone else. "I'm not surprised the governor would stoop this low, to use your entire family to locate the valley. He must be even more desperate than I thought."

"You're wrong, Ryder. We've left Sector 4 and that life behind for good. I want a new life for my family."

"And you want your new life to begin in the valley?"

"That's right. You were there when your father asked me to come."

"I remember clearly and I remember you said no. So, you must see how suspicious this looks."

"I'm going to be forty soon and you know what happens then."

"Oh, now I see. It's not that you've seen the error of your ways, it's that you're looking out for your own skin, now that your time is running out."

"I'll admit my age and pre-determined destiny did get me to thinking, but ultimately I want a better life for my family. I've done things I'm not proud of, but they were a means of keeping my family fed and safe behind the prison walls. Samuel's invitation gave me a glimpse of hope. This way I'll be able to see my grandchildren grow up."

"Almost convincing and well rehearsed. I don't like it, but I suppose there is only one thing to do, take you to my father."

Donna squeezed her husband's arm. He looked down to see her smiling, and he smiled back. Gant knew everything was going to be all right once they reached Samuel. "We're going to be okay," he told her.

"I just hope you're not playing us for fools. It would be bad for all of you," warned Ryder. After a brief pause, "We have a ways to go, so get something to eat over by the fire. And since they'll probably come looking for you, we'll leave as soon as our horses have had a chance to rest."

* * *

Chapter 19

That evening a member of the Guard search party returned to the compound, going directly to the governor's office. Damon noticed as a guard rushed by his living quarters. He hurried out, following closely behind. The guard knocked on the frame of the governor's door as the counselor caught up with him.

The governor looked up to see a guard at his door. "Yes?" answered Davis, not understanding why a mere guard would be disturbing his evening.

"Sorry to bother you, sir. I have news about Master Gant."

Damon, now standing beside the soldier, escorted him inside.

"Did you find him?" asked Damon. He couldn't have cared less about the rest of the family.

The governor's expression changed from one of

PARADISE

annoyance to one of being anxious now realizing why the man was there.

The guard looked back and forth between Damon and the governor, not sure who he should report to.

"We didn't find Master Gant... or his family, but we did find where it appears they met up with a few riders. Based on the tracks, the buggy continued south escorted by the riders. That's when I was sent back here to report. The rest of the search party continued to follow them."

"It sounds to me like our worst fears have come true, Gant has been kidnapped," speculated Davis. "What do you think, Counselor?"

"A kidnapping is a definite possibility," answered Damon, "it *is* rather dangerous out there, especially for a family. But suppose, for argument's sake, there is another possibility. What if it was an arranged meeting? Perhaps the riders were allies or even friends."

"That's Ridiculous!" declared Davis. "Why would he do such a thing? You can't possibly be suggesting Master Gant planned to leave. He has been loyal and dedicated to me since the beginning. He would never do something like that."

"Of course not, sir. I was just speaking hypothetically. I should never have mentioned it."

The guard was noticeably uncomfortable being in the governor's office, especially when it came to listening to accusations against Master Gant. Things he knew couldn't be true.

"Do you have any questions for this man before he's dismissed?" asked Damon.

The governor flicked his hand toward the door,

indicating he was through with him and he could leave.

"You're excused," said Damon.

The guard hesitated and then asked Damon, "Please, may I rejoin the search party, sir?"

Gant had been good to his men, treating them with respect and fairness even when they were given the most undesirable tasks, and they didn't want anything to happen to him.

"There's no need. You've done your part," said Damon.

"I'd like to, sir, with your permission."

"No. The search party has left us short-handed as it is, you need to stay and help here," said Damon.

The guard's shoulders slumped. "Yes, sir." He did an about-face, and sped away down the hallway.

* * *

Ryder and Darby led the way, riding side by side, while two others brought up the rear. They merged back with the main trail heading south. Gant recognized the familiar landscape. This was near where the Guard and Raiders had faced off.

"How much further to the valley?" asked Gant, wondering how close they had been when they had been there before.

Ryder turned in his saddle to answer, "Making a map?" he asked sarcastically, still not trusting Gant. Perhaps he should have blind-folded the whole lot from the beginning. It was too late now.

"Just curious," stated Gant. He felt better about their

PARADISE

situation, knowing they were on their way to see Samuel and that Ryder knew they were friends. His family was more at ease too, sensing his relaxed attitude, making small talk about his expectations in the valley. Gant was sure they were out of danger. Once they saw Samuel, he knew everything would be all right.

"We'll arrive there this evening," said Ryder, not turning around, "so, about another twelve hours at this rate."

Sighs of unhappiness came from the back seat of the buggy. The boys were cramped in the tiny space and twelve hours sounded like an eternity, but Gant and Donna had the opposite reaction. Broad smiles appeared on both their faces. They were within reach of their new life.

"We're almost there," he said, looking over his shoulder. "Instead of thinking about how uncomfortable you are, think about how good it's going to be once we get there." He glance back. Their eyes were closed.

Gant looked into his wife's eyes and smiled. This was the happiest he'd seen her in a very long time.

Ryder and the others heard a gunshot from behind them. Ryder halted the procession and rode back to the trailing riders, listening for another one.

*　　*　　*

Where the buggy had detoured off the main trail, the search party had split up, one group continuing to follow the buggy and the other one staying on the main trail. If one or the other saw the buggy or the captors, they agreed to fire a single shot and the other would come in a hurry.

They had played a hunch and it had panned out, the buggy *had* come back out to the main trail. Riding through the previous night, they had caught up. Seeing them in the distance, one shot was fired.

"Should we wait for the others?" asked one of the men.

The group's leader was looking through binoculars. "No. Master Gant and his family are in danger and I can only see four kidnappers. We outnumber them two-to-one. And they can't outrun us with a buggy in tow. We can take them."

"I just don't want the kidnappers to do anything drastic."

"We can't just sit here. We have to do something. And it's not going to change anything by waiting on the others."

"Then let's go. Maybe when they see us coming they'll tuck their tails and run away."

They whipped their horses into a full gallop, intent on saving Gant and his family. He'd been more than their leader, he'd looked out for them and they owed him for making their jobs bearable. There had been times when they had been ordered to do things for the governor that had turned their stomachs. Gant had helped them to see the big picture and get through it, to cope for their families sake.

*   *   *

Ryder didn't hear another shot, but he saw the dust cloud behind them, coming their way. The riders seemed to be slowing with the dust cloud settling. He recognized the

PARADISE

tan uniforms.

"We'll never outrun them," admitted Darby. "And there's too many of them."

"I know. So, what do you suggest?" asked Ryder.

Darby paused while he ran through their options in his mind. "Why don't we just leave them here? We don't owe them anything and the buggy can't go where we can. Besides, it's them the Guard are after."

Ryder didn't like the idea of deserting them and by their reaction neither did the Gants. Ryder needed to decide and to be quick about it. The Guard was getting closer. "Sorry, but I have to agree with my friend. We're going to let the Guard have you back." Ryder and his companions turned to ride away.

"Wait!" shouted Gant, his dream slipping away.

They stopped and Ryder turned back. "What?"

"Let me talk to them. We don't want to go back," pleaded Gant. "We can't go back."

Ryder was still suspicious of Gant's intentions. Was this another ruse to find the way to the valley for the governor? Just more deceit?

"We'll be one-half mile down the trail. If you can convince them to let you go, then you can catch up. Of course you realize that by doing so, you'll be labeling yourself as a traitor to the Guard and the governor.

"We'd already accepted that," said Gant.

"We'll give you half an hour. If you haven't convinced them by then, you're not going to. I don't suspect we'll see you again."

"We have to go!" urged Darby, watching as the Guard continued to close the gap.

All four riders turned and raced away. Gant and his family jumped down from the buggy, waiting for the guards to arrive.

When the Guard saw the kidnappers ride away, leaving the Gants in the middle of the trail, apparently unharmed, there were exclamations of victory throughout their ranks. They had successfully saved their mentor and leader. As they stopped abruptly behind the buggy, their cloud of dust followed, covering everyone there. The entire Guard unit jumped down from their horses, all smiles, rushing up to check on the condition of the family.

"Are you all right?" asked the leader, Jason. "We were afraid the kidnappers might do something drastic when they saw us."

Daniel and Donna exchanged glances. They weren't being captured, they were being rescued. "We're fine." Gant should have said thank you, but he couldn't. He would have preferred they hadn't pursued them at all.

"We're so glad to find all of you all right," said Jason. "After we rest we can head back. Everyone is going to be so glad to see you. Especially Governor Davis."

This was not the encounter Gant had envisioned.

Jason sensed something was wrong. Donna and the boys didn't appear happy or thankful, but almost disappointed. "What's wrong?" he asked.

Gant wasn't going to prolong the news, coming right out with it, "We're not going back."

The men broke out in laughter. He was joking and it wouldn't be the first time.

"I'm serious. We've decided to leave Sector 4." Gant wasn't smiling.

PARADISE

The laughter died away and grins were replaced by frowns of confusion.

"What about the kidnappers?" one rider asked.

"They weren't kidnappers, they were our escorts," explained Gant, "to a better place, where we intend to start a new life."

"You're not serious, are you?" asked another man, unbelief in his voice.

The other team of riders rode up, also glad to see Gant and his family were safe. They too became confused when informed of Gant's announcement.

A man from the second team, Travis, made his way forward until he was facing Gant. "Is it true?" he asked.

"Yes."

Travis turned his back to Gant, facing the other men. "We were ordered by the governor to find Gant and bring him back and that's exactly what we should do. Personally, I don't care if he comes back or not, but we have our orders. I'm sure the governor would especially like to see him now that we know he's a traitor."

"No!" shouted Jason. "If Master Gant goes back, it'll be his decision. We owe him that much. And I don't want there to be any more talk about him being a traitor."

"If you turn on your own people and go to the other side, you're a traitor!" shouted Travis, loud enough for all to hear.

Jason faced Gant to talk to him directly, "No one needs to know anything about your decision to leave. As far as everyone else back at Sector 4 knows you were kidnapped and we were able to rescue you. Just come back with us and everything will be just like it was before. No one here will say anything different."

"I… or we appreciate the gesture, Jason, but we've made up our minds," said Gant. "We believe there is something better out here."

Travis had always been gung-ho with a chip on his shoulder, although no one knew the reason why. His fellow guards had learned over time to keep their distance. He had made it clear early on he wasn't interested in making friends. His aggressive bullying had earned him a reputation with the citizens too, avoiding contact whenever possible. He was the one member of the Guard who actually enjoyed handing out punishment when it was called for.

"I don't know why you're even discussing it," said Travis, "we're taking them back with us because that's what the governor wants.

"No," said Jason, calmly this time, "it's up to them and they've made their decision."

Travis pulled his pistol and pointed it at Gant. "He's going back. Who else is with me?" he asked, looking for support from the surrounding guards.

There was silence from the others and then Travis felt a gun in his side. He looked down at it. "What are you doing?" he asked Jason. "I'll report you for this!"

Jason took the pistol from Travis's hand. "Report me for what? It's your word against all of ours. Who do you think the governor is going to believe? It's a shame we couldn't find Gant or his family. The kidnappers didn't leave a trace."

Travis couldn't believe his ears. "You're going to side with a traitor against one of your own? Then you're a

PARADISE

traitor too!"

Jason backhanded Travis with him stumbling and falling to the ground. Travis's face turned a bright red, not from being struck but from the rage that was building.

"You were warned. I told you I didn't want to hear that word again. And what we're doing is siding with friends," replied Jason who then turned to Gant.

"Thank you," said Gant, shaking Jason's hand, "from all of us. If I was able, I'd ask all of you to go with me. Maybe someday I'll be able to."

"Don't worry about us, we'll be fine. But keep in mind, the governor may send us back out to look for you again."

Travis refused to listen to another word as he picked himself up off the ground and stormed off yelling over his shoulder, "We'll see who the governor believes!"

Some of the men looked at Jason for direction as Travis strode hastily past them to his horse.

"Stop him!" he ordered.

Immediately, the men nearest Travis grabbed him, refusing to let go as he tried to fight free.

"You better go now," Jason told Gant.

Gant looked toward Travis.

"Don't worry about him," said Jason. "If we can't convince him to go along, he might have an accident before we get back." He paused. "I hope everything works out for you and your family. God bless."

Gant remembered Ryder had given him half an hour before they would leave. Time was running out. He had his family load back into the buggy, gave Jason and the others a smile and a nod, then drove away.

Donna had witnessed first-hand how much his men admired and respected her husband, willing to go out on a limb for him. It gave her a sense of pride. She could also see how it was affecting him. "You're very lucky to have friends like them," she said.

"I never wanted to get them involved. I owe those men."

"Maybe you'll have the opportunity to repay them."

"That would be nice. But first, I'm going to get you and the boys to the valley."

*   *   *

Chapter 20

Gant thought he could hear church bells begin to ring over and over in the near distance. He pulled back on the reins and stopped to silence the noise of the horse and buggy. His mind hadn't been playing tricks on him, they *were* church bells. A broad smile appeared across his face. They were close.

Ryder rode back to them. "Let's go. We're almost there."

Gant looked at Donna who was silently sobbing, tears streaming down her cheeks. He wrapped his huge burly arm around her and pulled her close. Gant looked to the back seat. His sons were asleep again in the most uncomfortable and awkward looking positions.

"Boys! Wake up! We're here!" he shouted.

Adam and Aaron awoke, slowly stretching their tired and stiff muscles as they sat up.

"I don't see anything," complained Adam.

"Yeah, Dad, me either. Are you messin' with us?" asked Aaron.

"Hear those bells? That's where we're going," answered their mom.

Ryder waited for them to start moving again while the others rode ahead. Gant flicked the reins and they once again began to move. He noticed the other riders had disappeared from sight. Ryder, who was now riding beside them, saw the puzzled look on their faces and smiled. It amused him every time he saw that same look from newcomers.

"You're about to see something truly amazing," said Ryder. Since he'd left to see what the rest of the world had to offer, he'd had a deeper appreciation for what he'd had at the valley.

Suddenly, the flat, sandy, desolate plain opened wide to reveal a luscious green valley with trees, grass, fields, and even a small lake.

Ryder realized he hadn't been fishing since leaving and he missed being able to relax. He loved coming back. Ryder led them down the switchback trail into the valley.

As they neared the bottom Gant and his family had a better view of what laid below the canopy of the trees, revealing neat rows of small houses and a small crowd of people coming toward them. The people were of all ages, young and old. Seeing folks with gray hair caused Gant and Donna to wonder about their own parents. Once the devastation of the quakes had started, they had lost touch, not knowing what had happened to them.

Everything Gant could see far exceeded what he had

expected. He was overjoyed to see Samuel, his old friend, leading the group of people toward them. He brought the buggy to a stop and jumped down, grabbing Samuel's hand and shaking it enthusiastically. "Thank you for inviting us, Samuel."

Samuel pulled him close for a huge hug. "I'm glad you changed your mind. You and your family are welcome in Paradise."

Gant had never heard anyone refer to the valley as that before, but saw how appropriate it was. He couldn't help but smile at their good fortune. Gant introduced Donna and the boys and Samuel introduced Emma. Several of the others were introduced, but they were so overwhelmed at the welcome, they didn't remember any of their names.

Initially, the crowd had been eager to meet the new family, but as murmurs spread through the crowd their attitude took on a chill and people began to turn away to return to their houses. Samuel noticed the change as did Gant and his family.

"Please, don't be shy. Come and welcome these new members to our community," encouraged Samuel.

"Why is he here?" I yelled from the back of the crowd. "It's Master Gant from Sector 4," informing the others.

The smiles on Gant's and Donna's faces faded away. He hadn't known whether he would be recognized by the people in the valley or not, but he had hoped he'd be given the chance to start over without being judged too harshly. Without knowing the outcome, he'd felt the rewards would be worth taking the chance. Evidently, his reputation had preceded him. Unfortunately, now here, some had recognized him and had chosen to voice their displeasure.

In a matter of minutes everyone in the crowd knew who he was, and he wasn't welcome. A murmur from the crowd grew into a rumble.

"He shouldn't be here," I shouted.

Samuel held up both hands high into the air to silence the crowd. As the rumble died away, Samuel climbed up into the buggy so everyone could see him. "Wait!" Some who had begun to walk away turned around, recognizing his voice.

"Is this any way to treat our new neighbors?" asked Samuel. "I happen to know some of you have pasts you'd just as soon forget. And you were accepted." There were a few individuals who looked sheepishly at the ground.

I made my way to the front of the crowd. "I don't know about anyone else, but I know he shouldn't be here. Not after the things he's done."

"You're not being fair, John," said Samuel. "I've known Daniel a long time and I can assure you he's a good man. I wouldn't have invited him here if he wasn't."

Hearing Samuel admit inviting Gant to Paradise stirred a sound of grumbling from the crowd. They hadn't known Gant was there by invitation. What had Samuel been thinking? How could he think they would go along with this, without asking them first?

"Doesn't everyone deserve a second chance?" continued Samuel, attempting to persuade the crowd to accept them. "He and his family just want a fresh start. Is forgiveness so hard to give? What do you say?" Samuel waited for a response.

Gant stood silently with his family close by, now apprehensive about their awkward situation.

PARADISE

Ryder shouted from off to the side while leaning nonchalantly against a tree, "I don't trust him. He works for Governor Davis. I agree with John, he shouldn't be here."

Samuel started to reply, but Gant asked, "May I speak?"

Samuel smiled and nodded. He climbed down from the buggy and Gant climbed up. Looking into the faces of the crowd, he could see they'd already made up their minds. Even so, they were all staying to hear what he had to say.

"Most of you don't know me, but you've heard of me. My name is Daniel Gant. And what was said is partially true, I did work for the governor and I have done some things I'm not proud of, but I'm not going to apologize. Everything I did was so I could take care of my family. But we left all of that behind. Now, I'm asking for a fresh start for me and my family. We'd like a chance to show you we're good people and that we can contribute to this community. We can't go back. Our future is in your hands. Please, give us a chance."

"Very touching," commented Ryder, clapping his hands in mock admiration. "It might mean more if your men hadn't been responsible for the disposal of everyone over forty, like John here."

"We were only following orders. I hated it and didn't always agree with it, but I also understood why it was done, so the young people could survive." The murmurs began again. "But, I couldn't be a part of it any more. It's one of the reasons why we left."

"I still don't think you should be here," repeated Ryder. "And if you're allowed to stay, I think it'll be a big mistake." He looked at his dad. "But it's not up to me. You were invited here by my father, and besides, I don't even live here."

Sarah joined me at my side. She had been listening from the back. "John, I'd like them to stay," she whispered. "Samuel let you come back to Sector 4 for us and gave us a chance for a fresh start. Maybe he knows something about Master Gant that we don't."

"It's not the same thing," he replied softly, confused by her reasoning.

"Yes, it is. And if he doesn't deserve a second chance, his family does."

He began to think about what she had just said as Samuel switched places with Gant on the buggy.

"You've all heard my son's opinion. Is there anyone else who would like to speak up?" There were a lot of looks exchanged between the crowd members, but no one else was willing to speak up.

"John?" asked Samuel, "How about you? Anything to add?"

"Yes, there is." I paused. "It's been pointed out to me that whatever is decided not only affects Gant but his entire family. And we shouldn't judge or condemn an entire family by one man's actions. My wife and I are willing to give them a second chance."

Samuel saw a few heads nodding in agreement. Ryder threw his hands into the air and stormed off. It seemed as though there were no further objections to the Gant's staying.

Samuel climbed back down. "Well then," he said to the Gants, smiling, "we need to get you settled in so you

PARADISE

can rest up from your long trip. Follow me."

Sarah came up to Donna and extended her hand. "My name is Sarah. Welcome. We're new here too. So, we know some of what you're going through."

Donna threw her arms around Sarah, tears coming to her eyes, while giving her a warm hug. "Thank you!"

The family collected the few items they'd brought in the buggy. Levi, who had been quietly standing nearby, took the reins to lead the horse and buggy off to the stable. Gant started to object.

"They'll be okay," said Samuel. "Levi will take good care of them. Gant nodded. Samuel took them to the community building where Emma had already prepared a meal. They ate quickly while Samuel and Emma looked on. They'd been hungry, but other things were on their minds.

"Let me show you where you'll be staying temporarily," said Samuel.

Gant and Donna exchanged looks, reading each other's minds. "We're too excited to rest," said Gant. "We want to see everything."

"Sure," said Samuel, understanding their excitement and just as anxious to show them.

Gant had tried to describe the valley to Donna and his sons just as it had been described to him, but none of what he'd heard had done it justice. They were overwhelmed with all the valley had to offer, bombarding Samuel with rapid-fire questions on their guided tour. The boys, growing up in the prison-wall environment for the last five years, had forgotten how much better it was to be in the outdoors, free and unconfined. They hadn't been allowed outside the compound walls unless accompanied by their dad. And here, the air had no lingering foul stale odors. They breathed in deeply. This had been a good decision.

When the tour was over, Samuel led them back to Town Hall where they would be staying in the same upstairs room where John and the others had stayed when they'd first arrived. Finding the cots inviting, Adam and Aaron were soon asleep, not a surprise to their parents. Gant and Donna were too excited to even try. They stayed late, sitting on the front porch, talking about their expectations and dreams for their new life. Eventually, they too grew tired, moved back upstairs, and fell asleep seconds after laying their heads down.

* * *

The Guard returned to Sector 4, after an understanding had been reached with Travis that there would be no trouble from him with no mention of seeing Gant and his family. And in return for his silence he wouldn't be beaten to a pulp and he'd be allowed to return to his duties without repercussions.

Jason pulled aside a few of the men and asked them to spread the word to keep an eye on Travis. None of them knew him well enough to trust him completely. He had always kept to himself. They had to at least consider the possibility he would turn on them. But as Jason had explained, it was his word against all of theirs. However, it would be best if a confrontation in front of the governor and the counselor could be avoided altogether.

After taking care of his horse, Travis headed straight

PARADISE

for his living quarters. He could sense watchful eyes following him. He entered his room, waited, and then peeked into the hallway. Empty, he crept toward the governor's office. Two of the guards stepped out into his path. He lowered his shoulder and hit the gap between them, knocking them aside. He went through a doorway, slamming and locking the door behind him. He stopped long enough to smirk at them through the door's reinforced window glass. The guards pounded on the door trying to make enough of a commotion for someone to notice and come to their aid.

Successful, heads popped out of several living quarter doorways as Travis ran by. Tentatively, one of the clueless individuals rushed to the door and unlocked it. The pursuing guards burst through the door, rushing past the other onlookers, continuing the pursuit. Travis was almost to the governor's office.

"Travis! Stop!" one of the guards shouted.

He ignored their hail, bursting into Davis' office.

Damon and the governor had been listening to Jason give his report on their rescue mission.

"What's the meaning of this?" demanded Governor Davis, extremely irritated.

Out of breath, Travis blurted out, "I have news for you, Governor. I…"

Damon held up his hand to stop him from saying any more. "We are hearing all the news we need to hear from Captain Hale."

"Captain? But, sirs, whatever Jason has told you is a lie."

The two guards appeared abruptly at the door. "We're

sorry he's disturbed your meeting, sirs. We'll take him away immediately." They gave Jason a look of apology as they grabbed Travis and began dragging him out.

In desperation, as Travis was almost out the door, "We found Gant!" he blurted.

Davis and Damon then gave him their full attention. "Hold him right there!" ordered Davis. He walked up close to Travis, glaring into his eyes. "What did you say?"

"We caught up to Gant and his family." He paused, still slightly out of breath. "But Gant didn't want to come back, so he let them go," said Travis, pointing to Jason.

Davis looked at Jason with an expression that demanded an explanation.

"I don't know what he's trying to pull," replied Jason. "Ask any member of the search party and they'll tell you the same story I've just reported to you."

"A story and that's all it is," said Travis. "Gant is on his way to the valley right now and he's not coming back. He was never kidnapped. He betrayed you! He's a traitor!"

Davis slammed his hand down on his desk and yelled, "Stop!" He didn't want to hear any more against Gant.

"You can't believe him," said Jason, sensing they were beginning to.

"If he's lying, why would he come to me with this?" asked Davis, not wanting it to be true.

"I have no idea, sir," claimed Jason.

"You two," with Damon directing his question to the guards, "Were you on the search team?"

"Yes, Counselor," they said in unison."

"And did you find Gant?"

"No," one of them said as the other shook his head.

PARADISE

"They're lying!" screamed Travis.

Damon looked at Davis and shrugged. Neither knew who to believe. They couldn't understand why either Jason or Travis would lie, but one of them was. Could they take the chance to ignore Travis? There was too much at stake to brush it aside. "Come here and sit down," said Damon as he directed Travis to a chair in the corner. "You other men are dismissed."

Jason wasn't sure the dismissal included him until Damon motioned for him to leave too. Jason and the two guards exchanged looks, fear flashing through their minds. If the governor and Damon chose to believe Travis, the future of all the guards in the search party would be in jeopardy. Their only prayer was that the governor would believe the many over the one.

Jason had his two friends spread a warning to the other men. Their stories had to agree if asked. If they'd only listened to their gut, they would have dealt with Travis on the trail, and there would be nothing to worry about now. Travis had always been a loner and hard to get along with. No one would have missed him and no one would have ever suspected them of letting Gant go his own way. Now, some were having second thoughts, afraid their actions could have deadly consequences affecting their families. If everyone stayed strong and united, there was nothing to worry about. But if the unthinkable happened, heads would roll, literally.

* * *

The next morning Jason was summoned from his

living quarters to the governor's office. His wife looked at him apprehensively. He had told her everything. He owed her that much. Whatever was going to happen was about to happen. The wondering would soon be over. She gave him a kiss and a lingering hug.

Two members of the Guard escorted him as though he was under arrest. He found it odd he didn't recognize either one of them. When he arrived, the two guards took up positions outside the office on both sides of the door. Governor Davis and Counselor Damon were waiting. Travis was there too with a smug smile, an unmistakable indication of how the evening had gone.

"Come in and have a seat," invited a smiling and cordial Damon, directing him to a chair directly in front of the governor's desk.

As Jason took a seat, so did the governor, sitting back in his chair, arms crossed, silent and expressionless. Damon stood by his side.

"Since we have no way of knowing who to believe concerning Master Gant, we've had to make a very difficult decision. Even if he," Damon pointed to Travis, "is lying. We can't ignore the possibility he's telling the truth and the conspiracy it would suggest. Either way, we must assume Gant will not be returning." He paused. "Therefore, changes are in order. So, as of this moment, Mr. Travis Peck, is now Master Peck. However, if it turns out Master Gant and his family were abducted, and we confirm it, Master Peck will suffer a most horrible and public death."

Jason couldn't believe what he was hearing. Somehow, Travis had swayed them in his direction.

PARADISE

"And you, Jason Hale, will no longer hold the rank of captain, but you'll be allowed to remain a member of the Guard with your former rank of Sergeant under the command of Master Peck."

"May I ask why you believe him over the word of the entire search party?" asked Jason.

"The governor doesn't have to justify his decisions, Mr. Hale," stated Counselor Damon. "But if you'd like to file a formal complaint, I'd be glad to give you the proper forms."

Jason remained silent, shaking his head slightly. He could predict how unbearable it was going to be, Travis giving him every undesirable task that came along, but he was thankful his family wouldn't have to suffer for his mistake. He began to argue his case, but Damon held up his hand, not wanting to hear it. If he had tried to plead his case, he would have only been digging his hole deeper.

"Along with his new command," continued Damon, "Master Peck has a few ideas for making improvements. Of those, security and manpower will be a priority with personnel receiving a complete makeover. Any member of the Guard who disagrees with the changes will be allowed to resign and take up residence back in Tent City where they were found. Appropriate jobs will be assigned at Master Pecks discretion. Is that understood?"

There was no point in saying anything. They had already made their decision and had already begun to implement the changes. Travis remained quiet in his chair, maintaining a smug smile of satisfaction. He must have been very convincing, thought Jason.

"You may go," said Damon.

After Jason had left the office, Damon walked over to Travis, leaned down and placed his hands on the arms of the chair, looking directly into Travis' eyes. "If I find out you *have* lied to us, I'll put the noose around your neck myself."

The smile on Travis' face never waivered. "That's not going to be necessary."

"And let me give you a little advice, whether you're telling the truth or not, you should probably watch your back from here on out since you just turned it against the entire Guard. I'd start replacing them with men you can trust, if there are any."

"I've already begun."

*　　*　　*

Chapter 21

Early the next morning there was a knock at Samuel's door. He was surprised to find a small group from the community gathered around his front porch.

"It must be important for all of you to be here so early," he commented, trying to lighten the mood after seeing their serious faces. "What can I do for you?"

Carl, a long-time resident, spoke up reluctantly, "We've been talking ... and we don't want a man like Gant living here." There were murmurs and nods of agreement from the group. "We've heard he's done terrible things and we think he'll bring trouble with him. Please, don't let him stay."

Samuel's ever-present smile disappeared, upset that they had such closed minds. "I'm disappointed in all of you? Don't you believe a person deserves a second chance?"

"Of course we do," said Carl. "It's just that ... he's Master Gant. The stories they tell about him are horrible. We're sorry, Samuel, but we don't feel safe with him here."

"I'm sorry, too," said Samuel with a sigh. "Sorry you feel that way, but you're entitled to your opinion. This is your community. Give me some time to come up with a solution. He and his family can't go back."

"We're not demanding you do anything, we're asking," clarified Carl. "We don't want anything to happen to any of them. But even if he doesn't pose a direct threat, danger follows a man like that. What if the Guard comes looking for him? Samuel, he's putting us all at risk. Take all the time you need to figure something out, but keep in mind, the chances of something bad happening increases the longer he's here." As they left as a group, Samuel overheard them plan to meet again later to talk further about the Gants. He shook his head in disbelief and sadness.

Samuel went inside and sat at the kitchen table. He didn't know what to do. He was the one to ask Daniel to come, to get him and his family away from the terrible situation they had been in, to start a new life. He couldn't just tell them they were no longer welcome and he couldn't just stand by and do nothing when the community was so concerned. He had responsibilities. Rather than go on his usual morning rounds, he decided to stay home to consider his options, something to satisfy both Daniel and the community.

Emma returned from taking breakfast to the Gants and cleaning up afterward. When she came through the door

PARADISE

she immediately sensed something was wrong. She'd never seen him this solemn and asked, "What's wrong?"

He told her about the visit he'd had from the committee earlier.

"You can't ask them to leave," she said. "I talked with them this morning. They're good people."

"I know, but what can I do? The community isn't even willing to give them a chance."

"You'll think of something. You always do." She smiled and kissed him on top of his head.

* * *

After breakfast, Gant and his family went on a discovery tour of their own, making an effort to talk with the people they met, only to be met with silence and a cold shoulder. It was the same everywhere they went, with one exception. Sarah saw them walking side by side down the center of the street, noticing by their posture something wasn't right. She asked if she could join them, which immediately lifted Donna's spirit. Sarah did her best to make them all feel welcome with some success in lifting their spirits. When she left them, she could tell she and Donna would be friends.

When the Gants returned to Town Hall, Samuel was waiting and he didn't look happy.

"I need to talk to you and your family, Daniel. Please, won't you all have a seat."

The family exchanged looks of concern as they took seats at the end of the table. "What's wrong, Samuel?" asked Daniel.

"I'm sorry, but the people of the community don't want you living here. I'm sorry, I didn't consider they would be so unforgiving."

"Are you asking us to leave?" asked Donna in disbelief. "You're the one who asked us to come here. We've risked so much." There was frustration in her voice.

"This isn't easy for me, but I have to think about the community." He paused. "I think I have a solution, if you're willing to hear it."

"I'm not surprised this is happening, just disappointed. I could see this coming," said Daniel, "after the comments yesterday and the cold reception we've been receiving all morning. I suppose we're at your mercy, Samuel. What 'solution' have you come up with?"

"There's another valley not far from here offering many of the same features as this one. The main difference is no one else lives there. We only pasture a few head of cattle there. You'd be entirely on your own, which could be a challenge. But then again, you wouldn't be bothered by anyone, so in that sense it could be a blessing. We'd be glad to help you with your new start and be available whenever you need help. What do you think?"

"Who else knows about this other valley?" asked Daniel.

"Only a select few."

They all sat quietly for a few moments. "I don't think I'd like being alone and isolated," declared Donna, an edge to her voice. "Would any other families be able to go with us?"

"Anyone can that wants to, but I don't know of any offhand who would. I'd be glad to ask around for you if you like," volunteered Samuel. "I'm so sorry it's come to this. I never would have mentioned coming here if I'd known you'd get this reception."

Donna perked up as though she had had a revelation. "I may know of someone who would go with us," she mentioned.

Samuel smiled for the first time all day. "Are you thinking of John and Sarah? I saw that you and Sarah seemed to hit it off. They haven't been here very long either."

"I don't know," stated Daniel, "John was very vocal against us, especially me, yesterday. I don't think he'd ever agree to it."

"You might be surprised," replied Samuel. "Do you think you'd be able to work with him?"

"I'd be willing to try if he is and it would be better than going alone."

"Would you like for me to talk to them?" asked Samuel.

Daniel looked at Donna. She smiled and nodded. "Sure," he said. "What do we have to lose?"

* * *

Samuel decided to wait until noon to go to John and Sarah's house. He arrived a little before noon, finding Sarah home alone. "John's not here, Samuel. They're all at their jobs, but they should be here at any moment for lunch."

"Mind if I wait for them?" asked Samuel, "I have something to discuss with all of you."

"Is there anything wrong?"

"No, not at all," he said, not elaborating. There was an awkward silence.

"Would you like to wait inside?" she asked.

"If you don't mind, it's so nice out I think I'll wait out here on the porch."

Since Donna and her family had arrived in Paradise, Sarah thought about how fortunate they had been to receive such a warm welcome, in contrast to the one the Gant's had received. As he sat down on the edge of the porch to wait, Sarah felt she needed to tell him so, "I'd like to thank you, Samuel, for taking us in and making us feel welcome."

He turned to face her. "It's been our pleasure, Sarah." Praise made him uncomfortable. He smiled and turned his back to her.

* * *

I saw Samuel sitting on our front porch as we approached the house. I smiled and waved.

"To what do we owe this pleasure?" I asked.

"I'd like to talk to you and your family," said Samuel. And seeing my puzzled expression added, "And, like I told Sarah, no, there's nothing wrong."

"I'm glad to hear it. Come on in the house," I invited.

We gathered around the rustic, plank-type table. It seemed Samuel was having a hard time saying whatever it was he had come here to say. "What's this all about?" I asked.

"It's about Daniel and his family." He paused. "A

PARADISE

group of concerned citizens came to me first thing this morning and informed me they don't want Daniel living here."

"I'm not surprised, with the things he's done," I responded.

"I don't know what things you're referring to, so I'm not going to judge, but I've known Daniel for many years and I know him to be a good man."

"Maybe he's changed since then," I said.

"Perhaps, but I don't think so. In talking to him yesterday and this morning, I believe him to be the same man I knew before. Perhaps he was forced to adapt to his circumstances. But that's not what I'm here to talk about. I'm afraid if he's allowed to stay, it could tear this community apart."

"You're going to make them leave?" asked Sarah, confused.

"I don't see any other option."

"But where will they go?" asked Sarah. "They can't go back."

"There's a place, another valley, similar to this one, only smaller, where they can go. I've already told them about it. No one else lives there. And they can have the fresh start they want."

"I don't understand. What does this have to do with us?" I asked suspiciously.

"I was wondering if you'd consider going with them?" asked Samuel.

"What?!" I exclaimed, smiling at the absurd joke. Then I noticed Samuel wasn't laughing. "You can't be serious. Why us? Did we do something wrong?"

"No, nothing like that. I just thought since both of your families are new, you're about the same ages, and since you both have children it might be a good match. And it would be much easier to start off with friends."

"Friends? Where do you get that? I don't even like the man. Why would I go off with him?" I asked in frustration.

"Well, since Sarah and Donna are getting along so well, maybe in time, you and Daniel could do the same."

I was feeling pressured and I didn't like it. Not that I could do anything about it. Samuel had the last word here about everything. "Do we have a choice?" I asked.

"Of course you do. You're our friends. We don't want to see you go, so it's completely up to you. I just hate the idea of Daniel, Donna, and the boys going it alone. I just want you to think about it."

"If it's our choice, I don't need to think about it. I choose to stay here where we've already put down roots," I declared.

"Wait a second, John," stated Sarah. "Maybe we shouldn't be so hasty. Let's do what Samuel suggested and think about it."

I looked at her as though she had lost her mind. "Are you seriously considering this?"

"I think their boys are kind of cute," said Cindy.

I could only shake my head.

Samuel slid his chair back from the table and stood up. "Well, I can see you folks need time to talk about it privately, so I'll check back with you later." He went to the door and let himself out. The four of us were already in deep discussion, unaware he had left.

PARADISE

* * *

That afternoon I had a hard time concentrating on my work, helping out with Christopher at the mill. We were grinding the wheat from the harvest and placing the flour in small sacks to be distributed to the households. Several times Christopher had to nudge me to get my attention, catching me daydreaming, which was a switch. Mid-afternoon Gant showed up in the doorway, standing there until I noticed him. Gant motioned me over. *What did he want now?* Reluctantly, I sat down the sack I'd been filling and slowly walked over. We went outside where it was quieter.

"Samuel thought we should talk," explained Gant.

"I don't think it's a good idea for us to go off together," I stated matter-of-factly.

"We'd really like for you and your family to go with us. I don't think we can do it alone. Our wives are becoming friends and our kids are about the same age. And I have to confess, I don't know anything about farming or construction."

"So, you just need us for your labor force? Is that it?" I blurted.

"No, just your guidance. We'll be right beside you all the way."

"I don't know if I can trust you, after seeing what the Guard has done over the last five years."

"I can't change any of that. All I can do is promise you things will be different, a fresh start for both our families."

Gant extended his hand. I had no intention of shaking his hand and just looked at it for several seconds. Gant didn't withdraw it. Finally, without knowing why, I took it. Perhaps it was because he was making an effort or maybe it was just a reflex action to get rid of him. Gant smiled.

"This doesn't mean I'm agreeing to go, just that I'm willing to think about it," I explained.

"I understand," said Gant. "If you'd like to talk, you know where we'll be."

I nodded and Gant left. I stared at my palm and then wiped it off on my pants. *How could we ever be friends?*

*   *   *

That night, lying wide awake in bed, I asked Sarah, "You really want to do this, don't you?"

"Just think of it," answered Sarah, "starting from scratch, from the ground up. The freedom to do it however we want."

"You do realize it'll be a lot of work. We'll have to clear the fields, plant the crops, harvest the crops, build our houses, and we'd have to do it with people we don't even know."

"Wouldn't it be wonderful?" she said, excitement in her voice.

I turned to look at her. There was a twinkle in her eyes. She was actually looking forward to going, treating it as though it would be some sort of a great adventure.

I was just about to doze off when I felt the bed shake slightly, almost imperceptible. But then it began to get stronger. I instantly came wide awake, sitting up, looking at Sarah. Her eyes were wide open, fear on her face. "Oh, John, not again!" I knew we were both remembering how it

PARADISE

had begun just like this at our home five years earlier. Sarah sprang from the bed and ran to check on our children.

It was the first noticeable quake we'd felt in four years. According to a talk with Samuel, I was surprised to learn that they'd never experienced one in the valley. His explanation centered on the faith of the community, but I speculated it had something more to do with the distance from any major fault lines or past disposal wells. After feeling the tremor, it was obvious the valley was not immune. If the pattern from before repeated itself, it would only get worse.

Sarah brought Christopher and Cindy to our bed. Even though the tremor had been weak and had only lasted a short while, we all had a hard time going back to sleep, until exhaustion finally took over.

* * *

The next morning when I got up, Sarah was already at the stove preparing my breakfast, singing cheerfully out loud to herself.

"How'd you sleep?" she asked.

"Not so good. What are you so happy about?" I asked, still waking up from the restless night.

"Oh, nothing," she said, smiling.

"How about you? Did you sleep okay?" I asked.

"Once I finally nodded off. The quake rattled me a little."

"I hope it was just a fluke." I sniffed the air. "Is that coffee I smell?" I asked with disbelief. Coffee had been one of those items not found at Tent City, but according to Paul had been plentiful within the compound walls for the privileged.

"I borrowed a small amount from Samuel. I thought you might like it."

I had a pretty good idea it had at one time been a part of the governor's stockpile of items. I breathed in deeply.

"And biscuits and sausage gravy? Okay, what's going on?"

"Nothing, Dear. Sit down and eat your breakfast."

I sat at my place at the head of the table. "Where are Christopher and Cindy?"

"They ate already and left for work." She let him start on his breakfast. She could tell he was enjoying it. "So, have you given any more thought to Samuel's idea yesterday?"

"It's all I've been thinking about." He set his fork down next to his plate, sat back, and let out a sigh. "That's what this is all about, isn't it?"

"John, what do you mean?" she asked innocently.

"You know exactly what I mean. You're trying to bribe me into agreeing to go." I paused. "What do the kids think about leaving here?"

"They didn't have much to say until this morning. The quake scared them last night. They asked me this morning if it'd be safer at the other place. I think they'd like to go now, but they'll go along with whatever you decide."

"So, I guess I can't use them as an excuse then, can I?"

"No." She could sense he was about to break. She cracked a smile.

I would do anything for Sarah. It looked like we were

PARADISE

going on an adventure.

"I guess we should inform Samuel and the Gants and start making plans. I just have one more question for Samuel. If things don't work out, I want to know if we can come back here?"

Sarah threw her arms around my neck and gave me a kiss. "Thank you. It's going to be amazing. You'll see." She kissed me again. "I'm going to tell Donna right now," she said as she ran out of the house, the screen door slamming shut.

I took a deep breath. After saying no, I had given in, and without a proper fight. And I was going somewhere I didn't want to go and with a person I couldn't stand. But it made Sarah happy and if she was happy, I was happy. I went back to eating my special breakfast and enjoying my coffee. It could be a while before I had something like this again. *What have I agreed to?*

* * *

Both families met with Samuel. It was decided they would leave in two days, plenty of time to prepare and stock up for the trip and soon enough to appease any of the community's concerns about Gant. The sooner they were gone the better.

Ryder came to his father's house after watching the others leave. He was still angry with John, not yet ready for a face to face. He greeted his dad without any of the usual pleasantries.

"I thought you'd left by the way you stormed off yesterday. Feeling better?" asked Samuel.

"Fine. I couldn't leave until I knew what you were going to do about the Gant situation," said Ryder. "Now, I hear you want to take them to one of the valleys. I think it's a mistake. John, I trust, but Gant... I think it could be trouble."

"I trust him," stated Samuel. "And that should be enough."

"Okay, Dad." Ryder didn't want to argue with him anymore and he knew he'd never change his dad's mind anyway. "Who's going to take them? You?"

"No. I was hoping you would."

"And why would I do that? I don't want them to go there at all," said Ryder.

"Because I'm asking you to, Son. Would you please take them or would you rather they stayed here?" asked Samuel.

Ryder didn't like either option. He believed most of the people in Paradise disliked Gant as much as he did, if not from personal experience, from what they'd heard. If Gant stayed, there could be a revolt against his dad, which he couldn't have.

"No, I don't want him to stay either. But, do they have to be taken to the valley. Can't you just provide them with some food, water, and a map and let them fend for themselves in the wasteland?"

Samuel smiled.

Ryder knew his dad would never agree to it. It went against everything his father had taught him. It didn't show any form of compassion. To let Gant fend for himself alone was one thing, but when his entire family was involved, it was different.

PARADISE

"Okay, okay, I'll take them."

"Thank you, Son."

"Just curious, but why couldn't Levi take them?" asked Ryder.

"Because I think you need to do this as much as they need you to."

"Still trying to teach me a lesson? You know I'm too old for that?"

Samuel continued to smile. "You think so?"

*   *   *

Gant and I had assumed Samuel would be taking us to the new valley. When he informed us Ryder would be taking us, there was obvious concern on Gant's face.

"Don't worry," said Samuel, in an attempt to put his mind at ease.

"I don't want to sound ungrateful," said Gant, "but I don't want to get waylaid on the way there. Your son hasn't been exactly discreet in hiding his feelings about me."

"I'm sure we'll be fine," I said, fairly certain I was right. "Ryder will do what he says he'll do. It's you I'm not so sure about." I was half-joking, with a trace of distrust still on my mind. During the two days of preparation Gant and I had talked frequently, each discovering we were more alike than I would have ever believed. Our common link was that our families were our primary concern. In time, perhaps I would learn to trust him, but first he'd have to earn it.

Several people from the community donated items to

both families to help us get started. Gant doubted if they would have been so generous if they had been going alone.

With help, we loaded a wagon with food, water, tools, and seed. Ryder would personally lead us on the half-day journey to our new home. As final preparations were being made and we were almost ready to leave, Samuel approached, carrying a crate of laying hens followed by Levi leading a goat for milk.

When we were ready to leave, the community came together to send us off. Gant mentioned he found it humorous how everyone, now that they were leaving, treated him and his family as best of friends. Samuel caught me off guard when he asked everyone to gather together and join hands to offer a prayer for us to have a safe journey and for the quakes to stop. It reminded me of the Sundays when we would go to church as a family. It was another thing moving into Tent City had taken away.

Sarah had taken Christopher and Cindy to the Paradise church on Sundays, but I'd kept my distance, not sure how I felt about God after all the crap we'd been through. I watched Sarah and Donna during the prayer, and they appeared to be sincere in their belief. Perhaps, in time, my faith would return.

After saying our goodbyes, we loaded into the wagon and buggy. The earth began to shake again, at first as a mild tremor, but then the intensity grew and panic appeared on the faces in the crowd. People in the crowd reached out for each other, fighting to maintain their balance and stay on their feet. We held onto each other and the sides of the wagon and buggy for protection as Gant and I fought to keep the frightened and skittish horses

PARADISE

under control.

As quickly as it had begun, the quake weakened and then stopped. Afterward, an audible sigh of relief came from the gathered people. There were nervous laughs, some from joy, some from fear. Several had dropped to their knees and were praying their thanks for being spared from damage and injuries. I overheard one prayer where the person was asking God to send Master Gant far, far away, before another quake came. I couldn't believe they thought the quakes were a result of Daniel coming here?

As soon as Ryder found out his mom and dad were alright he came to us. "Dad said we should go ahead and go as planned." We nodded agreement. No one had been hurt and there was no reason to delay.

The two recent quakes hadn't caused any damage, but if their frequency and magnitude increased as they had five years earlier, no place would be safe, not even a half-day's ride away.

* * *

Thank you for reading Paradise, the first book in the Aftershock Series. I hope it provided a great reading experience. I think you'll be as delighted with the second book, Exodus. Please check on the status at adventurewithmike.com.

Made in the USA
Columbia, SC
13 May 2025